SHULI MENSH

TOMORROW

JUDAICA PRESS

Tomorrow

ISBN: 978-1-60763-298-6

Editor: M. Jakubowicz
Proofreader: Hadassa Goldsmith
Cover design: Rivkah Lewis
Internal design and layout: Nachum Shapiro

The Judaica Press, Inc.
123 Ditmas Avenue / Brooklyn, NY 11218
718-972-6200 / 800-972-6201
info@judaicapress.com
www.judaicapress.com

Manufactured in the United States of America

"SORE TODAY ... STRONG TOMORROW."
— AUTHOR UNKNOWN

For my father
for being my hero and my biggest fan

For Alan
who has made my past and present so much brighter,
and with whom I want to share all of my tomorrows

A special shout-out to some special people,
with love—Ashira, Michael, Dovid,
Moshe, Meira, Avromi, and Sho

And a sincere thank you to Sarah Chicheportiche,
for all of her help with everything French

PROLOGUE

YESTERDAY

THE SUN SHONE BRIGHTLY in the Jerusalem sky. The air was fragrant, the children played noisily in the courtyard, and everything seemed as usual that day ... and yet, there was an air of melancholy that hung over them, a sadness that crept into their hearts and lay there heavily.

It was the very last day of seminary, and as hard as it was to believe, the year had come to a close. Machon Chana was a veritable bustle of whirling activity. Three nineteen-year-old girls sat on their beds, suitcases and duffle bags surrounding them, their possessions strewn everywhere. Though the hallway was filled with noise, their room was oddly silent.

No one spoke. Each of them was quietly reflecting on the previous year. It had not had an auspicious beginning at all. If anything, the three girls had rather disliked each other on that fateful first day, or so it had seemed.

Shari had entered the room to find another girl already there. The girl had tanned skin and hair streaked with blonde highlights, and she was bent over her Louis Vuitton bag, searching its contents furiously.

"Hi," Shari said cautiously.

"I'm Gali Gordon, from L.A.," the girl muttered. "I can't talk right now … I can't find my new lipstick. If I don't find it, I'm going to scream … My mother will have to fly here to bring me a new one …."

Not knowing quite how to respond, Shari just stood there awkwardly.

"You can take that bed over there," Gali said.

Shari obediently made her way to the bed in the corner. It was a crowded spot, with a shelf right above it and a small closet right next to it. How would she put away her things? It seemed like a nearly impossible task. She would have infinitely preferred the other bed closer to her new roommate, which also happened to be near a large window, but Gali was obviously saving it for someone else. In any case, it was probably better not to make demands right away. After all, they didn't know each other.

"I have an extra lipstick I could give you," she offered, in what she hoped was a reasonable, friendly tone.

Gali stood up and stared at her like she'd just sprouted wings.

"I only wear Chanel," she said.

Well.

So that was how it was going to be.

Before she could collect her riotous thoughts, another girl entered the room, all curly hair and hand gestures, bringing with her a bustling, take-charge attitude.

"Hi, I'm Tova Miller," she said in a loud, hoarse voice. "Oh, Gali, you're so sweet for saving me a bed by the window! And what's your name?"

She stared pointedly at Shari, waiting for an answer.

For a split second, Shari was terrified that her voice wouldn't come … but it did.

"Shari Weiss," she managed.

"Shari?" Tova repeated. "That's such an unusual name, I just love it!"

"Thanks."

"Is it short for anything? Like Yeshara or something? Wait … don't tell me. Let me guess! Um … Shari … Shari …" Her face brightened. "Oh, is it Sharsheret?"

Gali, who at that exact moment discovered her missing lipstick, said quickly, "That's not a name, Tova."

"Of course it is! It was the name of our production in camp, remember?"

"Yeah, a link in the chain … No one would name their kid that!"

"Why not?" Tova retorted. "It's a name filled with meaning."

"Meaning? It sounds like a chain-link fence … There's no way that's her name."

Shari couldn't help but smile. The two girls arguing over the origins of her name was actually pretty funny.

Gali shrugged. "That's not your name, right?"

"Right. Uh … so you two know each other?"

"Yeah, from camp a few years ago," Tova said. "We were bunkmates for, like, two or three years in a row."

"Two years," Gali clarified.

Not one to drop things, Tova continued her barrage of questions.

"So what's it short for, anyway? It's not Yeshara, it's not Sharsheret … Uh, is it, like, a Yiddish name or something?"

Shari sighed. "It's short for Sharona. It's an Israeli name. My parents are both Israeli."

"Sharona!" Tova gasped. "I never would've guessed! So you grew up here in Israel?"

"No," she replied. "I was actually born in Flatbush."

"Oh." Tova looked a little disappointed.

"Where are you from?" Shari inquired politely.

"Detroit ... nothing too exciting there. So you know Ivrit perfectly, I guess? It'll be amazing, Gali—she can translate for us!"

Was it Shari's imagination, or was Tova deliberately asking questions to avoid revealing any information about herself?

"Um, I don't really ... I mean, I understand it really well, but I don't speak it that much. We always talked English at home."

It was quiet in the room after that, with each of them putting away their clothing and getting themselves organized. Shari had a sinking feeling. The two of them obviously knew each other, and she was an outsider ... Gali was apparently a privileged princess. Tova seemed to be a friendly out-of-towner, and not her type either. It was going to be a very long year ....

BUT IT HADN'T BEEN a long year at all. In actuality, the year had simply flown. Gali wasn't at all the spoiled, frivolous California girl that Shari had first imagined her to be; she had a depth to her that wasn't easily observed by the casual onlooker, a loftiness and generosity of spirit that, once revealed, was hard to ignore. Furthermore, Tova was far from a clueless, bumbling type. It had become clear from the start that her intelligence level was off the charts; she was possibly the most academic student in the entire seminary. Shari's initial impression of both of them had been completely, utterly wrong.

Chanel lipstick-wearing Gali had proven herself to be a loyal, trustworthy friend, who sat by Shari's bedside with a bucket when she had a nasty bout of food poisoning in April. Tova had accompanied Shari for Shabbos to distant relatives whom she'd barely known. Not only had Tova made the visit less awkward with her presence, she'd made it a lot of fun.

And when Gali suddenly lost her grandfather in March and had to return to L.A. for two weeks, the three of them had shared a taxi to the airport, with Tova and Shari reassuring the sobbing Gali the whole way. The three of them had become inseparable throughout the entire year, so much so that everyone commented on the incredible connection that they'd forged. One of their teachers had even been inspired to give an entire lecture on the power of friendship, citing the multiple examples of special friendships in Jewish history.

They were more like family than just friends.

And now that it was time to say good-bye, the three of them felt that they couldn't bring themselves to do it.

And just as suddenly, it occurred to them that they didn't really have to.

"Wait a minute," Tova said. "Why do we have to say good-bye? We'll always be together, no matter where we are …."

"No matter what tomorrow brings," Shari agreed.

"If you guys even *think* of not coming to my wedding …," Gali sputtered, tears seeping from the corners of her eyes.

"Of course we'll come," Shari said quickly. "It's not even a question."

"All the way to L.A.?" she asked tremulously. "It's a six-hour flight from JFK, you know. And sometimes the flights are really expensive."

Tova shrugged. "I don't care if I have to *walk* there! I'm *coming*, I tell you!"

Shari nodded her head in agreement. "I really always wanted

to get married right here in Yerushalayim. I want to live here permanently—you both know that. Talk about expensive! I guess I'd understand if you guys couldn't make it, but I really wish that you could, somehow ...." Shari's voice was wistful.

"We'll be there—period," Tova said.

Gali nodded her assent.

Oddly enough, Tova hadn't mentioned any dreams for her own eventual wedding, but the others knew not to press her. She'd already hinted during the course of the year that marriage was not something she was ready to experience in the near future, and they'd let it go at that. They'd learned to tread lightly when it came to details about Tova's background, since strangely, she hadn't talked about her own family the whole year. Photos of any kind were curiously absent from the wall by her bed, and whenever the topic had come up, she'd consistently veered it to a different direction. The others had been loyal and understanding, giving her space and the freedom to choose what she wanted to share with them. They figured that whatever she was hiding, she'd tell them in her own way, in her own time. And if she chose to never disclose personal information about her family life, well, then, that was fine with them, too. Gali and Shari had never discussed it with one another either, as it was simply none of their business.

They were sisters, the three of them, since in actuality none of them had sisters of their own. Though Tova was remarkably restrained when it came to personal matters, the others knew that she was an only child. Gali had three older brothers, and Shari had, in fact, been an only child for quite some time. When she was nine years old her parents had brought home the most wonderful surprise from the hospital: two identical, adorable twin boys whom she'd loved from the beginning with an almost primal force. They were the famous Avi and Gavi, though they hadn't been given rhyming names on purpose. One was named for Shari's maternal grandfather, Avraham, and the other was named for her paternal grandfather, Gavriel. They grew to be a rambunctious pair, an endearing tag team of terror, and they were now almost ten years old. Shari had missed them this past year with an incredible intensity. Gali and Tova grew to love the twins, as well, and enjoyed hearing stories about their latest antics, just as they'd shared everything throughout the year.

And so it was on that day, the very last day of seminary, that those three remarkably mature, good friends decided then and there that they'd all be there for each other their whole lives through.

Whatever tomorrow would bring …

No matter when.

No matter what.

THREE YEARS LATER

TODAY

CHAPTER ONE

SHARI

AS SHARI ADLER SAT on the bus on the way home, the doctor's kindly voice reverberated in her mind.

Just think about something else. Trust me.

Dr. Miriam Schwartz, a specialist in the field, had repeated the line quite a few times, in fact.

Think about something else ....

There's nothing wrong with you ....

All the tests came out perfectly normal ....

Just think about something else.

It was difficult to define her reaction to the doctor's visit. On the one hand, she was overwhelmingly relieved that everything had checked out so well. Many of the tests themselves had been more than a little uncomfortable, not to mention the tortuous waiting for results. That had seemed interminably long, and there had been many nights when she simply couldn't sleep from all of the anxiety. She was understandably grateful that it was all over, but ...

But.

The results, albeit wonderful, just hadn't quelled the desperation inside her.

If everything was in perfect working order like the doctor had said, why wasn't she expecting a baby?

That had been her unasked question. She hadn't needed to verbalize it since it was etched in her face. It was then that Dr. Schwartz had reiterated the importance of not dwelling on the fact that she'd been married for nearly three years. Thirty-two months, to be exact. Thirty-two months without a pregnancy.

Trust me, sweetie. You're very young ....

"I'm twenty-two," she'd interjected.

The doctor had smiled at that.

See what I mean? You're putting too much pressure on yourself. It will happen on its own ... when you least expect it ... you'll see ....

Think about something else.

If only ...

If only it could be that simple.

How could she think of anything else? What else was there to think about?

After all, her own mother had experienced secondary infertility after she was born. It had taken nine long years until Gavi and Avi were born.

Did that mean she was destined to have similar difficulties?

The doctor certainly didn't seem to think so. She'd been poised and articulate, and confident in her belief that all was well.

If her doctor believed so, then who was she to argue?

Shari noticed with a start that it was almost her stop. She'd nearly missed it; she'd been so engrossed in her thoughts. She quickly stood up to exit the bus, and saw a familiar face outside the window. It was her husband, and he was standing near the bus stop.

Checking her watch, she saw that it was almost four o'clock. He was always in yeshiva at that hour, and she wondered why he was there to meet her. She'd already called him to tell him the results. His relief had been palpable over the phone, so it couldn't have been about the doctor's visit.

The doors opened, and she walked down the steps to the curb.

"Simcha," Shari said. "What are you doing here?"

"Waiting for you." Her husband smiled. "I have amazing news."

"Really?" She thought she'd already received good news that day; did she dare ask for more?

"Of course, nothing is better than the news you've already received," Simcha added quickly. "But this is pretty terrific news, I have to say."

"Okay, you've certainly got my curiosity going. What is it?"

They were strolling toward their apartment when Simcha said, "Let's turn left instead."

"What? Why?"

"You'll see."

She followed her husband, confused. They were walking in the opposite direction, away from their apartment. They were heading toward Rechov Paran in Ramat Eshkol.

"Where are we going?" she asked.

"You'll see" was all he would say, with a strange smile on his face.

Shari frowned. She disliked surprises.

Just what was this all about?

For a wild moment, she had the panicked thought that perhaps his mother had come to visit. She hadn't visited them even once since they were married, but she'd often intimated that she might drop in on any given moment, which had set Shari's nerves perpetually on edge.

Oh, no, she thought. *That would just about ruin what started as a very good day.*

She wanted to go back to their apartment, as tiny as it was, and just … be. She needed time to digest things, to absorb the news she'd been given. She'd been so worried that there was something very, very wrong with her. She hadn't slept in several weeks, tossing and turning all night long, positively convinced that the doctor would tell her that she'd be unable to ever have children. She wanted to call her parents, to tell them what had transpired, to unburden her heart, which felt remarkably lighter than it had in weeks. At that moment, she couldn't deal with her mother-in-law, who always had a way of dampening her spirits.

"Just tell me that she isn't here," she found herself saying.

"Who? Who's here?" Simcha asked.

"Your mother. Is she here? Did she come to visit? Is that what this is all about?"

To her relief, her husband laughed at the worried expression on her face. "No, Shari, she'd never do that to you, especially with everything you've been through these past few weeks. Just relax. She'd never just show up, unannounced. My mother is probably in her office in Manhattan, like she always is. Trust me."

They walked in companionable silence.

Trust me.

The doctor had used the very same phrase, but it wasn't all that easy to do. Still, Shari forced herself to be patient, a virtue that eluded her much of the time, and tried to enjoy the stroll.

Though it was already almost January, the weather was much warmer than usual. Stores were open and cafés were filled, and as they crossed the busy intersection, there were people everywhere. She never tired of the bustling surroundings. In fact, she sometimes had to pinch herself that she was really there, living in Yerushalayim, since it had been her dream since she was a young girl. She knew that she was so fortunate to have met her husband quickly, and from the start, he'd also talked of his dream of living in Eretz Yisrael. They'd shared that goal and had so many others in common, and she'd instantly known that she'd found her destined match.

It hadn't been all that easy, though. In the nearly three years that they'd been there, they had to move four times. Rental apartments were scarce, and each time the owners wanted their apartment back they had to move again. The apartment in which they were now living was unbearably tiny, no bigger than a storage unit. It had a makeshift bedroom in the back, with a small bathroom and kitchen. Still, there was a small window in the kitchen, which made it a bit cozier.

Before long, Simcha turned to her and, with a flourish, said, "Well, here it is."

He was pointing to a lovely apartment building, a bit older than the other buildings beside it but well-maintained, on Ma'avar Hamitleh, just to the left of Paran.

"I … I'm not sure I understand."

He pointed to the second-floor balcony. "See that apartment? It just became vacant, and here's the best part — the owner is willing to sign a two-year lease. Two years!"

Her mouth opened. "Are you serious? I've never even heard of a two-year lease these days. That's unbelievable! How did you find out about this? Are you sure it's available?"

"Not only is it available, but we have an appointment with Mr. Aaron Bergstein's assistant tomorrow to sign the lease," he said. "I told you it was amazing news."

She was incredulous. Of course, she'd heard of the famous Aaron Bergstein, an incredibly wealthy businessman who owned around half of Manhattan, and who also owned multiple rental properties in Yerushalayim. Still, she'd never dreamed of renting an apartment from him.

"Can we afford this?" she asked.

"You won't believe this, Shari ... This is such *yad Hashem*. It has two bedrooms, and it's actually only four hundred shekel more than what we're paying now ...."

That wasn't a large sum at all. It seemed too good to be true.

"Are you sure?" she asked dubiously.

"Yes, I'm sure. And I have the key." He showed it to her proudly. "Would you like a tour?"

It was surreal. She had never dreamed this could happen. Two years! Two years without having to move. The mere thought of it was such a luxury.

Didn't they say "Meshaneh makom, meshaneh mazel"? When people move their physical location, their spiritual mazel changes as well. Maybe the timing was right ... a new start, a fresh beginning ...

As they entered the building, her husband explained to her that one of his *chavrusa*s had mentioned the apartment, and he'd called Aaron Bergstein himself several days earlier to discuss it. He hadn't wanted to tell Shari anything at first, but now that they'd gotten the doctor's news, it all just fit into place.

"The earlier tenants went back to America or something," he explained. "Well, here we are."

It was on the second floor, a short walk up. The miniscule apartment in which they were now living was on the fifth floor, which was a difficult climb. This, in comparison, seemed like a breeze. The building was in better condition as well, with freshly painted hallways. It even had a fresh smell, like someone was baking bread.

They stood outside the door. It had all happened so fast that Shari felt as if she were dreaming.

Simcha turned the key in the lock.

The door opened, and Shari eagerly led the way in.

"Oh, it's beautiful," she exhaled.

And it was. It wasn't an incredibly large apartment, but it was bright, open, and airy, with a very modern, small kitchen off the living and dining area. It was spacious and clean, and they walked around as if in a daze. Compared to the apartment in which they were living, it seemed like a palace.

"This is too good to be true," she whispered.

There was a large *mirpeset* off the living room, with a lovely, tree-lined view. The bedrooms were definitely on the smaller side, but there were two of them. They walked through the whole apartment, clearly thrilled with what they saw.

And then Shari got a closer look at the kitchen, which had sparkling white quartz countertops and stainless-steel appliances. She knew she'd enjoy cooking there and hosting guests.

"I just can't believe this," she kept saying.

"It just goes to show you, Shari. Hashem is looking out for us and He knows what's best. This apartment just became available. Timing is everything—*lakol z'man v'eis.*"

Simcha's dual meaning was not lost on her. *A time for everything, and for everything a time …*

This apartment was there, right now, waiting for them.

Simcha's words echoed her thoughts. "Can you imagine two whole years without having to move? And who knows? Maybe we can even extend the lease for longer. We'll have such peace of mind … We won't have to worry about a thing …."

Shari's eyes roamed the apartment, imagining their small wooden table in the dining room and their black leather couch, which was now in storage, taking its rightful place in the living room.

It would feel like a real home.

"We'll even have room for visitors," she said, hastily adding, "Uh … like my parents, I mean. When they come here for Gavi and Avi's bar mitzvah in May."

Simcha laughed good-naturedly. He knew what she meant.

"Stop worrying," he said calmly. "My mother absolutely hates traveling alone, so she never goes anywhere."

That was true. One of the bonuses of moving to Eretz Yisrael, besides it being her lifelong dream, had been the realization that there was a very large ocean and several continents between Simcha's mother and herself.

Which was exactly how she preferred it.

"Well?" Her husband was waiting for a reply.

"I say we should go for it," she responded enthusiastically.

He nodded in satisfaction and they took one last look around. It was a truly lovely apartment and they couldn't believe their good fortune.

They left the apartment together, buoyantly talking about their exciting plans. There was so much to do—packing yet again, organizing—but this time, it wouldn't seem like such a chore. It would feel like they were going home, at long last.

Shari was naturally organized and punctilious by nature, which was necessary for her job as an accountant. She still had all of her lists from the previous moves. Everything was alphabetized; she had it all down to practically a science.

What a relief it was to know that they would finally be *settled*. The apartment would be theirs, and all would be well.

As they arrived outside in the sunshine, Shari turned back to look at the building one last time. The apartment loomed over them in the afternoon sun.

"That's funny," she muttered.

"Huh?"

"Oh, it's nothing ... I just thought I saw someone staring at us from that window over there." She pointed.

Her husband looked up. There was an open window in the apartment next to the one they had just seen, and a filmy curtain was floating in the breeze.

"Nah ... it's just a curtain," he said, as they quickly made their way down the street. "It's been a long day, Shari."

It *had* been a long day, filled with twists and turns of every possible sort. Things were looking up, indeed, and she felt so grateful.

Still, Shari couldn't shake the strangest notion that there was someone behind the swaying curtain, watching her. It was as if she could feel someone's eyes boring into her back, but surely, that just wasn't possible.

There was no one there.

But she kept glancing back, all the way down the street, until the apartment was out of her view.

IT WAS THREE WEEKS later.

After a restless night spent tossing and turning, Shari drifted into a deep sleep toward dawn. She'd had a peculiar dream, unlike any she'd had before, not that she was much of a dreamer. In the dream, she found herself standing on a long, dusty road ....

She was completely alone. There was no one around, just a long, winding, impossibly dusty road before her. There were no cars or people of any kind. Why she was there was a mystery, but she accepted this with equanimity as she walked slowly down the road. As she walked, the sky above her seemed to grow dark and foreboding. It appeared as if a storm was rapidly approaching. Looking up, she noticed a squall of black birds circling above her head. Fearful, she began to run. At that moment, an enormous, evil-looking black bird swooped down and pursued her, flapping its massive wings, its talons almost reaching her ....

She awoke with a gasp, her heart beating wildly. Glancing at her watch, she saw that it was almost seven o'clock in the morning.

The black bird had almost had her in its clutches ....

It had seemed so terrifyingly real ....

Though the dream had started to recede somewhat, it still seemed so vivid and frightening that she found herself looking around the tiny bedroom, trying to calm herself. There were no black birds anywhere, real or imagined. There were just masses of boxes everywhere, nearly floor to ceiling. She was wide awake now, with the horrifying dream already fading. There was no time to think of it now since there was so much to do.

It was moving day.

Simcha had noiselessly left the room to go to Shacharis, but she wanted to be prepared when he came back. Rising quickly, she made a pot of coffee, which she knew he'd appreciate. He'd been up half the night as well, packing all of the last-minute items.

Shari was extremely proud of the detailed lists she'd made, along with the color-coded labels on the boxes that were alphabetized for easy future reference. This move had been the easiest so far. She'd done her job well. Now it was up to the movers to do their job, and she knew she had little control over the outcome. The company Simcha had hired was reputable and honest, so she hoped everything would go smoothly.

She was standing in the cramped kitchen, in her faded robe and snood, when there was a loud knock at the door. She wondered if Simcha had forgotten his key.

Making her way toward the front door wasn't all that easy, since she had to navigate through towers of boxes and leftover piles of newspapers that they'd used to wrap the more fragile items. She opened the door, saying, "Simcha, did you forget your—"

The words died on her lips.

All coherent thought vanished.

She just stood there, stupidly, staring ....

"Well, aren't you going to invite me in?" her mother-in-law demanded.

"Of course," she answered weakly. "Please come in."

Eva Adler walked into the crowded apartment with a general air of disdain. Though she was as thin as ever, with a black *sheitel* cut in a severe bob and the latest, fashionable clothing, her prying eyes and cutting remarks had always made her thoroughly unattractive in Shari's eyes.

"This place is a mess," she muttered. "It looks like you've never even unpacked, and you've been here for months, haven't you?"

"Uh, we're actually moving today. To a bigger apartment. Didn't Simcha tell you?"

Her mother-in-law glared at her.

"No, he didn't, as a matter of fact," she bristled. "And how much is this going to cost?"

"Well, I—"

"Not that it's my business how he uses his trust fund money, of course, but what's wrong with *this* apartment?"

"Well, it's very small—"

"So? So what? It's only the two of you," his mother continued, with a pointed look at Shari's stomach.

Shari swallowed. The awful nightmare that she'd had just an hour before had inexplicably come true. With her small, beady eyes and pointed nose, Eva Adler truly was like the threatening black crow of her dream, swooping down to devour her prey.

"Far be it from me to tell him how to spend his money," she said. "He's an adult now. If he wants to make mistakes, there's nothing I can do to stop him."

Ouch. What was she saying?

Was she trying to convey that Simcha's marriage to her had been a mistake, too? It was obvious that she'd thought that from the start.

Shari said nothing, though she inwardly burned with resentment. *If only Simcha could witness this exchange, then maybe he'd understand ....*

She could never truly explain her complex feelings to Simcha, in any case. This woman was his mother, after all. And she had a tendency to be on her best behavior around him, her only child.

"Have pity on her, Shari," he would say. "She's had a difficult life, losing her husband at a young age, building up the real estate business ... It hasn't been easy for her, believe me."

At the very beginning of their marriage, Shari had tried hard to give Eva Adler the benefit of the doubt. It was true that her mother-in-law had been dealt a heavy blow with the passing of her husband, and she'd raised a young son while building up a very successful business.

Shari had told herself numerous times that Simcha's mother had a hard, cynical edge because life had been cruel to her, and she'd had to forge a tough outer layer in order to survive. In all probability, she was an insecure soul, and her denigrations made her feel all the more powerful. Shari's rational side understood this very well. Still, her softer, more vulnerable side couldn't deal with Eva's overly critical nature.

And the questions ... The hundreds of prying, detailed questions that set Shari's heart racing and her teeth on edge.

"Where are you planning to stay?" she asked aloud, as politely as she could.

"Well, I was hoping to stay here, but I see that's impossible," she answered in an irritated fashion. "I guess I'll have to stay at a hotel."

You never told us you were coming, Shari thought. *It's your own fault, lady.*

At that moment, Simcha bounded up the stairs and through the front door, which was still ajar. He was her savior, her knight in shining armor ... Shari had never been happier to see him.

He stood there, utterly confused.

"Ma? What are you doing here?"

Eva glared at her son.

"You call that a welcome?" Her voice rose. "I flew halfway

across the world to come and visit you. I was at the airport at five this morning, I'm totally exhausted, and all you can say is, 'What are you doing here?'"

"Sorry, I guess I'm just a little—"

"Surprised? Well, I am, too. You never told me you're moving again," she said accusingly.

"Yes, we—"

"Why do you people feel like you have to move every few months?"

You people.

Ugh.

"What a waste of money! It doesn't grow on trees, you know. You have to save for the future ... maybe you'll actually have kids some day."

She looked again at Shari, who wanted to shrink into the floor—anything to get away from her mother-in-law's small, razor-sharp eyes. Although Eva was a businesswoman, she was a consummate prosecutor who had looked deep into her daughter-in-law's soul and found her guilty. Guilty of what, she didn't know.

What had been her crime? What was her exact transgression? What had she ever done to make Simcha's mother hate her so? All she'd done was marry her son—was that so terrible? They were very happy together. Didn't she see that? Why couldn't she be happy for them?

A new, disturbing thought came to her. She wondered why she'd never thought of it before. Of course, that was it.

She was jealous.

She was jealous of the happiness they'd found together.

"Well, Simcha, aren't you going to offer me something to eat or drink?" she demanded. "Shari hasn't offered me a crumb since I got here."

"Which was what, five minutes ago?" he retorted. "You still have your coat on."

Shari looked gratefully at her husband.

Perhaps he understood things, after all ....

"I have a pot of coffee on," Shari offered.

"I never drink that awful stuff," Eva answered. "Poisonous ... It's what killed your father, Simcha."

"Coffee?" he said incredulously.

"Oh, he was addicted to it, absolutely. All that caffeine—it's just not healthy at all."

"He was killed by a drunk driver, Ma. What does that have to do with coffee?" Simcha shook his head.

"With all that caffeine in his system, his injuries were just too much for his body to handle. Maybe he'd have pulled through if he hadn't had ten cups of coffee in him."

The rationale was so outrageous that Simcha fell silent. Over the years, Eva had blamed her husband's death on such a variety of things that he'd lost count. He'd heard tales of bad weather, traffic, terrible driving conditions—everything except where the blame really lay—with the drunk driver who himself had been killed instantly.

Still, coffee was a new one.

"Sorry, Ma," Simcha said, "but there really isn't much to eat. Everything is packed."

"I could make you a cup of tea," Shari offered.

"Tea? Again, caffeine! Is caffeine all you people drink around here?"

You people, again.

"What about some good, old-fashioned orange juice?" Eva demanded.

Shari and Simcha looked at each other.

"You know, for vitamin C," Eva added.

"We don't have any juice, Ma," Simcha said weakly. "You sort of came at an awkward time ... Why didn't you tell us you were coming?"

"Since when do I have to tell my own son that I'm planning to visit? I should be welcome any time of day or night, am I right?"

"Of course, you're welcome to—"

"No, I'm not," she retorted. "You should have seen the look on this girl's face when she opened the door! She looked like she saw a ghost!"

I'm still in the room, Shari wanted to say. *I'm standing right here ... Stop talking about me like I'm not even present.*

Simcha looked at his mother with something akin to anger in his eyes. Her husband, the most mild-mannered person Shari had ever known, actually appeared to be ... *angry.*

"Ma, Shari has been up half the night. Actually, she hasn't had a decent night's sleep in weeks—"

"If she wouldn't insist on moving every three minutes, you wouldn't be in this mess," Eva said coolly. "Your father would roll over in his grave ...."

"What are you talking about? This move was entirely my idea."

"But why? I just don't understand, Simcha."

"Ma, what is there to understand? This apartment is no bigger than a shoebox, and besides, our lease is up soon. This new apartment has a two-year lease and is much bigger, and not that much more expensive. Aaron Bergstein owns it, as a matter of fact."

"The famous Aaron Bergstein?"

"Yes, he actually owns the whole building. It just makes sense for us."

"Oh, whatever ... suit yourself," she said as she began to remove her fur jacket. "I told your wife that you're an adult and you can make your own mistakes."

Simcha said nothing, but a muscle tensed in his jaw and his eyes flashed with resentment.

Just then, his cell phone rang. Reaching into his pocket, he answered it.

"Hello?"

Shari could tell from his side of the conversation that it was the moving company, and that they were on their way.

"I'd better get dressed," Shari said self-consciously, wanting to slip away to the privacy of her room. Anything to escape ...

"It's already almost eight o'clock—better late than never," Eva remarked.

Simcha ended his phone call and looked at his mother.

"So what's this all about?" he asked. "Why are you here? I mean, really."

"Can't a mother just pop in to visit her son?" she asked innocently.

"You haven't done it in the three years that we've been married," he answered. "You hate traveling alone ... I think that something's going on. What is it?"

She was quiet for once.

"Actually—" She cleared her throat. "— I wasn't alone. There were several people I knew on the flight, but you're right. There's a little teensy-weensy something I'd like to discuss with you."

"Which is … ?"

"Well, I wanted to tell you in person," she continued vaguely.

"Okay, Ma, now you're here."

"Yes, I'm here, and I just cannot believe that you're moving again—"

He held up his hand. "Ma, please. The moving truck will be here very soon, so maybe you should just say whatever it is you came to say."

Simcha was in a touchy, combative mood. He was exhausted, and he didn't appreciate the disparaging tone his mother had used with his wife. Really, after everything Shari had been through, she just didn't deserve this tirade.

There were so many riotous thoughts churning inside his mind that he was thoroughly unprepared for what his mother said next.

"Simcha … actually, I'm thinking of getting married …."

CHAPTER TWO

TOVA

TOVA TIPTOED INTO THE apartment and locked the door behind her. The overhead lights were off, with only the dim light over the oven illuminating the small kitchen. She wearily sat down on a chair in the living room and massaged the back of her neck, which was knotted and uncomfortable.

As a matter of fact, her whole life seemed knotted and uncomfortable, and it had been that way ever since she could remember. She usually prided herself on being a strong, resilient individual, but after tonight, her resolve was beginning to wane.

She just couldn't do this anymore.

She found herself looking around the darkened living room. An ornate grandfather clock stood majestically in the corner, and the patterned afghan on the couch was comfortably worn. She tried to keep her thoughts on specific, mundane details. Anything to distract her from truly *thinking* …

This was getting ridiculous.

It was no use. She couldn't sit on the couch forever. She checked her watch. It was only ten minutes to eleven, but her grandmother had obviously gone to bed hours earlier. She was debating whether or not she should call the *shadchan* when her cell phone rang.

So soon …

Her heart sinking, she answered.

"Hello?"

The *shadchan*, Faigy Davis, was a sweet, inexperienced young woman who was, in all probability, not much older than Tova herself. She also happened to be the daughter-in-law of Tova's boss, Dan Davis, who was a senior partner at the accounting firm in which she worked.

Tova knew what Faigy would say before she actually heard her utter the words. Still, the familiar pit of dread that was ever present in her chest threatened to overwhelm her as she heard the apologetic note in her voice. "He said he really admires you, with all you've been through and everything, but he just doesn't think it'll work …."

"I understand," Tova replied, in what she hoped sounded like a positive, upbeat tone of voice.

"I really hope you're okay," Faigy said tremulously. "This never happened to me before. It started out so great and everything, but I'm sort of new at this, and I'd hate for you to be upset …."

"No, not at all," Tova lied. "Besides, it's not your fault. I really do appreciate that you took the time to think about me, and everything …."

"Don't worry, we'll keep thinking!" Faigy said, sounding genuinely relieved.

"Thank you so much. I really do appreciate—"

But she'd already hung up.

Tova looked at the cell phone in her hand and felt the familiar hot tears well up in her eyes.

It's no use crying, Tova thought.

The amount of tears she'd shed over the years was simply unimaginable, and if anything, her circumstances had gotten only more difficult with each passing year. She sighed, and reached for the well-worn *Tehillim* that was in her purse.

Tehillim was her lifeline. *Tehillim* was her therapy. She knew the entire *sefer* by heart, and as she murmured the words soundlessly, her inner turmoil quieted somewhat. The heaviness in her heart seemed to lift slightly. Each time she uttered the holy words, she felt Hashem's presence hovering over her, which calmed her very soul.

She would never forget the day the nightmare had started. It had never been easy, of course, but she remembered the exact day that events had spiraled out of control.

It had been just the two of them, her and her mother, after her parents had divorced when she was around four years old. At first, her father had done his best to be a solid presence in her life, knowing that her mother was, unfortunately, an unstable individual. But a few years later, he'd remarried, and the distance between father and daughter had grown—first figuratively, and then literally, when he and his new wife settled in Chicago. The reality was simply that he had a new life, with a new wife and children, and whenever Tova visited for a Shabbos or Yom Tov, though they did their best to accommodate her, she felt awkward and out of place. Strangely enough, at those times she actually preferred her solitary existence with her mother, even though there were times when her mother would fall into a depression and take to her bed for days on end. Tova would turn into her mother's caregiver, making meals and running errands for her.

Tova had always felt a measure of pity for her mother, who

was also an only child, born to elderly parents who were Holocaust survivors. Her grandfather, who'd been much older than her grandmother, passed away when her mother was a mere teenager. Tova had been named for him, since his name had been Tuvia. Her mother had cared for her own mother for several years, and Tova had often wondered about the toll it had taken on her, and whether her mother's upbringing had anything to do with her declining mental health ....

Miraculously, none of her friends had known about any of this. She was a popular, integral part of many extracurricular activities at school. She'd even been the head of the school production. Her teachers also hadn't realized that anything was amiss, since she was an outstanding student. The only thing that was a bit peculiar was that Tova never invited anyone over, making excuses, but her friends had accepted this with equanimity and invited her over to their houses instead. Her life up to that point had not been easy, but it did have a certain consistent rhythm, with her going to school and taking care of the house, even paying the bills and taking care of the finances. When her mother felt well, she managed to work from home doing medical billing, which covered most of their expenses. When bills came that Tova knew they couldn't afford, she'd call her father, who quietly covered the cost. So life had worked somehow, for the two of them, albeit in an unusual way.

Until that fateful day.

The day had actually started out like any other. She'd been sixteen years old, and her carpool had dropped her off after school in front of her small house in Oak Park. She had let herself in with her key, knowing that her mother usually napped during the late afternoons. Her mother had never been a tidy person, but the scene that awaited her had been something out of a horror film. The sofa cushions were overturned, all of the drawers in the kitchen were opened with the contents spilling out, food from the refrigerator was on the floor, and the door to the fridge was ajar. For one wild, terrifying moment, Tova thought that their house had been burglarized and ransacked … *and where was her mother?* Panic seized her as she searched frantically, running from room to room, only to discover her mother in the bedroom, on the floor, underneath an overturned mattress, looking disheveled and muttering to herself.

"Mommy?" she said, tentatively inching closer. "Is everything okay? What happened here?"

Her mother looked at her without really seeing her and kept muttering, "Can't find him … can't find him … tried to find him, but can't find him …"

Tova looked at her mother with a mixture of pity and fear. She'd always been a bit unbalanced, but this was a different, frightening realm that Tova had never before experienced.

"Who are you looking for, Mommy?" Tova tried to keep her voice level, though she was terrified. She knew in her heart that something was terribly wrong, that life as she'd known it was forever altered, never to be the same again.

"My husband," her mother babbled. "I can't find my husband … looked everywhere … can't find him, can't find him …"

Tova stared at her, hot dread rising. As young, naive, and inexperienced as she was, she knew in her innermost heart that her mother had suffered some sort of severe mental breakdown.

She'd wondered all along if it would ever come to this, since her mother had been teetering precariously close to the edge for so long. It seemed like the day she'd been secretly dreading had finally come.

Details after that were a bit blurry, but she recalled Hatzalah members speaking in soothing tones to her mother as they gingerly placed her on a stretcher and took her away ....

Because of her age and the grave state of affairs, Tova hadn't been allowed to visit her mother during those first few days. One of the Hatzalah members had acted as a liaison between the doctors and herself, explaining to her that they were trying a combination of medication and therapy. At first, he seemed hopeful when he gave Tova daily reports. As the weeks wore on, however, he gently informed Tova that her mother's prognosis looked bleak, indeed. She'd suffered such a serious setback, he wasn't sure if she'd ever recover enough to be able to live independently.

In her naïveté, Tova had said, "But she doesn't live independently, she lives here with me." He'd just shaken his head and looked at her sadly. "I'm sorry to tell you this, Tova, but there's no way she'd be allowed to live here, in your care. She needs real full-time care, and you're only a minor. The state wouldn't let it happen, even if she could manage on her own, which she can't."

Tova had gone to live with her grandmother after that—her father's mother, who tried her best to fill the void in Tova's world. However, she was quite elderly and had her own health issues to contend with. She was set in her ways, preferring a quiet environment. She went to sleep at nine each night and Tova tiptoed about, trying not to disturb her.

Those days had been tense and difficult, and it had been a huge relief for both of them when she'd gone to seminary.

That had been the best year of Tova's existence. Her roommates had, simply put, been gifts from Heaven. Shari and Gali had become closer to her than the imaginary sisters she'd tried to conjure as a child, yet that year she did not disclose her burdensome secret, even to them. Shari and Gali were so normal, their lives at that point had been untouched by crises. Surely they would've treated her differently had they known, and she didn't want to be the object of anyone's pity. It had been such a relief the whole year to act like every other normal girl, seemingly without a care in the world. She often thought that she was a combination of two people: the extroverted, outgoing Tova, who was blessed with an engaging personality and vitality—and most importantly, a life like everyone else. And then there was the inner Tova, whose sadness was a crushing weight on her heart, as she carried a terrible burden that no one knew ....

But that was three years ago. Tova had to face her dismal reality and readjust to her lonely existence as soon as she stepped off the plane. Since then, she'd shared more of her background with Shari and Gali in phone conversations—it was easier to do on the phone than face to face. They'd been wonderfully understanding and supportive, but they couldn't begin to fathom what her daily life was like, and Tova was careful to avoid painful details. Though her grandmother's health had thankfully remained status quo, the elderly woman was unusually fearful and went to doctors on a regular basis. On average, she frequented the gastroenterologist every two months, the podiatrist every six months, and the cardiologist every three months. That was not including the numerous visits to her general practitioner, and biweekly trips to the physical therapist for the nagging pain in her hip. Tova dutifully drove her to nearly every appointment, studying for her CPA exams while endlessly waiting in doctors' offices. That had been her routine: studying, driving, errand-running, caregiving ... followed by more studying, driving, errand-running, and caregiving.

There were four parts to the grueling CPA exams, each of them seemingly more difficult than the previous one. The first exam she'd taken was BEC, followed by Regulations. She'd passed those two on the first try, which was a feat that most couldn't even attempt. Later, she'd taken FAR and Audit, and her score had been unusually high on each of those as well. Passing all four parts in rapid succession was a tremendous achievement, and it hadn't gone by unnoticed. Dan Davis, a respected *askan* in the community, who also happened to be a senior partner and manager of a large accounting firm, had offered her a job, which she'd accepted. The pay was phenomenal, but the hours were long and arduous, and kept her very busy.

Tova hadn't had a moment to think about herself or her future life during those first few years after seminary. It wasn't such a bad thing, since as the weeks turned into months, and the months turned into years, it had become clear that her mother would never fully recover. It was painfully obvious that she'd have to stay in the group home in which she'd been placed, possibly forever.

Each Friday, Tova visited her, bringing with her two small loaves of homemade challah for Shabbos. Her mother barely spoke, and when she did, her words were garbled and incoherent, but Tova would sit and chatter about the latest tests she'd taken, her course load, and her grandmother's latest medical results. There were times when her mother seemed to listen. It wasn't clear how much she understood, yet Tova still found it reassuring to fill her mother in on the details of her life.

The last several months, though, had undoubtedly been the most challenging for Tova. The world of *shidduchim* was daunting enough, even to a girl who had no external issues. Tova, on the other hand, had devastating issues, and all of them were through no fault of her own. The facts were stark and plain: her parents were divorced, her mother had a seemingly incurable mental illness, and no one was interested in meeting her. Although she had sterling qualities and a brilliant mind, her dismal predicament seemed unbearable, with no end in sight.

She was twenty-two and had never gone out on a date—until just a few weeks earlier.

Dan Davis's daughter-in-law had graciously thought of an idea for her—a cousin of hers, Avi Koenig. He had lost his father at a young age, his mother had remarried, and he'd had hurdles of his own to overcome. Miraculously, he had given her a yes, and for once things had started looking up for Tova. She had liked him from the very beginning. He was kind and mature, an excellent learner with a sharp mind, and he attended law school in the evenings. From the start, they'd shared a friendly rapport, and Tova had felt that this could truly lead to something wonderful.

But she knew what she had to do. On the fourth date, as her *rav* had directed, she was obligated to share with him the painful details of her mother's condition.

So she did.

He'd asked many questions, trying to clarify where things stood. She wasn't in the habit of discussing such personal matters, and she'd grown more and more uncomfortable. After that, the conversation had been stilted and awkward, and things hadn't been the same between them. To make matters worse, Tova had a sneaking suspicion, though she'd never know for sure, that his mother had been pressuring him to end things with her. And that very evening, which had been their sixth date, that's exactly what he did.

She could hardly blame him for wanting to run. There were days when she wanted nothing more than to run, run … and never stop. She wanted to run away from her own life, she wanted to wake up one morning living a completely different life, with a different identity … with all of her problems solved.

But the rational side of Tova knew that even with a different identity, she'd have problems. And she would want to run away from those, as well …

Running wasn't the answer, she knew. She further knew that one day, she'd no longer have the urge to run … one glorious day when she'd be settled, and no longer alone. Just when that day would magically appear remained a mystery, and the uncertainty of it all seemed a bit much for her to bear.

It was well after midnight, and it was cold in the room.

Was it the cold January weather, or was it a different coldness that had settled inside her heart? Tova snuggled into the afghan's warmth, and still clutching the *Tehillim* in her hand, she fell into an exhausted sleep, right there on the well-worn couch in the living room.

She was walking through a long hallway … high ceiling, very ornate walls, with marble flooring and gold leaves everywhere … Tova kept walking … walking … She appeared to be in a palace … Her footsteps echoed on the polished floors … very beautiful, very grand … there was no one about … she kept walking ….

Suddenly, there was a man … an old man, very old, with a white beard, yet he seemed spry and his movements seemed young … He was smiling … he looked familiar ….

She looked at him closely.

His eyes were her own.

"Are you … my grandfather?" she asked tremulously, instinctively knowing that he was her mother's father, Tuvia.

He nodded, smiling.

He looked so peaceful … his face radiated such light … he looked so happy … Tova knew that all would be well … He was surely there to tell her that all would be well ….

She felt at peace … They were walking, she knew not where, but she was content to walk along with her namesake ….

When she was younger, her mother had often told her about her grandfather, saying that he was a tzaddik who had lived his life without complaints, although it had been fraught with hardships.

"Where is this place?" she asked as they walked together.

Soundlessly, he gestured toward the Tehillim she still clutched in her hand.

"Where do you think?" he said gently. His voice was both gentle and deep, with no discernible accent, confident but without a trace of arrogance ….

She thought before answering, but she knew in her innermost heart exactly where she was ….

"In David Hamelech's palace? Is that where we are?"

"Of course, my sweet girl, you are correct. You are in the palace of the king, and most people don't merit ever seeing it. But you, Tova, have a special zechus. Your devotion to Tehillim … your emunah … don't think it has gone unnoticed. Everything is noticed. Everything …"

Tova's eyes filled with tears.

"Will Mommy ever recover?"

"You're a special girl, my dear one, to ask about someone else before yourself. However, this is a secret that cannot be revealed …."

Suddenly, they were in a large room. It appeared to be a library, with floor-to-ceiling gold bookshelves, filled with sefarim of every kind.

Her grandfather sat behind a large mahogany desk.

She sat down as well on a gilt-edged chair.

"I have so many questions, Zeidy …."

"You can ask me your questions, but I'm afraid there will be few that I can answer. There are secrets, secrets that aren't allowed to be revealed …."

"Have you learned all of those sefarim, Zeidy?" she asked, motioning toward the endless bookshelves. "Is that how you know so much?"

Her grandfather smiled and nodded.

"But there is always more to learn," he murmured. "There is always more to know."

"Zeidy, the boy I was going out with said 'no.' I thought we would get married …."

"You will, my sweet girl. Just not to him."

When he said that, with such kindness in his shining eyes, she felt a measure of peace that had alluded her, perhaps her entire life.

She would get married. She'd just been given the assurance that she would.

"Really, Zeidy?"

He nodded and smiled.

"When will it be my turn, Zeidy? When?"

"These are secrets I cannot tell you, my dear one. Just know that all is good. You do believe that, don't you? I wouldn't be here if you didn't …."

Though his words seemed cryptic, she understood what he was saying. Through it all, her emunah had not wavered, and that was why she was fortunate enough to talk to him, the grandfather she'd never known in life but with whom she shared a kindred bond, having been named for him.

"Yes, of course I believe it's all for the good. It's just so hard sometimes ...."

"I know it's hard, and although you cannot get married now, it's all part of a plan ...."

"But I'm all alone," she cried.

He shook his head kindly. "That is untrue, dear Tova'le. You must know that you are never alone. In fact, you're being watched over very, very carefully."

"Then why can't I get married now?" she persisted.

He shrugged his shoulders and smiled at her.

"In the World of Truth, it's really very simple. It's only down in your transient world that it seems complicated."

Tova was quiet for several moments before responding softly, "But Zeidy, that's the world I'm in right now. I just don't understand why I can't get married at this point in my life."

Her grandfather again nodded and smiled with a serenity that quelled her nagging fears.

"Let's just say that as of this moment, he's married to someone else ...."

She awoke with a start, her heart pounding wildly. Sunlight streamed in through the balcony doors into the living room. She could hardly believe that she'd slept on the couch, in the same position, the entire night.

But it no longer mattered to her. The only thing that mattered was that she'd been granted the privilege of seeing her saintly grandfather, who had assured her that one day she would marry. One day, all would be well ....

The night before, her spirits had been crushed, her world confusing and hopeless. Everything had seemed so impossibly bleak.

The end of her hopes, the end of her dreams.

But then she'd had the best dream of all, which had reawakened her hopes for a happy and fulfilling future destiny. This morning, she felt a lightness, a buoyancy of spirit that she had never before experienced.

Tova didn't know why she'd been granted this tantalizing glimpse into realms never before imagined, but she had—and it had been so amazingly, comfortingly real. She wanted to remember every detail of the dream, since parts of it were already beginning to fade, but there was one large, glaring element that she didn't think she'd ever forget.

Her future husband was currently married to someone else.

What did it all mean?

CHAPTER THREE

GALI

"GALI!"

Everyone was calling her name, hugging her. The house was brimming with people. All Gali wanted was to sneak away with her *chassan*, to get away from all the well-wishers with their curious, prying eyes. She lifted her head for a glimpse of her *chassan*, but he was swarmed by his friends in the living room. He seemed to be enjoying himself.

Her mother knew how to throw a party, that was for sure. She'd hired the famous Mindy Weiss of Beverly Hills to design the affair. Their house was the perfect venue for it, since it was a stately stone mansion that took up almost an entire city block in the heart of tony Hancock Park. Mindy had put lanterns with candles on either side of the graceful flagstone steps leading up the loggia to the front door. The high-ceilinged rooms were draped in sheer white fabric, and there were enormous orchids in large marble vases everywhere. Waiters in white gloves walked around with hors d'oeuvres on silver trays, and everyone seemed to be enjoying themselves immensely.

Everyone except Gali, that is.

Though she enjoyed the finer things in life and didn't consider herself to be a low-maintenance type of girl, she'd secretly wanted a small, intimate affair—not this lavish, city-wide extravaganza. It was almost like a mini wedding, and in Gali's mind, it took away from the Big Day. But she knew better than to voice her opinion to her mother, who'd been planning this event for years, ever since she'd laid eyes on Yigal Ben Ezri when Gali was sixteen years old and decided that he would be the perfect husband for her daughter.

Gali had to admit to herself that her mother had been so right about that. It was just so obvious—she'd known from their first date that he was the one for her. Even though he was six years older than her and had just completed his residency at Cedars-Sinai, there was an easy comfort between them that they'd enjoyed from the very start. He was stable, grounded, and mature, and that had further appealed to her. He seemed so familiar, as if she'd known him all her life. In all truth, he lived on the next block over, and she'd known of the prestigious Ben Ezri family for years, since Yigal's parents had built the large, imposing shul in the area and her parents had donated a wing to that very same shul.

It was a perfect fit.

They would make a great team, Gali knew, with their home open to all.

Dr. and Mrs. Yigal Ben Ezri.

How she liked the sound of it.

She remembered how when she was nineteen and recently returned from seminary, her mother's hopes had been crushed when Yigal's engagement was announced to a girl from the Nes Or family in New York, a very well-known, prestigious Sephardic family. Gali hadn't been upset at all. She'd shrugged it off at the time, figuring that he just wasn't destined to be her soulmate. But a few short months later, news of his broken engagement spread like wildfire across the L.A. neighborhood that they both shared. Different smatterings of stories had been strewn about, but no one really knew what had happened, since the Ben Ezris hadn't said a word about it.

In Gali's opinion, they'd shown class and taken the high road.

As far as she knew, he'd been busy with his schooling and hadn't dated much since. But when her neighbor recently suggested the match to her parents, her father had looked into his broken engagement. To his credit, her father didn't divulge too much to Gali, saying only that his findings had revealed that there were undisclosed issues with the Nes Or girl, and that Yigal had been correct to end things. Never one to gossip and being disdainful of idle chatter, Gali hadn't asked too many questions. She knew that Yigal had appreciated this while they were dating, as he didn't enjoy dwelling on that painful period of his life.

In any case, it no longer mattered. They were starting fresh, her and Yigal.

Together.

It had been a whirlwind courtship, with her *chassan* seemingly at times a bit distant, but only because he was immersed in the dizzying vortex of medical school. She was so proud that at twenty-eight, he was a doctor, and an accomplished one at that. He was such an integral part of the close-knit Sephardic community to which she belonged as well, which was so important to her. They shared the same customs and had similar backgrounds.

And the icing on top of the cake was that it didn't bother him in the least that she hadn't yet finished her degree and had, in fact, gone a rather unconventional route in terms of a career.

Like Tova and Shari, Gali had been in school for a while. But while the others were studying for their CPA exams, Gali was studying to be a speech therapist. Then one day, she'd decided it was futile. She didn't really want to be a speech therapist. In fact, she'd suddenly decided that she hated everything having to do with speech therapy.

She'd cheered on Shari and Tova as they both passed their CPA exams, but deep down, she always knew what she wanted to do and it had nothing at all to do with speech therapy. And so one day she walked into the kitchen of her spacious home and, in a sense, never left. She'd been a remarkable chef ever since she was a young girl, and she began to create recipes that others would never have dreamed to attempt.

And just like that, word got around. Gali was hired as a private chef for birthday parties and anniversary dinners, even though she didn't have a true culinary background. Though she'd kept her burgeoning catering business small, her popular food blog had enjoyed an unusual meteoric rise in the blogosphere, with over twenty thousand followers. What had followed were food demonstrations at schools, speaking engagements and charity events, and even a cookbook in the works.

She was Chef Gali.

And she was pretty famous—practically a household name.

She loved what she did since it was varied, and always new and interesting. And her hours were flexible. One day, she wanted to stay home with her children, and Yigal would provide for his family. They'd both agreed on this and Gali was the happiest that she'd ever been. It had taken three years of searching, but Yigal had been the one all along—right there on the next street.

Everyone at the *vort* was exclaiming how the *shidduch* was perfect. Gali and Yigal just seemed so right together. Even their names seemed to mirror one another's ....

Gali and Yigal.

The actual proposal that night had been surreal. It had been special, sincere, and private, just between the two of them. And that's what truly mattered. Later, the house had filled with people, and the extravagance had been unmatched. Everyone there knew that this would be the wedding of the century, with no expense spared. It was a sensational fete, with people she didn't even know *ooh*ing and *aah*ing and showering *brachos* that to Gali sounded a bit hollow. Really, all she wanted was to find a private space to be with her *chassan*, and later, when the party was over, she'd call Shari and Tova.

"Gali! Come here!"

It was her mother, looking triumphant, dressed in a Prada gown. "We're taking pictures!"

Gali obediently followed her mother to where the photographer stood in the two-story foyer, taking pictures with her parents and her older brothers with their wives and kids, followed by her soon-to-be in-laws.

Gali was also wearing couture, of course, a frothy Valentino creation that her mother had flown in from Milan. It was somewhere between a pale pink and a shimmery silver, and it swirled around her ankles. She knew she had never looked better, but on the other hand, she'd never before worn a dress with a price tag of $7,000. She had always wanted her wedding dress to be the most sensational creation, and she had no idea how she would ever be able to top this. She couldn't help but feel that the entire evening was a colossal waste of time and money.

But before long, the photographer led her to where her *chassan* was standing. And there was Yigal, so tall and handsome, his face wreathed in smiles when he saw her.

She felt like a queen.

Maybe the whole affair wasn't a waste of time and money, after all.

"*Chassan*, what do I have to do to get you to smile?" the photographer joked.

Gali looked over at Yigal.

The smile on his face came from his very soul. The two of them stood there as the photographer took pictures, their happiness coming from a place that was as bright as the sun.

With Yigal beside her, Gali felt herself begin to relax a bit. Before long, she, too, began to enjoy herself ....

LATER THAT NIGHT, AROUND midnight, Gali called Shari, knowing it was around ten o'clock in the morning in Yerushalayim.

The screaming that ensued could probably have been heard across the ocean, though Shari had known that Gali was on the verge of becoming engaged for weeks already.

"I'm coming in for the wedding!"

"Of course you are."

"Did you call Tova?"

"I'm going to call her as soon as I hang up with you."

"So I'm hanging up right now so you can call her!"

Gali laughed.

"When's the wedding?"

"Oh, probably in June, I guess. Yigal will have some time off then, after the boards."

"I'm going to be there," Shari reiterated.

She apologized that she needed to hang up, but she had to prepare lunch for her mother-in-law, who was visiting. Gali felt a twang of pity for her, for though she'd never said anything, Gali had sensed that there was tension between the two.

Gali then called Tova, figuring that even though it was after three o'clock in the morning in Detroit, she'd want to be called.

A groggy Tova answered the phone.

"Hello?" she whispered.

"Sorry for waking you up, Tovs, but I have something to tell you."

Instantly awake, Tova blurted, "You're *engaged*?"

"Yes!"

Tova screeched, "To Yigal What's-his-name?"

"Yes!"

"The doctor?"

"Yes!"

"You mean the one who your mother predicted you'll get married to one day, but then he got engaged but then he broke it off, and now you're engaged to him?"

Gali giggled. "Yes!"

"Are you only capable of giving one word answers?"

"Yes!"

And the phone call went on like that for much of the night ...

THE NEXT MORNING, YIGAL was on his way to the hospital. He was on the freeway, and traffic had slowed to a standstill. Nothing was moving in either direction. Traffic in L.A. was always bad, but that day it was much worse than usual. He checked his phone, and sure enough, there appeared to be a messy car accident involving a tanker truck. The lanes would be closed for a while. Ordinarily, he would've been upset, but he was in too good a mood to care. He was in such a grateful frame of mind, it didn't bother him in the least.

Gali was the right girl for him, there was no question about that. The absolute certainty gave him a measure of comfort that he had never before experienced, and it was a relief to feel such calm after weathering such an awful storm.

He'd told Gali very little about his first engagement, not wanting to go into detail about once weighty issues that no longer mattered. And to her credit, she had a maturity and depth to her. She hadn't pried, knowing that he wasn't the reason for the breakup. Sure, the split had been his doing, as he'd told her, but the reasons behind it had been inevitable and no fault of his own. He leaned back in the driver's seat of his car, stuck in traffic that wasn't moving, and allowed himself to remember.

It wasn't something he did often. It was a closed case, ancient history, and he hadn't allowed himself to dwell on it for the last two years, at least. Now, though, with Gali, he felt far enough removed from it all to recall what had really happened.

The whole, miserable story had begun innocently enough, with a phone call from his mother's cousin, who lived in the Five Towns.

"She lives on our block," this cousin had said. "Everyone has heard of the Nes Or family, a very prestigious Syrian family. They own the largest chain of shopping malls in the Tri-state area. Their oldest daughter, Leah, would be perfect for Yigal ...."

And, truth be told, it had started out well enough. She was a pretty girl, polite, and she'd been very agreeable, easy to date. There had been nothing about her that seemed unusual, and he'd actually been relieved that his dating life had gone so smoothly, which had allowed his foray into medical school to continue uninterrupted.

But then …

But then …

They had been engaged, he and Leah Nes Or, when he'd begun to notice certain things that bothered him a great deal. Some things had been benign, irritating, to be sure, but nothing major. Then, there had been a troubling series of events and he hadn't known what to make of it.

Unbeknownst to others, there were times when she lied to him inexplicably. Sure, the fabrications were over minor things—but they were lies, nonetheless. He'd caught her in several exaggerations and deceptions that left him baffled and confused.

And more than a little upset.

"Just tell me the truth," he'd said, feeling that she often distorted things in order to tell him what he wanted to hear. Her tendency to be purposely unclear had bothered him, but not enough to end things.

Until one day, when the final straw had finally come.

He'd been in New York for an extended weekend. His school had spring break, and he wanted to take Leah out to dinner that Thursday night. At first, she seemed less than enthusiastic about the idea, and then she finally told him that she couldn't make it. When he asked her why, she told him that she'd promised her little sister, Ora, that she'd take her out for her birthday. He felt a little uneasy at this answer since it seemed manufactured, and as of late, he was always on his guard.

Somehow, he felt that he couldn't trust her.

Sure enough, the next day, when he came to deliver flowers for Shabbos, he saw Ora, her nine-year-old sister, playing with her friend on the wide, stone steps of their house. He wished her a happy birthday, and she looked at him, confused.

"It's not my birthday," she said. "My birthday is in November."

He remembered feeling a hot wave of anger rising in his face as he blindly took the steps two at a time and pounded on the front door. The housekeeper answered the door, and with one look at his alarmed expression, went upstairs to get Leah. She'd come downstairs leisurely, unaware and unapologetic, and even raised her eyebrows when she saw the look on his face.

"What's wrong?" she asked.

He looked down and saw that he was still holding the flowers he'd brought. He forced himself to remain calm, but the sinking feeling he was experiencing was threatening to overwhelm him.

"You tell me," he challenged.

"I don't understand."

"Your sister, Ora, told me that her birthday is in November."

She gave him a blank stare, not comprehending. He examined her face, wondering for the first time how he'd ever thought her pretty. Sure, her facial features might have been aesthetically pleasing, but her inner nature was confounding … even ugly.

"So what?" she answered.

"SO WHAT?!" he shouted, unable to stop the maelstrom of emotion from surfacing. "You lied to me! Again! If you didn't want to go out last night, why didn't you just say so? Why all the lies?"

The color rose in her face, and understanding dawned on her for the first time. At once, he realized that she was so used to being dishonest, it was a pattern, and she was unaccustomed to being reprimanded for it.

And if there was anything he simply could not abide, it was a liar.

"Sorry," she said. "It was just—"

"WHAT?!"

She looked like she was struggling with something, and finally came to a decision.

"I had a yoga class. I want to look perfect in my gown, and I know how you feel about yoga, so I made up a little story. It's no big deal . . . you don't have to shout at me!"

He vaguely recalled telling her on one of their dates that he thought yoga was a silly waste of time, or something along those lines . . . .

And for that, she had to fabricate an entire story?

She couldn't have just told him the truth?

"You don't think lying is a big deal?" he asked her.

She looked at him and giggled, her hand over her mouth. "No, not really. What's your problem?"

At that moment he realized that something about her was somehow off, somehow unbalanced. And all at once he knew with stunning clarity that he could not marry this girl—not then, not ever. If she could lie about such trivial things directly to his face and not be bothered by it, how could he trust her to be a partner in the raising of his children?

It was unthinkable.

And there it was, looming large and uncomfortable in the room with them, a chasm so deep that it couldn't be ignored. Later, when she realized the seriousness of her mistake, she'd alternately begged and screamed hysterically, making her seem all the more shrewish and unbalanced. He'd called his father and his rav, and after explaining the situation, they'd both agreed that the only recourse was to end the engagement, and end it quickly.

Her parents had been livid, shouting that he'd made a mockery of them, the powerful Nes Or family, and they'd even threatened to drag his family to a beit din to clear their tarnished name. That had never materialized, thankfully, but nothing had prepared him for the vile, hysterical conversation that ensued between just the two of them that very last time.

She'd called him every vulgar name in the book, even going so far as to threaten him with spreading false rumors about him.

"If you break the engagement, you'll be sorry you were ever born. I'll make you pay for what you've done to me!" she'd shrieked, appearing completely unhinged.

And then, miraculously, it had been over. He'd returned to the West Coast, the invitations that had been printed were never mailed, and the clothing for the wedding hung in the closets unworn. He'd thrown himself into his schooling with an intense fervor, glad to be spared from further drama.

That had been three years earlier.

He didn't know what had happened to her, but he secretly hoped that she'd married since and no longer blamed him for the breakup. He felt guilty for causing her any humiliation, but he knew in his innermost heart that he'd done the right thing, that something about her hadn't been quite right, and he'd very luckily dodged a bullet.

The traffic started to pick up, and his phone rang.

It was Gali.

He smiled and answered the call.

CHAPTER FOUR

SHARI

SHARI WOKE UP COMPLETELY disoriented. It took several minutes for her to remember where she was, and suddenly, all the details of the previous day came flying back at once.

They had moved into their new apartment yesterday … Simcha's mother had dropped her little bombshell on them ….

She groggily put her hands over her eyes, recalling every detail of the previous day. It had seemed like one of the longest days of her life, between the move itself, the boxes, the unpacking ….

Not to mention her mother-in-law's watchful, sharp eyes that didn't leave her for a moment.

Toward evening, when some beginning semblance of order had been made, they'd gone out to dinner with Simcha's mother to a place in Mamilla that Shari usually enjoyed. Not that evening, though. The food had been delicious and exquisitely presented, but it had been a strained and tense meal. Shari picked at her pasta dish, devoid of appetite, and Simcha was also unusually quiet and restrained. It was Eva who kept the conversation going the only way she knew, with a constant barrage of questions.

"So, Shari, how's work going?" she'd asked, in a strange, syrupy sweet voice. Shari supposed that in her own way, she was trying to extend the olive branch and be cordial, for which she was grateful.

"It's going well," Shari answered. She would have said more, but a quick glance from Simcha made her hold her tongue. It was obvious that her husband didn't want his mother to know more about her job than was absolutely necessary.

And she couldn't have agreed more. The last thing she wanted was to be fodder for her mother-in-law's conversations with her friends.

"Are you still doing accounting?" Eva probed further.

"And payroll, yes."

"For the bakery café?"

"Yes."

"What's the name of the place, again?"

She couldn't recall ever telling her mother-in-law the name of the bakery, but there was nothing she could do about it now. She had asked a direct question, and it couldn't be avoided.

"Petit Patisserie," she answered.

"It's on Rechov Yaffo?"

"Yes."

"And you like it there?" Eva asked dubiously.

"Yes, I do."

"How many people work there?"

Shari swallowed a forkful before answering.

"Just a few."

"Oh, so it's a small business, is it?"

"Yes."

Simcha, to his credit, tried valiantly to change the topic, but to no avail.

His mother forged on. "And you have no interest in pursuing a real job? At a large firm?"

The words just wouldn't come.

No, I love my job. And it fits our needs very well. The pay is great and the hours are flexible and the people are so wonderfully nice.

Unlike you.

But she swallowed her words and heard Simcha thankfully say, "No, Ma, Shari has a great job. And she's great at it."

Truth be told, she really did have a dream job. Several years earlier, an elderly Jewish couple from France had moved to Yerushalayim to be closer to their many children who lived there, leaving behind only one married son who lived in France. The Marcianos had been accomplished bakers in France, with a very popular *patisserie* on the famous Rue de Rosier in France, which they'd owned for years. Their son took over the business when they moved, and they'd opened a small *patisserie* in Yerushalayim filled with the most heavenly, mouthwatering French confections. Their specialty, though, was their impossibly flaky, buttery croissants, which they filled with every possible filling, both sweet and savory.

The small French bakery had been an instant hit.

Unable to keep up with the large demand, they'd recently moved to a larger corner space on Rechov Yaffo. They'd hired Shari and another young *kollel* wife to run the business office in the back of the store, while the couple and their adult children tended to the customers. They'd added more tables and chairs and expanded their menu to include iced coffees, milkshakes, and hot chocolate, as well as their famous pastries.

For the past year, Shari had been fortunate enough to spend

her days working in a warm, relaxed atmosphere. She'd become fast friends with Sarah Klein, a New Yorker like herself, who was in charge of ordering supplies and keeping the enterprise running smoothly. Working in the cozy office together, they'd enjoyed an easy camaraderie. The pay was excellent, and as an added bonus, the Marcianos had just taken an entire month off to travel back to France with their family to celebrate their 50th wedding anniversary. Their son in France apparently had a wife who wasn't well, and couldn't travel to Eretz Yisrael to be with them.

In fact, from the hushed whispers and frantic phone calls that had recently taken place, Shari was secretly worried about the Marcianos. It seemed that their young daughter-in-law was seriously ill, and Shari's heart went out to them. They had decided to close their store for the duration of their trip, and would reopen it upon their return.

The timing had actually coincided perfectly with their move, since Shari would have time to get organized and adjusted before the Marcianos returned in two weeks' time.

Everything had been going so well of late — the doctor's reassuring news, the spacious apartment, the time off from work ....

Everything until her mother-in-law's unexpected visit.

"How long will you be staying?" Simcha had asked his mother at dinner.

"You want to get rid of me already?" she retorted.

"Look, Ma —"

"I can clearly see where I'm not wanted. I just hope that you won't be as rude to Shmiel Goodman."

Simcha's eyes widened.

For what seemed like a long time, no one spoke. Shari looked from her husband to his mother, and then back again. They were both still, unmoving.

"Shmiel? That's who you're marrying?"

"It sure looks that way," his mother said dryly.

"You mean, the accountant?"

"The one and the same."

"He's done your taxes for what—twenty years?"

"Oh, at least," she replied. "He's a very honest man."

Again, there was silence. Shari looked over at Simcha, who was chewing his food thoughtfully. She knew that if he'd been asked to describe the food he was eating at that very moment, he'd have absolutely no idea.

This news couldn't have been easy for him. On the other hand, he'd lost his father when he was just three years old, so it wasn't like he remembered him at all.

Shari found herself wondering what type of man would appreciate Eva's difficult, somewhat abrasive demeanor, then blushed at the uncharitable thought.

Maybe her newfound happiness would make her … different.

More tolerable.

It would take a miracle, but one could only hope ….

"So I guess you'd like to know how this all came about," Eva said. "It's a fascinating story, if I do say so myself."

They waited.

"Well, do you want to hear it or not?"

"Yes," Simcha said.

Shari nodded, which she hoped indicated her agreement.

"You know, Shmiel lost his wife around two years ago. Very sad, actually … She was a wonderful woman."

"I think I remember her," Simcha said.

"Yes, I'm sure you do. Anyway, Shmiel fell into a depression. He couldn't work—it was just a disaster. I didn't realize how bad it was until I got a threatening letter from the IRS. I was behind on my taxes and they wanted to know why! Not the kind of letter anyone likes to receive, I can tell you."

Simcha paused, his fork in midair.

"He didn't file your taxes?" he sputtered.

"No," she said. "Naturally, I was really angry. I mean, what was I paying him for? To go to jail?"

They waited. She would no doubt tell her story in her own way, and in her own, interminable time. She looked like she was enjoying herself for once, with an audience listening to what she had to say.

Shari found herself imagining what her mother-in-law would look like in a prison uniform, but quickly gave up. Her brusque manner, coupled with her up-to-date clothing and fashion sense, made the image quite impossible to conjure, even for a second.

"So what happened next?" Simcha asked politely.

"Well, I called him up and basically gave him a piece of my mind. Believe me, I read him the riot act, poor man."

I believe you, Shari thought. *Poor him.*

"I told him that I was dumping him and getting a new accountant. Which I did, of course, the very next day. I don't take these things lightly, you know."

Of course you don't, Shari thought.

"So who's the new accountant?" Simcha asked.

"Let's just call him Mr. X," she responded coyly. "You'll see why in a minute—I'm getting to that. You won't believe this, but it turns out that he was an unscrupulous, scheming sort. He had a stellar reputation, of course. How these people maintain their reputations is just beyond me. He was a thief, and not a very smart one, at that. He started skimming off the top almost as soon as I hired him."

"Skimming off the top?" Simcha said doubtfully.

"Embezzling," Shari clarified. "In the business world, it happens all the time, unfortunately."

"Exactly," his mother agreed. "Oh, that's right, Shari, I guess you know a little bit about these things."

Excuse me, but I have a CPA, and I know a lot *about these things,* she wanted to say.

But she said nothing. She just sat there, seething with indignation, and waited to hear the rest of the uninteresting story and end the dinner.

"So after months of this, when I finally realized what was going on, I called up Shmiel in a panic. Someone else would have hung up on me, am I right? After the way I'd treated him—but no, not Shmiel. He sounded so contrite, telling me that it was all his fault I'd had to use another accountant in the first place. Which was true, of course. Not that I'm blaming him—he had enough problems of his own. In any case, he went to work right away. It took a long time, but we're finally all squared off with the IRS. The whole chapter is behind us."

"But whatever happened with Mr. X?"

"Oh, Shmiel was magnificent. He told him off. Boy, was he scared, and rightfully so."

"Are you going to report him to the authorities?"

"Shmiel asked his *rav*, and he said to wait, for now. So we're keeping him under surveillance. Believe me, any whiff of anything not right, and Shmiel will report him to the authorities at once—and he knows it."

"But—"

"He knows that we're keeping an eye on him. Believe me, he'll think twice before scamming others. I mean, I hope so. I wouldn't want this to happen to other people … I couldn't stand it if anyone else had to go through this …."

So benevolent of you, Shari thought. *So kind.*

"Well, that's quite a story," Simcha said. "Still, you never mentioned how this all came about … you getting married, I mean."

"Oh, that was just a week ago. Shmiel dropped off some papers, and almost as an afterthought, he mentioned that he thought we should get married!"

"Just like that?"

"Yes, just like that. It had never occurred to me, of course. He's so much older than me, you know. He's probably at least ten or fifteen years older."

"Which one?" Simcha asked.

She raised an eyebrow. "What do you mean?"

"Is he ten years older? Or fifteen?"

She vaguely responded, "I'm not exactly sure."

Shari had a sneaking suspicion that he was around the same age as Eva, but since she'd never told them how old she was, they'd never know for certain.

She cared very much about retaining a youthful appearance, and Shari had a further sneaking suspicion that she'd had quite a bit of work done to her face to achieve the effect she wanted. The permanently frozen look over her eyes was most probably a result of Botox, and the smooth, pulled back appearance of her cheekbones was the unfortunate result of too many facelifts.

Did she care?

Not in the least.

"Anyway, I told him I'd think about it."

"And?"

"And I decided it would be a good idea, after all."

"So what did he say?"

"I haven't told him yet. That's why I'm here—I wanted to discuss it with you, my only son."

Eva had an insidious way of making Shari feel very small and insignificant, as if she was an outsider. And an unwanted outsider, at that. She made it a point of saying phrases like "my only son" quite often in Shari's presence, as if she didn't even exist.

They talked of other things at dinner, but that had been the main topic, so to speak. After all, that was why she'd come to visit them, albeit with awful timing.

She'd wanted to receive her son's blessing, and he'd given it to her.

Thankfully, she hadn't asked Shari for her input, and so she'd been able to remain blessedly silent. But inwardly, she pitied poor Shmiel Goodman, whoever he was. First he lost his wife, who undoubtedly had been a good woman, and now he'd be chained to this woman for the rest of his life. It was unfathomable.

Shari knew that her uncharitable thoughts toward her mother-in-law, vile as she was, went against everything she believed in. And though she'd never outwardly verbalized it to anyone, she knew that the resentment in her heart wasn't very good for her own soul.

But Shari was human.

And she had limitations.

It was amazing to Shari how the next morning, she could still recall last night's conversation word for word. She'd have to grit her teeth and play the gracious hostess by entertaining her mother-in-law for the next several days, whether she liked it or not.

She knew that soon, Simcha's mother would travel back to America, they'd get acclimated to their new home, and all would be well.

If she'd just survive the next few days.

Shari got up quickly and dressed. After being up till the wee hours of the morning, and being unable to unpack as many boxes as she would've liked, she was chagrined to discover that it was later than she thought. Simcha was undoubtedly in yeshiva, and she wanted to prepare some sort of lunch for his mother, just in case she dropped in, unannounced, like she'd done the previous morning. As she went down the stairs, it occurred to her again how wonderful it was that the *makolet* was right downstairs. As a matter of fact, their apartment was so conveniently located, it seemed that anything she could ever need was mere seconds away. Adjacent to the *makolet* was a fruit store, dry cleaners, a bakery, and a store that sold housewares. Further down the street was a large supermarket, and there were also restaurants and take-out places.

Going down the stairs quickly, she bought orange juice, cereal and milk, yogurts, and some fresh bagels and spreads, and went back upstairs to set it all up as attractively as possible.

Her cell phone rang as she was walking briskly toward her apartment, hoping that her mother-in-law wouldn't be waiting in the hallway of her building.

It was Gali.

It was the phone call she'd been waiting for, knowing the history behind Yigal Ben-Ezri, and how right it had felt for Gali from the beginning.

After the screaming had died down, she said, "I'm coming to the wedding!"

AN HOUR LATER, THE table was set beautifully. Shari had even managed to find her placemats in one of the boxes, and the table looked inviting and festive. She hoped that Simcha's mother would notice the effort she'd put in and be pleased with her, for once.

But, as it turned out, she needn't have bothered.

Simcha bounded through the front door and grinned when he saw the beautiful spread.

"Is this all for me?"

"Well, I thought your mother might drop in," she admitted sheepishly, feeling guilty that she'd never prepared such an elaborate lunch for Simcha in their three years of married life.

"Well, she isn't coming," he said.

"How do you know? You spoke to her?"

"She called me a few minutes ago. She said she's jetlagged or something, and she'll stop by tonight when I come home from yeshiva."

As soon as the words left his mouth, Simcha felt contrite. He thought his wife would be happy that his mother wasn't coming by until later, but he saw the look of humiliation on Shari's face, and understood it all too well.

"She hates me," Shari whispered.

"No, she doesn't. That's just the way she is, Shari ...."

It was the same conversation that had been repeated and replayed so many times. The truth was, Simcha felt that his mother had been unusually harsh toward Shari the day before, and it pained him. It was undeniable that his mother had had it hard all these years, and she'd forged a tight bond with him, her only son. He knew that it couldn't have been easy for her to "share" him with Shari, and she was undoubtedly jealous that her position had been usurped.

Still, it didn't give her the right to be rude.

"Let's just change the subject, okay?" Shari suggested. "I'm technically still on vacation, so we can eat together for once. I have so much to tell you."

He was glad to oblige and grateful to his wife for letting the matter drop, at least for the time being.

They sat down to lunch and Shari said, "Gali called. She's engaged!"

Simcha grinned. "To the doctor?"

"Yes, Yigal Ben Ezri. She's over the moon. And you know what this means."

"It means you want to go to L.A. for the wedding," he replied. "You all promised each other that you'd be at each other's weddings, no matter when and no matter what—whatever tomorrow would bring, right?"

Shari smiled at him. It was uncanny how in sync they were, how well Simcha knew her. She knew that she was so fortunate to have him as her best friend and ally. It was so comforting that he knew everything about her and they had no secrets between them. The fact that his mother was … difficult … was just something that she'd have to endure.

It wasn't easy, but then, what was ever easy?

Simcha was worth it, after all.

"Exactly right."

"So when will it be?"

"She said it'll probably be in June, after all of the medical boards, or something like that."

A shadow of concern crossed over Simcha's face.

"Uh-oh. What's wrong?"

"My mother said that's when she wants her wedding to be … and she wants us to be there, in New York. And she wants us to stay at a hotel."

A sinking feeling crept into Shari's stomach.

Oh, no. A wedding in June with Simcha's mother and new stepfather? Just watch … Gali and Simcha's mother will probably get married on the same day.

It was too much. When her voice came, it was unexpectedly sharp. "Excuse me, but I am *not* going to miss Gali's wedding. I *refuse*, and I'm not going to change my mind. Period."

Simcha gaped at her in shocked silence. Shari was usually easygoing and well mannered. She rarely lost her temper and most certainly never spoke to him in such a way.

"Sorry, Simcha," she said contritely. "But your mother …"

And she burst into tears.

Simcha looked at her with sadness in his eyes. Secretly, he'd always assumed that his mother and wife would be on great terms, but nothing was further from the truth. In fact, the tension between them had become almost unbearable.

And, deep down, he knew that it was his own mother who was to blame.

He was just getting up from the table to get her a tissue when there was a knock at the door.

Shari began to rise from her seat when he waved her back down.

"I'll get it," he offered. "You just sit and relax …."

He went to the door and opened it. Shari couldn't see who it was from her vantage point since there were still mountains of boxes everywhere, but she could hear a woman's distinctively loud voice.

"I'm Rachel Marcus," the woman boomed. "Your next-door neighbor. I hope I'm not intruding …."

"Actually, it isn't a very good time—" he said apologetically.

"Oh, of course, I know you've just moved in and everything, but I wanted to check in and see how things are going, and introduce myself, and all that."

"Yes, thank you, maybe some other time—"

Shari couldn't hear the rest of the unintelligible conversation, since it had ostensibly taken place in the hall, but miraculously, Simcha was able to soon close the door and rejoin her in the kitchen.

"Sorry, Shari," he murmured.

"You mean, about the neighbor?" she sniffled, blowing her nose into the tissue he offered.

"No, about my mother," he said quietly. "I've always been sympathetic to her because she's had it so rough, but I think you've been treated unfairly—I really do. I'm sorry that she's hurt you so badly."

The words were lodged in her throat, but she wouldn't have been able to articulate them, in any case. She just made quiet, whimpering noises as she cried miserably into her stack of tissues.

Her emotions had been running high, with the doctor appointments, moving apartments, her mother-in-law's unexpected visit … she'd been going on sleepless nights and pure adrenaline, and this morning it had all culminated in a maelstrom of tears, which wouldn't stop.

Simcha didn't press her and instead, let her cry it out.

He understood the difficult predicament in which they found themselves, and most importantly, he understood his wife.

It was cathartic for her to cry. The tension of the last few weeks had risen to a crescendo, with the mere thought of missing Gali's wedding pushing her over the edge. Sure enough, after a while, the tears ebbed, and Shari took a deep breath and sighed.

Simcha looked at her sympathetically.

"Better?"

She nodded, her eyes red-rimmed and puffy.

"Thanks," she whispered.

"No need to thank me, Shari. We're in this together, you and I."

"I know," she said gratefully.

"Remember that."

"I will."

Wordlessly, they got up and began to unpack the boxes that surrounded them. The task seemed overwhelming, but as long as they did it together, they felt they could handle whatever would come their way.

CHAPTER FIVE

EVA

AS SHE WEARILY BOARDED the enormous plane, pulling her expensive pilot's case behind her, Eva sighed. She wasn't as young as she used to be, and traveling was simply exhausting. The worst part was that the week-long visit with her son had not gone as well as she'd planned. And there was one glaring reason why.

His wife.

She knew that the visit had been unannounced and unexpected, but the hostile, frosty welcome had truly been like a slap in the face. From the moment she'd arrived, the reviled look on her daughter-in-law's face had been all too obvious. The girl wanted nothing to do with her, and for no good reason. In her estimation, she'd always tried to be nice to the girl, but it was difficult, with them being so many miles away. And she was a very busy woman, which didn't leave much time for idle chitchat. She wasn't one to pick up the phone and call the girl just out of the blue.

Besides, she wasn't a phony person by nature. Her true feelings about her daughter-in-law had to come out somehow, she knew, no matter how she tried to keep her emotions in check.

It just wasn't easy. The girl was so … so …

Meek.

Mousy, even.

Oh, she wasn't a bad-looking girl, nothing like that, she admitted to herself. In fact, she was actually a pretty girl, but in an unassuming, nondescript sort of way. Actually, if Eva was to be perfectly honest with herself, Simcha's wife was a *very* pretty girl with lovely features, but … but …

She was just so timid.

She lacked confidence and personality. There were times when she seemed scared of her own shadow, and Eva simply had no patience for it. She felt that sometimes she had to goad Shari just to get her to say something. She didn't enjoy needling her, of course, but sometimes it was the only way to get her to respond. Deep down, she knew that her goading and teasing wasn't perhaps the best approach, but still …

The girl was like a little mouse, never speaking her opinion on any topic, so as her mother-in-law, she had no way of knowing how she felt about nearly anything. She truly had no idea if they had anything in common, which she secretly doubted. In the beginning, Eva had thought that there was intelligence behind those large, brown eyes, but her daughter-in-law's words always seemed so measured, so guarded.

At least when Eva was around.

It was almost as if the girl had built a very large, brick wall between them, and no matter how valiantly Eva tried to scale that wall, she was unable to do so.

It truly wasn't her fault. For instance, when she asked Shari in a reasonably friendly way about her job, she received one word answers. Eva thought her short, clipped answers to be unwarranted, even rude. She was just trying to make friendly conversation, and what was wrong with that? Nothing at all, surely. She was just showing an interest in the girl's life, and come to think of it, did she ever ask *her* anything about her own life?

Did she ever ask *her* about the real estate business that she'd turned into a multimillion dollar empire?

Did she ever ask for any details about Shmiel Goodman?

The girl had never said a word. In fact, she'd appeared completely disinterested when she'd divulged to them the exciting news about her future wedding plans. It was as if the girl didn't even care.

Which, in all probability, she didn't.

In fact, Eva would have liked to disclose more to them about Shmiel's current medical situation, but Shari had looked so disinterested, she'd dropped it. Even Simcha, her own precious boy, had seemed less than enthused. It had been such a subdued meal, that she'd told Simcha the following day that she'd meet them for dinner, and his wife shouldn't expect her to drop by before then.

It had been a relief for her to not have to deal with her daughter-in-law.

The very thought of even having to *look* at her was too much.

She thought of all of the people she knew who were already grandmothers. It was a club that she wanted desperately to belong to, but even that was denied her. In all probability that was the girl's fault as well.

She was so thin, and honestly, the way she picked at her food ....

She certainly didn't seem like a robust girl with a hearty appetite. She was a mere slip of a girl who never seemed very hungry. Surely, she could stand to gain a few pounds.

Eva felt very virtuous that she had never mentioned the girl's weight to her son and the obvious correlation between being underweight and fertility issues. She considered it unfair that she'd never received credit for being *good.* She was only censured each time she said something that came across the wrong way. It wouldn't have mattered, in any case, since Simcha's wife would probably have looked down at the floor and said nothing.

Eva rubbed her eyes. She was so *tired.*

But after everything that had transpired that night, she knew that she'd never be able to sleep on the plane.

She'd been on the defensive, that was all. Simcha had come to her hotel room several hours earlier ostensibly to say good-bye, but it wasn't long before she realized that he had other things he wanted to discuss as well. He'd caught her off guard, that was it.

That was most probably the reason for the entire debacle.

He'd had the nerve to basically blame *her* for the lackluster relationship between her and his wife, and then he'd even gone as far as to ask her for an apology. As if *she* was the one who was at fault.

Honestly, if he'd taken a knife to her heart, it would've hurt less.

An apology.

It would never happen.

She hadn't done anything wrong.

Eva had never thought things would evolve this way between them, but it had undoubtedly been the result of a natural progression. It was obvious that her daughter-in-law hadn't liked her from the very beginning and wanted nothing to do with her.

As she tried to settle herself in her first-class seat, she leaned back and wished for what must've been the millionth time that

Simcha had married a more outgoing, likable girl, such as the Roth girl. But the rational side of Eva knew that wishing was futile. It was simply too late.

The Roth girl lived around the corner from Eva, and she'd watched her grow up, in a sense. She was a beauty, of that there was no doubt. She had gone to the best schools, dressed beautifully, and had an enviable, outgoing personality and a certain confidence to her that Eva admired. She was pursuing a degree in the medical profession—a Master's degree in physical therapy, she believed—and would no doubt one day get a prestigious, lucrative job in the city.

And she was still single.

Eva recalled word for word the awful conversation she'd had with Simcha just before she left for the airport. It just wasn't fair since the conversation hadn't been planned, and it had come out all wrong.

Oh, why had she said anything?

She hadn't meant to hurt his feelings, her only son whom she treasured above all else, but she knew that she had done just that. Oh, why had she said anything?

"WHAT? What are you saying?" Simcha had bellowed.

"Simcha, there's no need to shout at me. I just don't think that you look very happy, and I'm worried about you. All I said was that I wish you'd have married the Roth girl!"

As soon as the words had flung, unbidden, out of her mouth, she knew that she'd made an awful mistake.

Her son's mouth had become a hard line.

His face, so young and handsome, had taken on a bright red hue.

"I can't believe you just said that," he whispered.

He had turned to leave but then turned back around and pointed his finger at her in blazing anger, a deep-rooted anger that she had never before witnessed.

"You know who's perfect for me? My wife, Shari. It's unbelievable that you can't see that … It's INSANE!"

Shakily, she'd responded, "Oh, for goodness' sake, Simcha. Lower your tone, please. I'm just worried about you, that's all. It's been three years, like you said, and there are no children, you both look miserable … I just care about you, that's all."

His tone was icy. "Ma, I think it's time for you to leave. There's nothing left to say."

"But, Simcha—"

He'd already left, slamming the door behind him.

She leaned her chair back and closed her eyes. She really shouldn't have said anything, she knew, but it was futile to wish that she could take the words back. It was almost as if she'd opened the proverbial Pandora's box … She hadn't meant to mention the Roth girl—it had just spilled out. She was an honest person, and surely, he should know how she felt about the matter. She was his mother, after all. If she couldn't be honest with her own son, then with whom could she be?

After her husband, Shimon, had died so suddenly and tragically, something inside her had died as well. She used to have a spark … a joie de vivre … but it was extinguished the very instant she received that ominous call from the police station.

She'd never forget that awful night, even though she'd willed it out of her mind countless times over the years. It was a pain that would be permanently etched in her, and it would never fully go away.

Her only solace, her only reason for living, was her son, Simcha. He had been so young at the time, a cherubic little boy. She'd vowed to herself that he would not grow up a "case," an outcast, a *nebach*. That would've been more than she could bear.

She was determined that he would be well cared for, and have every creature comfort that every other boy had. He would go to the best yeshivas and camps, and lack for nothing. And so she'd thrown herself into her husband's real estate business, working day and night, and made it into an incredible success. Her offices in Manhattan were spacious, chic, and modern.

Simcha had grown up in as normal an environment as she could manage, which had been her goal. They were not pitied by others at all. In fact, they were most probably envied, which gave Eva an extra measure of satisfaction. They'd lived in a large, spacious corner house on one of the best blocks in Flatbush, and Simcha had excelled in every yeshiva he'd attended. He was a popular boy and well-liked by all. When it came time for *shidduchim*, the offers had been fast and furious. Simcha was known for his sharp mind, his *hasmadah* in learning, and his *middos*. He was also tall and good-looking, and was it her fault that she'd wanted the very best for him?

She'd thought from the start that he could have done better, and well, now he knew exactly how she felt. She'd always danced around the topic, but now there was little doubt as to how she felt about his meek, mousy wife. He was angry, of course, but he needed to realize that she had his best interests at heart. One day soon, he would come around and forgive her. He always did.

The plane gathered speed and lifted into the air, and Eva forced her mind off the unpleasantness between Simcha and herself. It wasn't her fault that she'd wanted better for her only son. It just didn't seem fair that after everything she'd been through, she couldn't have a better daughter-in-law. She deserved it. Her thoughts drifted to the girl that Shmiel's son had married.

Devora.

Devora Goodman was a bubbly, effervescent young woman, who managed to care for Shmiel with a devotion that was truly touching, just as she'd cared for her mother-in-law during her brief illness.

She was a nurse, and she also managed to raise three adorable children. She even had Shmiel over for nearly every Shabbos. She was an angel, a lovely young woman, and she always looked at Eva when she spoke to her. She was exactly the kind of daughter-in-law she'd always wished for.

Wait a minute ....

When I marry Shmiel, she'll be my daughter-in-law, too.

The thought made her lips turn up at the corners. How she'd never before made that connection, she had no idea. Shmiel's two sons would be hers, as well. The older one lived in Toronto, so she wouldn't see his family as much. But she'd surely see Devora and Daniel quite often, and she looked forward to being a *bubby* to their children, at least, since it remained to be seen if Simcha would ever have children of his own.

The dreadful conversation still rankled. An apology, of all things ...

An apology for what?

For saying the truth?

She would have infinitely preferred him to take a knife and stab her in the heart, and just get it over with. An apology would not be forthcoming, thank you very much.

Not that night, and not ever.

Let him apologize to her, his long-suffering mother who only wanted what was best for her son.

She set her jaw firmly as she looked around, noticing the people around her with disdain.

There was an overweight businessman in the next row over who had begun to snore the very second the plane took off the ground.

There was a young couple with two small children on the other side of the aisle. The children appeared to be around eight and six years old, perhaps. They were well-behaved, but Eva inwardly disapproved of the way the parents were raising their children.

Really … Flying with kids in first class … They'll become spoiled, unmanageable. Children need to realize that money doesn't grow on trees. One has to work for a living, and work hard ….

And so the scrutiny continued. Eva glanced at every person that her vantage point would allow and wondered at their stories. Of course, it wasn't nice, but she wasn't in a nice mood. The rational side of her knew that she was judging, and judging unfairly, but she didn't care.

She couldn't recollect the exact time she had stopped caring, but it had happened years ago. After everything she'd gone through, she had every right.

She had every right to just … not care.

She wasn't a fool, and she was well aware that she had a hard edge to her. She even recalled how, five years earlier, she'd taken a so-called friend's disastrous advice and gone to see a therapist. She even remembered his name.

Dr. Don Fischer.

Trust me, her friend had said. *He's brilliant. He's a frum man. It'll be so helpful … so freeing.*

She hadn't spoken to her friend since.

Or to the self-righteous Dr. Fischer, for that matter.

Though it had been five years earlier, she could still recall their meeting. At the time, she'd had the sneaking suspicion that Dr. Fischer's piercing blue eyes beneath his horn-rimmed glasses could see right through to her very soul, and it had disconcerted her. In the space of three minutes, he'd had the nerve to tell her that she seemed *bitter.*

"Excuse me?" she'd bristled.

"Oh, please don't take any offense," he said. "It just seems that you're seething with an inner anger, a bitterness … You were so right to come to me."

"Oh, and I suppose you have all the answers," she replied sarcastically. The man was preposterous. Here she was, a polished, put-together woman, expecting advice from a man whose shirt was rumpled and his glasses askew. His tie hadn't even matched his shirt. How his wife had allowed to him to leave the house was beyond her.

"No, I don't think anyone has all the answers," he'd answered amiably.

"So what am I paying you for?" she'd challenged.

He'd smiled and paused.

"Maybe we can find out those answers together."

She'd raised her eyebrows at him and inwardly thought, *Ugh, what arrogance. He thinks he understands me, and he doesn't even know me … What a total waste of time.*

"I have some questions to ask you," he'd continued, seemingly unaware of the venomous rage that was brewing within her.

She'd wanted nothing more than to rip down his highbrow diplomas from the wall and smash them over his egotistical head.

"Question one, how often do you find yourself angry?" His syrupy, soothing voice was grating on her nerves. It was surely all an act—no one was that nice.

"You mean, how often do I get angry at someone?" She rolled her eyes.

"No," he clarified. "Not necessarily at a person. Just angry in general … angry at the universe at large."

Her eyes narrowed, and when she'd replied, her answer was brusque and clipped.

"Every second of every day."

And, with that, she'd picked up her pocketbook and got up to leave his office, never to return. On her way out, he'd called after her jovially, "You'll be back."

Had that been some sort of threat?

"I doubt it," she'd responded coldly.

For some strange reason, she still had his card in her wallet, though true to her word, she'd never returned.

Eva reclined as far back as her seat would allow and kicked off her heels.

No one understood her.

She wondered if even Shimon had understood her. It had been so long ago, and she'd been a different person then. Their marriage had been so brief, it was almost hard to remember what it had been like. She hadn't been married for ages, and she'd relished her independence for such a long time.

Was she willing to give it up?

Curiously enough, she didn't think her independence would suffer at all, being married to Shmiel.

Shmiel was a hardworking, private man who would let her do as she pleased. Furthermore, he'd recently become confined to a wheelchair, which others would have viewed as less than ideal, but not Eva.

To her, it made him seem even less threatening. The thing she abhorred above all else was feeling intimidated, and with Shmiel, there was absolutely no intimidation. With Shmiel, what you saw was what you got, which Eva appreciated. And it wasn't as if he was fully incapacitated, either. He was able to get around by himself, more or less, and he worked from home. She'd be able to continue her life in much the same fashion, no doubt, without Shmiel or anyone else breathing down her back.

There would have to be some minor revisions to the layout of her home, she knew, but she was willing to make some allowances. The one thing she'd have to be adamant about, though, was the fact that she didn't want to be the one to move.

She would insist on that point, if it came to that, and she felt reasonably sure that Shmiel would see things her way.

Hers was the larger of their two homes, and she'd decorated it exactly how she wanted. Spending time in Shmiel's first wife's kitchen was just not something she was willing to do. However, she was willing to make some minor changes in her own home in order for him to maneuver around.

The wheelchair was a result of an accident that had occurred years ago. He'd been hit by a car one Friday night when he was walking home from shul. His left leg had been crushed from the sheer force of it. Because he'd been injured so badly, his leg had required several operations. Infections had set in, resulting in even more operations. Years later, when his leg had become more clumsy, specialists in the field were consulted, and further surgeries were needed to reverse the earlier operations, which had been unsuccessful.

His leg had never fully healed. The muscles in his lower leg had atrophied to the point that he needed a motorized wheelchair to get around. He'd actually won a large settlement years earlier when the hospital admitted to negligence and wrongdoing in his case, which helped defray the cost of his living expenses.

Eva knew full well that he wouldn't be walking to the *chuppah*. He'd get there in his wheelchair, but for some reason, it didn't bother her in the least.

She was tired of being alone.

And Shmiel, though he certainly wasn't perfect, was a kind, decent man. She thought they could work well together, or at least coexist peacefully, and at this stage of her life, it sounded just fine.

Surely, her friends would be surprised at her decision. They'd be shocked, even, and a part of her received some satisfaction from the thought of shocking them.

They were mere acquaintances, really. Early on, she'd shunned close friends because they could not possibly understand what she'd been through, and they always managed to say the most inappropriate, callous things. So she'd kept most friends at bay, preferring instead a circle of acquaintances who were boring, but safe.

Deep down, she didn't much care for them, with their ordinary lives.

Nothing about her own life had ever been remotely ordinary. And certainly, when she married Shmiel, her life would become even less typical … and that was a good thing.

There was a part of her that reveled in being different. Different meant exciting … special.

She wondered if that was the reason why she resented and despised her daughter-in-law so much. Could it be that she'd disliked her from the very beginning because she was just so typical? There was nothing about the girl that was unique, nothing at all. If Shari had been an ice cream flavor, she'd undoubtedly be plain, old vanilla.

Boring.

And if there was anything Eva prided herself on, it was the fact that she was not boring at all, and nothing about her life had ever been boring, either.

Her son would come around. He'd forget about their unpleasantness ….

Wouldn't he?

He had to.

He always did.

She leaned back in her seat and closed her eyes. It was a *fait accompli.* Her mind was made up.

When she got back to New York, she would meet with Shmiel and give him a yes.

CHAPTER SIX

GALI

GALI WAS BROWSING QUIETLY in the Jewish bookstore on Pico Boulevard. The store was mostly empty, except for a few customers. She was looking for a Jewish medical tome, an encyclopedia of sorts, with medical advice primarily from the world's greatest medical source, the Rambam. She had been passing by the store, doing errands, and she realized that Yigal had mentioned this particular book on more than one occasion. Naturally, she wanted to buy it for him, but disappointingly, it wasn't on the shelves.

She went over to the counter and inquired if they had it in stock.

"Oh, sorry," the man said. "That's been out of print for a while. It's an intense *sefer*, very complicated. Once in a while, a doctor will ask me about it, or someone in the medical field. It's not for the layman."

With a surge of pride, she replied, "Oh, my *chassan* is a doctor."

At this, the elderly man smiled understandingly.

"Oh, of course," he said. "You're the Gordon girl, right? I know the Ben Ezri family very well. *Mazel tov* to you!"

"Thank you so much."

"Yigal is really a wonderful young man. You know what, it's a tough book to find, but I can try to order a copy from my brother-in-law in New York. Do you want me to try?"

"Yes, that would be great. I really appreciate it."

She gave him her name and cell phone number, and he said he'd let her know if he was successful in tracking down the book. She turned to leave, after thanking him again for his help. But she hadn't walked more than a few feet when she felt a light tap on her arm. She turned.

"Excuse me," a girl said quietly. "I couldn't help but overhear ... are you the famous Chef Gali?"

Gali smiled. "Guilty."

The girl was slender, pretty, and looked to be the same age as her. Since she'd never seen her before, Gali figured that she must be a tourist.

Echoing Gali's thoughts, the girl said, "I'm just in town for a few weeks, visiting my aunt, but I've been following your blog. Your food looks really interesting."

Interesting?

Now was that supposed to be a compliment, or not?

Gali wasn't quite sure.

"It's always nice to meet one of my fans," she replied. "Have you ever made any of my recipes?"

"No, no, I haven't," the girl admitted. "I never cook, but your blog is very interesting."

There it was, the word *interesting* again.

Gali found herself wondering what could possibly be interesting about following a food blog if one never cooked, but she figured the pictures might have looked appealing. Trying to be friendly, Gali said, "So you're in the L.A. area for a few weeks? Have you ever been here before?"

"Once, but it was a while ago. Maybe you can recommend some interesting places to see? I'm here all by myself, and it's been a little boring."

They left the bookstore and walked outside together.

"Yeah, sure, I really don't know too much about sightseeing stuff, but if you're looking for shopping, there's always the Grove."

The girl made a slight face. "Been there, done that."

Gali tried to rack her brain for something interesting for the girl to do. Clearly, she seemed less than enthusiastic about her trip, which was such a shame. There was so much to do in L.A., but for some reason, Gali's mind went blank.

"I'm really sorry I can't think of anything," Gali apologized. "I just got engaged a week ago and I guess I'm a little scatterbrained right now."

"Oh, *mazel tov*," the girl said. "That's actually what I'm here for, in a way. A *shidduch* ... well, you know how it is. Anyway, don't worry about it—you have more important things on your mind."

Something about the way she said it gave Gali a stab of sympathy. Here she was, prattling on about her recent engagement. The poor girl was here to date, and it was obvious from her demeanor that things weren't going all that well.

Suddenly, she had an idea.

"You know what, every Wednesday morning there's a really nice farmer's market in Santa Monica," she said. "I usually go."

"Really?" The girl looked doubtful.

"Well, I go for my business, of course, but still, it's fun to walk around to all the vendors, even if you don't cook. The produce is amazing, everything is so fresh, and they have the best flavored pistachios from Santa Barbara. It's right near the Third Street Promenade in Santa Monica, which is really nice."

The girl looked thoughtful. "Wednesday? That's tomorrow."

The girl looked so forlorn, so out of place, that kindhearted Gali took pity on her and found herself offering, "I can pick you up, if you'd like. Would you like to go together?"

The girl looked relieved. "Only if you're going anyway. I wouldn't want you to bother on my account, or anything."

Gali nodded. "Yes, I was planning to go, since I was hired to do a fiftieth anniversary dinner in two days. The couple only eats vegetarian, so I'm going to buy produce and get some fresh ideas for the menu. It's going to be a pretty small event, less than twenty people. Just family and a few close friends."

"Are you sure?"

"Of course, it's really not a problem at all."

"I guess I could tag along, then."

"Oh, good. I'll probably leave at eight or eight-thirty in the morning. Should I pick you up?"

"Uh, no, I have a car ... I can just meet you there. I'll use Waze."

Gali smiled. "Good idea. By the way, what's your name?"

"Leah ... Leah Rosen."

"Rosen?" Gali repeated. "You're not by any chance related to Shari Weiss, are you? I think her cousins are Rosens ... Shari Adler is her married name."

The girl hesitated. "Yeah," she finally replied. "I think we're cousins, like second or third, or something like that."

"Oh, my goodness, what a small world! Shari is my closest friend in the world ... I'll have to tell her that I met you."

The girl seemed flustered. "Well, thanks so much. I'll see you tomorrow."

As she walked away, Gali felt like she'd done an easy mitzvah. She was going to the farmer's market anyway, and this girl looked so happy to be included. It wasn't lost on Gali, the girls who were still struggling in the complicated world of *shidduchim*, and the fact that this girl was a bit shy surely didn't help matters. Even for more confident girls, such as her older cousin, it was rough going.

And then there was Tova, of course.

Nothing in life was a race, but Gali's heart felt full as she thought of Tova, who had been through so much. She didn't know all the details, but she knew enough to feel sorry for everything Tova had endured at such a young age. She knew that Tova wished her every happiness with her whole heart. And Gali knew that she would daven for Tova under the *chuppah* with every fiber of her being. Surely, Hashem had someone wonderful in store for Tova. Like her name, she was just so ... *good.*

THAT DAY WAS A busy one for Gali. She had errands and appointments, and that night, Yigal was taking her to her favorite restaurant in Oxnard, California, which was a little over an hour away. The award-winning restaurant was on the ground floor of the famed Baron Herzog winery in Oxnard, and though she hadn't been there too often, she remembered the outstanding food she'd eaten the last time she was there.

It was truly a special place, with attentive service and incredible ambiance, and Yigal had told her that he wanted to take her there to celebrate their engagement, just the two of them.

So all through the day, as she hopped around town from errand to errand, she was looking forward to their evening together. He said he had a surprise for her. She couldn't fathom what it could be … She felt that he'd already given her so much. Just being a presence in her life was the greatest gift of all.

She was just leaving the cleaners when her cell phone rang. It was her mother.

"Gali," she said in exasperation. "Where have you been all day?"

"I'm out doing errands. I have an anniversary dinner coming up on Sunday and I need to get things in order—the tablecloths, the centerpieces, the chafing dishes …"

"Gali, you're a *kallah*!" her mother chided. "You aren't supposed to be running all over town by yourself."

"Why not?"

"It's just not done. This is the time to be planning your own *simchah*, not someone else's!"

"Ma," Gali said, in the most patient tone of voice she could muster. "We've talked about this. This is my job. I know it's unusual, but running errands is a part of it. And tomorrow morning, I have to go to the farmer's market in Santa Monica again."

"Not Santa Monica again!" her mother wailed.

Gali's mother had a flair for the dramatic. She'd once read that there was a large homeless population in Santa Monica, and she'd conjured in her mind an image of Santa Monica being a dangerous place. She'd been worried about Gali going there ever since.

"You don't need to worry, Ma," Gali soothed. "I'm not going alone. I'm taking someone with me."

"Who?"

"Oh, a girl I met today. She's actually a cousin of Shari's.

Anyway, she's here visiting with relatives and I told her I'll take her with me. So you don't have to worry."

"Well, that's a relief, at least," her mother replied. "Just don't take all day, Gali. You know we're going to have a million appointments soon. Between the caterer, the florist, the band … I'm just so overwhelmed, I don't even know where to begin."

"Why don't you hire Mindy Weiss again?" Gali suggested. "Ma, you're the mother of the bride. Let someone else handle all of the details."

"Oh, I would, but she's booked for the next two years. She only did the *vort* for us because she's the friend of a friend …."

"Well, what about someone else? She can't be the only wedding planner in town."

"She's the only good one in town," her mother clarified. "I have standards, you know."

How well she knew.

"Just don't worry," Gali reiterated. "It'll all work out."

She hung up with her mother, not even realizing how prophetic her statements would seem later, when she reviewed the day's events later that evening.

IT WAS AFTER EIGHT o'clock, and they were finally seated at their table in Gali's favorite restaurant. Everything about the place was inviting, from the serene decor to the upscale food, beautifully prepared. Their appetizers had just arrived at their table—a seared fresh tuna pizzetta for Gali and a pulled beef wonton dish for Yigal.

Forgoing the traditional fork and knife, Gali lifted the crisp pizzetta, which was essentially a homemade cracker, and took a bite. It was sheer perfection, and she knew she'd write about it on her food blog. The fresh lime, cilantro, and hint of spicy mayo were a perfect counterbalance for the rich, velvety tuna. It was a small appetizer portion, but a lovely bite, nonetheless—a tantalizing taste of the meal to come.

After the tensions of the day, Gali was just beginning to relax and unwind when Yigal leaned forward and said, "So I have an idea."

Gali waited.

"How badly do you want to get married in L.A.?"

If there ever was a question Gali thought he might ask her, that was not it.

"Uh ... I'm not sure I understand the question."

"Okay," he continued. "Let me rephrase that. If there was anywhere in the world you could choose as the venue for your wedding, where would it be?"

Gali didn't hesitate.

"Yerushalayim, of course. But that's out of the question."

Yigal smiled.

"Really? Why?"

"I mean, everyone is here. Our relatives, our friends ..."

"Oh, really? Your friend Shari is there, right? My sister Simi is in seminary there, and my aunt lives there—my mother's sister that I told you about, remember?"

Gali did remember hearing about his Aunt Livnat, his mother's only sister, but she still wasn't sure where he was going with all of this. Still, he had her undivided attention.

"She actually called my mother this morning. Did I ever mention what she does?"

"What she does?"

"Yeah," Yigal replied. "For a living, I mean."

"I don't think so."

"Well, she happens to be the wedding coordinator at the Waldorf Astoria. In Yerushalayim."

Understanding began to dawn in Gali's eyes ....

"She's the wedding coordinator? You mean ..."

"Yes. Flowers, band, food ... We could have a beautiful wedding at the Waldorf, and everything will be done for us. We just need to show up as the guests of honor. In Yerushalayim Ir Hakodesh."

Well.

Well.

How many people had *that* opportunity? No one she knew. As a matter of fact, Shari had gotten married in New York, after all, which had been easier for her at the time, but really, she didn't know anyone from L.A. who'd had the privilege of getting married in Yerushalayim. The very idea seemed surreal.

Finding her voice, Gali sputtered, "I can't believe it, I just can't ..."

"Would you want to?"

"Me? Of course I would! But my mother ..." Her voice trailed off. She knew how much her wedding meant to her mother, since she was the only daughter. Handing over the reins of her special day just wasn't something she thought her mother would agree to.

"Trust me, my Aunt Livnat will make it beautiful."

"You mean, she's like the Mindy Weiss of Yerushalayim?"

"That's the planner your mother hired for the *vort*, from Beverly Hills?"

"Yes, she's really famous. She took care of every detail."

"Yes, that's exactly what my aunt does."

"You mean, she'll take care of the flowers?"

"Done."

"What about the band?"

"Done."

"The centerpieces?"

"Done."

"What about the tables? Who arranges all the seating?"

"Uh, I'm not sure there are set tables in Israel. Everyone just takes a seat and sits down."

At this, Gali burst out laughing. "That's amazing. Why can't we just do that here?"

"I have no idea. But I was at a wedding there … Trust me, it was done in the best of taste."

It wasn't just exhilarating to think that she could get married in the sacred city of Yerushalayim, it was overwhelming to even think of such a wondrous thing.

How many people, much greater than herself, had vainly tried to reach the holy city, never able to attain their dream? Why was she, little Gali Gordon, able to merit such an incredible opportunity?

Her eyes filled with tears.

"I just can't believe this, Yigal! I can't believe your family would agree to this …."

"Believe me, my mother would be very happy to come as a guest. Every detail will be taken care of, and it'll be incredible."

Gali laughed. "I feel sorry for your aunt. My mother might want to help her plan the wedding, if you know what I mean."

Yigal grinned. "Livnat can take care of herself, don't worry."

"So it's decided?"

"Only if it's okay with your parents, of course. And with you."

For herself, Gali couldn't have dreamed of a better surprise. She loved every facet of this incredible opportunity that was being presented to her on a silver platter, and felt humbled by it all. But though she knew her father would be on board, she was unsure how her mother would react to the idea.

Her mother had often expressed her desire to create for Gali the Wedding of the Century. Ever since she could remember, her mother had talked about her future wedding. Gali was their youngest child, after all, the only daughter after three sons, who had all been married for years. On the other hand, the extravagant *vort* had truly been like a mini-wedding ... Would it be enough for her mother? Truthfully, the thought of planning a wedding with her mother for the next several months didn't sound all that appealing.

She hoped her mother would acquiesce to her and Yigal's wishes.

Gali smiled. "Oh, don't worry. I'll work on them ... You know, that was an incredible surprise—the best surprise I could have wished for."

Yigal raised his eyebrows in question.

"That *was* the surprise, wasn't it?" she asked.

He shook his head. "No, Gali."

He suddenly produced a small, black velvet box out of seemingly nowhere and placed it on the small table between them. She opened the box and gasped.

"That's the surprise," he said, beaming.

An emerald cut diamond ring, around three carats, shimmered in the light. There were no other stones on the setting, and it was magnificent in its utter beauty and simplicity.

"It's beautiful," she breathed, again humbled at how she'd been blessed with her dreams coming true. The diamond was truly breathtaking, but it paled in comparison to the true gem she had been given. Yigal was everything she could've hoped for in a mate, and she could hardly wait for their future life together to begin.

She wanted to express her innermost feelings to him, how incredibly fortunate she felt, how humbled she was, how grateful to Hashem, but found that she had a lump in her throat and the words just wouldn't come. Then came the tears—hot, salty tears that rolled down her cheeks unbidden.

"I'm just so happy," she whispered. "And so grateful."

He leaned forward in his chair and looked at her with shining eyes.

"I know, Gali," he said, reading her thoughts. "I know."

"How? How do you know?"

He smiled. "Because I feel the same way."

CHAPTER SEVEN

MOSHE

MOSHE MARCIANO WALKED UP the narrow flight of stairs and opened the door of his apartment on Rue Buffault. The apartment itself was small but sunny, with large windows that faced the street below. It was in an excellent location, in the Ninth arrondissement in Paris, France, where he'd lived his entire twenty-nine years. Actually, his birthday had been several days earlier but he was quite unaware of the fact. With all that had transpired, it was inevitable, after all.

He'd always loved this particular street. The shul was on the very same street, and though the *patisserie* that he'd inherited from his parents was on Rue de Rosier, in the fourth arrondissement, it wasn't at all a long distance to work each day.

The well-known *patisserie* was closed at the moment, and he wasn't sure when it would reopen. Or if it would reopen.

He couldn't think about that now; he couldn't think of anything just now.

He sat down on the sofa in the front parlor, defeated, and put his head in his hands. With everything he'd been through, he felt so much older than he was. It seemed like ages ago, a lifetime ago, but how well he still remembered his joy, their initial excitement when they viewed this very apartment together nearly six years earlier. He'd been twenty-three then, a young man, and he was newly engaged to the lovely Dalya Bitton. They'd viewed the apartment together with emotions that resembled near bliss. It was the symbol of the beginning of all their hopes and dreams.

Now, Moshe returned to the empty apartment alone, after driving his parents to Orly Airport so they could wearily return to their home in Jerusalem. He'd noticed the stoop of his father's frail shoulders as he helped his wife toward the terminal, the sad, defeated countenance of his dear mother as she waved good-bye, and his heart ached. His parents were elderly people, and he worried about the tremendous toll this had taken on them.

"*Non, non, mon chere fils*," his mother had soothed him, her youngest son. "Do not worry about us. It's you who we are most concerned about. You must eat, you must take care of yourself … Dalya would want that."

Yes, it was true. His wife had always put his needs above her own. She had been selfless, in fact, valiant and courageous through every *traitement* that the finest specialists in France could think of.

The specialists had to think out of the box, since in addition to her dreaded diagnosis, her health had been further compromised by type-1 diabetes. But the *traitements* hadn't been enough, in the end. At least, not in France. There actually had been a new, promising clinical trial in Baltimore, Maryland, that had met with much success, but in her weakened state, she had been unable to fly ….

They had waited too long.

If only, if only …

A single, salty tear coursed down his cheek, and he wiped it away with something akin to surprise. Another tear … surprising, indeed, for all the while, he'd thought that he hadn't any tears left to shed.

His precious little girl, Naomie, was still at the neighbor's house, where she'd been for the last several weeks. Thankfully, she was very comfortable there, in their cozy, happy home. She was only three years old, far too young to understand what had happened. It made Moshe grateful, in a way, since she would never mourn what she'd barely even known.

Well.

A searing, devastating loneliness settled upon him like a thick, murky blackness. He knew he couldn't succumb to the despair he felt, for he had to go on. There was Naomie to consider, after all.

She'd never remember her wonderful mother, and that fact caused him great worry, for every daughter deserved a loving mother, and it was a role he knew he couldn't fill.

Perhaps his parents had been right. Perhaps it was time to leave and join them in Yerushalayim. He would do there exactly what he did in France, baking in the family *patisserie*. Most importantly, Naomie would be surrounded by his own, loving family. It made sense.

He could actually envision, in his mind's eye, working alongside his brother in the *patisserie*, Naomie playing nearby with her cousins. He could smell the freshly baked bread, the rolls, the croissants … it was what he'd done his entire life. Naomie would have a family and a future.

Then why had he resisted the very thought for so long? Was it because he was afraid to start over?

It would be a new land, a new home … so many changes, all at once. But it was more than that. He was terrified that in a new place, his memories of his old life would begin to fade. Perhaps, even his memories of Dalya would slowly fade.

And he didn't want that to happen, not ever.

He'd promised his mother that he'd think it over, and he would. And in his innermost heart, he knew it was a fait accompli. The move was inevitable, but he wasn't quite ready to make that leap just yet. Instead, his thoughts traveled back to when they'd first been married, and they'd eaten their first dinner at their apartment, just the two of them.

Dalya had been feeling well at the time, her diabetes under control. He'd opened a bottle of wine with a flourish, and the table had been cozily set for two.

They'd sat and eaten the lovely meal that Dalya had prepared, and Moshe could even now recall how it had tasted. They'd had thick, juicy rib steaks, perfectly cooked, with small fingerling potatoes.

In the candlelight, Dalya's face glowed, exultant in her new role as a wife, and indeed, as a cook. He recalled how nervous she'd been, having no culinary skills whatsoever, or so she'd claimed.

"*C'est deliciux,*" he'd exclaimed. "The best steak I've ever eaten."

"*Merci,*" she'd beamed. "It's the very first meal that I've prepared. I can't believe it came out so well."

He'd teased her that she'd set the bar very high. She'd playfully retorted that it would be all downhill from then on, which of course, it was not. Her prowess in the kitchen had been unmatched, but more importantly, her generosity of spirit and sunny disposition had made him a very happily married man. Two years later, their daughter, with her angelic countenance and blonde curls, was born, and their joy had been boundless. They'd arrived home from the hospital, exhausted but exhilarated, ready to tackle parenthood with the same love and commitment with which they had each been raised. He recalled one particular night, he arrived home quite late from the bakery, thoroughly worn out. The baby was sleeping, and Dalya had kindly prepared for him the same meal as their very first meal together, steak with fingerling potatoes.

The meal had tasted even better that time, for the appreciation he now held for his wife, a new mother, had expanded his heart in ways that he couldn't before fathom. How well he remembered lingering at the table, the two of them, over that transcendent meal. It was a memory that had been etched in his mind over the grueling last few years. It seemed like every time he needed some spark of happiness to cling to, he would recall that special moment.

Moshe looked up from his reverie. It was growing dark already, and there were dark shadows already slanting on the walls. The days were growing a bit longer, but the chill in the air was still there, and it would soon be time for Minchah. He decided to pick up Naomie after shul and finally bring her home. She deserved to have a sense of stability, to sleep in her own bed, to feel cared for and cherished.

In his innermost heart, he knew that it would be best for his young daughter to be near his relatives, to grow up with a family, and not to be so isolated. But it was too soon, much too soon for him to seriously contemplate. Just the thought of the painstaking task of going through all of their belongings in order to move was simply too overwhelming. So much had happened, and their apartment, with all of the memories they'd shared … as painful as it was, for now there was no other place he'd rather be.

CHAPTER EIGHT

GALI

THE SMOG THAT USUALLY enveloped the city of L.A. was unfortunately no different that morning, its gloom hanging in the air, making the stellar views hazy and distant. Still, it was an upbeat Gali who walked around the Santa Monica farmer's market that morning, sampling the juicy peaches, wondering if she should prepare a peach galette for the special anniversary dessert. The vendors that day were many and varied; it actually seemed that there were more vendors out than usual. The streets were lined with white tents on both sides, and the lovely array of fresh fruits and vegetables stretched for blocks. She carried her small leather notebook with her, which she used to jot down ideas and inspiration for the upcoming dinner.

As Gali walked, she thought of the conversation she'd had with Yigal the night before, and she couldn't help but smile. To think that their wedding might take place in Yerushalayim ... she hadn't spoken to her parents yet, but she thought they'd be flexible. Her mother, after all, had created the *Vort* of the Century, and she'd just commented the day before that she felt more than a bit overwhelmed. Surely, she'd be mollified with the thought that everything would be taken care of in the most spectacular fashion.

In the most spectacular place of all.

Gali scanned the crowd but saw no sign of Leah Rosen, the girl she'd met the day before, so she opened her notebook. Her clients' anniversary was mere days away and she had a menu to plan. On the top of the page, she wrote *Meet Leah Rosen*, but other than that, the page was blank. A peach galette was out of the question, that much she knew after walking around, since the peaches weren't exemplary at this time of year. Her mind was usually such a swirling maelstrom of ideas, but today it seemed as blank as the paper before her. So she took out her cell phone and dialed Shari, who answered on the first ring.

"Hi, Gali," Shari said breathlessly.

"Hey, you sound out of breath."

"Just a little," Shari panted. "I just got off the bus with some packages. The bus was so packed, you can't imagine …."

Gali was well able to imagine the crowded bus in Yerushalayim, and Shari in the midst of it all.

"I wish I was there, too," Gali replied. "Are you back at work? Did the Marcianos return from France?"

There was a pause on the other end.

"Yes, they've returned, but I don't start for another week. Something terrible happened to their family."

All sorts of frightening images crowded Gali's mind, but she was unprepared for the devastating news that Shari now confided to her.

"I feel so sorry for them," Shari said, her voice welling up with emotion. "I just wish there was something I could do. They're the most wonderful people, Gali, really warm and kind. Everyone calls Mrs. Marciano '*Maman.*'"

"That's just so tragic. Is their son going to stay in France, or join them in Eretz Yisrael?"

"They want him to join them here, but I'm not sure if he will. The rest of his family is all here, though. I actually have a feeling that he'll join them here one day soon."

Gali was quiet, thinking of the dreadful reality that the family she'd heard so much about was now facing. It was just too awful to contemplate.

Wanting to lighten the mood and cheer up her friend, Gali said, "Shari, I have incredible news that I think you'll be very happy about."

"Really? What?"

Gali paused a few seconds for effect. "What would you say if I told you that you don't have to schlep all the way to L.A. for my wedding?"

Another pause.

Shari said cautiously, "What do you mean?"

"What would you say if I told you that we're thinking of having our wedding in Yerushalayim?"

"WHAT?"

"Yes," Gali giggled. "Can you believe it?"

If there was anything that Shari wasn't expecting her to say, that had to be it. She suddenly recalled the conversation they'd had on the last day of seminary, when they'd been so certain that she'd be the one to get married in Yerushalayim. Instead, she'd gotten married in Brooklyn, and now, three years later, it appeared as if Gali's wedding would take place in the sacred city. Shari was so awed, she was speechless.

"Yigal's aunt happens to be the wedding coordinator at the

Waldorf," Gali said. "If I can persuade my mother, that's what Yigal and I really want to do."

"That's amazing news!" Shari exclaimed. "I just can't believe it! You know, Gavi and Avi's bar mitzvah is coming up and they're having it here, too. We don't have to go anywhere."

"What? It can't be their bar mitzvah already … I can't believe it, the famous Gavi and Avi? I still think of them as the little boys you had plastered all over your wall in seminary."

"Yeah, those two little boys are turning thirteen in the beginning of May."

"Wow, that's only a few months away—time really flies. Well, our wedding can't be until June, after the boards, but we're making it easy for you to attend. Remember when—"

"Of course I do! And I'm sure Tova does, too."

Gali agreed. She then proceeded to fill Shari in on more details, and to describe her ring. It felt so good, so right, to talk things over together. Although they were half a world away from one another, in ways that were both abstract and tangible, it didn't seem that way to either of them.

Gali was eagerly explaining to Shari the ideas she had for the floral centerpieces when Shari said, "Uh, Gali? Could I call you right back? There's someone at the door."

"Your mother-in-law?"

Shari paused for a fraction of a second.

"No, she left. I think it might be my neighbor, actually. This is the third time she's knocking and I don't want to be rude."

"Of course, of course. I'll talk to you later."

As if on cue, Gali had just hung up when she spotted the girl she'd met the day before. Oh, she'd forgotten to mention her to

Shari ... hadn't the girl mentioned that they were cousins?

Walking toward her, she waved. The girl didn't wave back. Was it her imagination, or did she seem to stiffen? Remembering that she was shy, Gali tried to tone down her naturally exuberant personality. She didn't want to scare the poor thing, after all.

"Hi!" Gali exclaimed, bustling with her packages. "So nice to see you again."

"Here I am," the girl replied. "So this is the farmer's market."

"Yes, it is." Gali felt bewildered. *The girl seemed so nervous, like it was the last place she'd rather be. So why had she come?* Gali hoped that she hadn't felt obligated. She was just trying to be friendly.

"Did you have a lot of traffic on the way here?" Gali asked, in what she hoped was a friendly tone.

"Not more than the usual."

"Where did you park? There's a public parking garage right around the corner, right off of Wilshire."

"Yeah, I found it."

Well, that was a relief, at least. The poor girl had found her way here, parked her car, and wanted to see the sights. The least Gali could do was try to be cordial, but it was more awkward than she'd expected, since the girl was so painfully shy.

"I actually was just on the phone with your cousin," she said.

"My cousin?" the girl stared at her blankly.

"Yes, Shari Adler. Her maiden name was Weiss. Didn't you mention that you're cousins?"

The girl look flustered. "I'm not sure how we're related ... It's a long story."

Gali waited expectantly, but when no explanations were forthcoming, she decided it would be best to drop the matter.

Had she imagined that the girl had said Shari was her cousin?

The girl's whole demeanor seemed peculiar. Still, Gali had offered to help her, and she was determined to show her a good time. They walked around, mostly in silence, with Gali commenting on the freshness of the fruits and what she planned to make for the gala anniversary dinner for her clients.

"It's nice that they're having a wedding anniversary," the girl said finally, albeit reluctantly. "At the rate I'm going, I don't think I'll ever have one."

So that was it.

The labyrinth-like maze of *shidduchim* was difficult for nearly everyone, but Gali could well imagine that for such a shy girl, it must be torturous. She once again felt a wave of sympathy for her.

"You'll find someone soon, I'm sure," she said earnestly. "It always happens when you least expect it."

"That's easy for you to say," the girl muttered bitterly.

Gali was surprised. Here she was, trying to be helpful and friendly. Surely she didn't deserve to be judged unfairly.

"No," she said carefully. "No, it's not just words. Everyone has their share of problems, and *shidduchim* is a tough one for almost everyone. It hasn't been easy for me, either. But don't give up ... You'll see, it'll all work out."

The girl was quiet.

"What type of boy are you looking for?" Gali asked gently. "Maybe I could try to think of someone."

The girl turned to Gali, and for a fleeting moment the look on her face was distraught and filled with ... Gali couldn't be sure, since it was a fraction of a second, but it looked almost like ...

Defiance.

Gali was taken aback. She resolved at that moment not to mention the delicate subject again, which was obviously more painful than she'd realized.

Maybe she'd just received a "no."

Maybe she'd had a date that had gone badly.

Maybe she'd arrived in L.A. for a date that had never even materialized.

The possibilities were endless. They walked on in silence, and Gali felt more miserable with each passing step. She hadn't meant to hurt the girl's feelings, she was only trying to help ... she couldn't help but feel that their entire outing was a huge, abysmal failure.

"Look, I'm sorry if I offended you. I was just trying to help—"

"I don't need your help, thanks," the girl muttered.

"Of course you don't," Gali said soothingly. "I was just trying to—"

Mercifully, a large trumpet blared, introducing a new song from a street band, so Gali never had to articulate what it was that she'd been trying to do.

As for the girl, she seemed to forget that Gali was even there, so engrossed was she in the live music and the fresh, kosher cotton candy that they were giving out for free. Gali stood awkwardly next to her in line, waiting for her free sample of cotton candy, as well. Never had she felt so foolish.

Somehow, the girl seemed inexplicably younger than she'd initially surmised. Gali had originally thought her to be around her age, but she must've been mistaken. She didn't seem more than eighteen or nineteen.

The gooey, sticky cotton candy seemed to help matters a little bit, at least. They didn't have to talk, so Gali didn't have a chance to say the wrong thing, which was helpful.

Still, it was with a huge sigh of relief when their tour of the farmer's market came to a close. They had perused the entire nine blocks and there was nothing left to see. The girl muttered a quick "thank you" under her breath for Gali's time and began to beat a hasty retreat, saying "See you," or something to that effect. She clearly hadn't enjoyed their little outing, but still, Gali felt quite relieved to have done her duty. There was something a bit odd about the whole encounter, but she'd done her best. Now she was free to take care of more errands while she was in the area.

After another hour or so, she was finally ready to go home, unload all of her packages, and create the perfect menu for the upcoming dinner.

Menus were always a thorny problem, to be sure, but since these clients were vegetarians, it made matters far more complicated. The menu couldn't be too pretentious or stuffy, but it still had to be five-star dining. They were paying for it, and quite a large sum, at that. She had to deliver—she had a reputation to uphold, after all.

Gali often found that once her menu was finalized and she had a clear path set before her, the hardest part was over. The actual cooking was something she genuinely enjoyed. She thought it over during the entire drive from Santa Monica to her home in Hancock Park, conjuring up ideas and just as quickly rejecting them. The ideas came fast and furious, her mind churning. Since the menu would be dairy, it made the main course trickier than usual. At last, she decided to serve a chilled spiced gazpacho for an appetizer, along with her famous parmesan crisps. It was a simple yet elegant appetizer, and she knew the flavors would stand out. The cilantro in the trunk of the car was so fragrant, she could smell it from the front seat.

When she tried to decide on a second appetizer, though, she got stuck. Mushrooms were so pedestrian, she just didn't want to go that route. Anything with puff pastry was simply out of the question. If these clients had been meat eaters, she would've served her smoked lamb lollipops, which had been a huge success at her last event. However, the fact remained that they were vegetarians, and she'd have to adjust accordingly. She seriously contemplated a tuna tartare tower, but then rejected it. She couldn't guarantee the freshness of the sushi-grade tuna the morning of the event, and by then, if it wasn't perfect, it would be too late to think of something else. No, it just wasn't practical. It was also a bit overdone these days, and Gali liked to think out of the box.

She was a few blocks away from home when the idea came to her. A lovely second appetizer would be arancini, a rice and cheese ball mixture in a lightly breaded crust, with a dipping sauce on the side. And the more she thought about it, the more a fresh pasta dish sounded appealing for the main. Ravioli in a fresh tomato basil cream sauce, with grilled ramps and sweet potato mousse … Yes, that would be exactly right. For dessert, she'd serve hot churros with cardamom ice cream, with a swirl of lime curd and some macerated blueberries. The tartness of the lime curd, combined with the sweet blueberries and spicy ice cream … Yes, she knew that the flavors would mesh well together. Perfect.

Pleased with her decision, she pulled into the large, circular driveway of her parents' home. It was interesting that she already considered it her parents' home, and not her own. When had *that* happened?

Mercifully, no one was home yet. She still had to broach Yigal's idea to her mother. In fact, she thought she'd do it that very night, when her father would be home, before she lost her nerve. She'd seat them down in the family room and explain it all to them ....

Yigal thought it would be a great idea to get married in Yerushalayim ....

No.

Yigal and I thought it would be a great idea to get started in Yerushalayim ....

That was a bit better, but ...

I have great news ... Yigal thought that we could get married ...

Guess what? Yigal's aunt is the wedding coordinator at the Waldorf in Yerushalayim ....

Ma? You know how you said that Mindy Weiss can't plan our wedding? Well, here's the thing ....

She murmured a silent prayer to Hashem for the right words to say as she bent to retrieve the fresh fruits and vegetables from the trunk of her car.

Since there were so many packages to bring in, and her curved driveway was so expansive, she was on her second trip into the house when her neighbor spied her.

"It's the *kallah*!" Judy Rubin, her neighbor, chided good-naturedly. "You shouldn't be carrying packages, you're the *kallah*!"

"I know," Gali replied. "It's just that I'm planning an anniversary dinner on Sunday night and have tons to do, Mrs. Rubin."

A shadow of concern crossed Mrs. Rubin's face. "You know,

Gali, I think a friend of yours was looking for you earlier. I guess no one was home, so she left."

"Really?" Gali said. "Who was it?"

"I've actually never seen her before," Mrs. Rubin commented. "But she seemed around your age, so she must've been looking for you. She was looking through the dining room windows, over by the shrubbery. The gate was open."

She pointed to the large, diamond-pane windows on the left side of the house.

"That's strange," Gali murmured, mostly to herself, since Mrs. Rubin's cell phone had started to ring and she went back indoors to answer the call. Kindly Mrs. Rubin had been their neighbor for ages. Gali couldn't recall a time that she hadn't lived in the palatial home next door. Of course, Mrs. Rubin knew most of her friends.

A girl around her age looking through her dining room windows?

Gali found herself picturing Leah Rosen doing just that.

But *why?* And how did she know where she lived?

It was certainly odd.

Gali entered the kitchen and placed all of the packages on the enormous granite island.

"Elizabeth?" she called.

With a sigh, she realized that their housekeeper wasn't home either, and was most probably out doing errands. She settled herself on a comfortable kitchen stool and took out her notebook. It still said *Meet Leah Rosen* at the top of the page, and the rest of the snowy white paper was still blank. But now she wrote:

chilled gazpacho, parmesan crisps
arancini, dipping sauce

ravioli, tomato basil cream sauce
grilled ramps
sweet potato mousse
churros
cardamom ice cream, lime curd, macerated blueberries

She was looking at her menu while sitting under the skylight in her kitchen, feeling pleased. The sunlight felt warm on her back, the house was blissfully quiet, and all seemed right with the world, when suddenly a chill went down her spine and she looked at her notebook again.

No. It couldn't be.

It wasn't the menu that caused Gali's blood to grow cold.

Instead, her eyes fixed on the words that she'd carelessly scribbled into her notebook that very morning, the impossible dawning on her.

Meet Leah Rosen.

She stared at the name Rosen ... it just couldn't be.

Her heart began to pound furiously.

With a shaking hand, she took a pen and wrote the name Rosen backwards.

Meet Leah Nes Or.

Her whole body was shaking now.

It couldn't be, it simply couldn't.

Could it?

CHAPTER NINE

TOVA

LOOKING DOWN AT THE floor, she noticed for the first time how some of the tiles in the corridor were a dark purple shade, though most of them were a light, sickly green color. Funny how she hadn't noticed them before, since she'd been seated on the uncomfortable chair for what seemed like many hours. Massaging her neck, she looked around. There were faded greenish curtains on the windows, as well, ostensibly to match the nasty tiles. Tova found herself wondering if the decor had ever looked fresh and new. It was hard to imagine the decrepit hospital surroundings as anything but old and forlorn.

She knew that she was just focusing on mundane details because it kept her mind from wandering back to the predicament in which she found herself. Still, she felt that the diversion was necessary; she'd even recently read up on the subject of mindfulness as a way to de-stress. Paying careful, mindful attention to the tiles on the floor, the curtains on the window—whatever it took to keep her mind from drifting back to the evening before.

When she'd come home from work at around eight o'clock that night to find her grandmother on the living room floor, breathing but unconscious.

She got up from the chair in the narrow alcove of the hallway and walked around a bit in the cramped space, continuously kneading the tight muscles in her neck as she walked. There wasn't much space to stretch in the intensive care unit itself. The large room was filled with machines of every sort. The hospital bed was in the center, with machines on all sides. She was only allowed to be there for minutes at a time, and so she found herself on that very chair around the corner for much of the time. Her grandmother's oxygen machine emitted a gentle *thrrrp*, *thrrrp* sound every few minutes, but other than that, the room felt utterly quiet and still. The monitors had blessedly ceased their cacophony of riotous beeping since the previous night, for which she was grateful. It meant that her grandmother's condition had stabilized somewhat.

The doctors weren't sure what had caused her cardiac event, as they called it, but the fact that she was still alive was surely a miracle. Her vital signs were so weak that the doctors hadn't believed she'd live through the night. They felt that the next forty-eight hours would be crucial. If she gained consciousness, there would be a chance she'd survive. If.

It was a very big *If.*

There had been oxygen deprivation, of that they were certain.

Tova had approached one of the nice nurses in the ICU the previous evening.

"The fact that she's still unconscious ... does that mean she's in a coma?" she'd asked.

"Not exactly, dear," the nurse had responded kindly. "We call it a twilight—she can awaken at any moment. The longer it takes, though, well ... the chances become slimmer."

"I understand."

The empathetic nurse looked at Tova with genuine concern. "Look, dear … my shift is over in ten minutes. I'd be happy to answer any questions you might have then, all right? My name is Laurie, by the way."

"Thank you, Laurie," Tova whispered. "I'd really appreciate that."

She'd waited in the very same hallway the evening before, and true to her word, the nurse had joined her there after ten minutes or so, sitting on the chair opposite hers.

Tova had a very analytic, sharp mind, and the very first question she'd asked was what had caused this to occur.

"She hasn't been complaining of any chest pain or anything," she explained. "I live with my grandmother, so I would've known. She's been complaining of other things, digestive problems mostly, but I never thought she'd have a heart attack …."

The sweet nurse, with her serene face and kind eyes, had answered honestly.

"Well, she didn't have a heart attack, dear."

"She didn't?" Tova asked incredulously.

"No, she went into cardiac arrest."

"Isn't that the same thing?"

"People seem to think so, but they're very different," Laurie explained. "A heart attack is caused by a blockage, which temporarily stops blood flow to the heart. What your grandmother suffered was cardiac arrest—that's when the heart's electrical system malfunctions. People often confuse the two terms because they're related, but they aren't the same thing at all."

"I see," Tova said. "What causes the electrical system of the heart to malfunction? Is there anything I could've done to prevent this?"

The nurse smiled. "At her advanced age, it was most likely due to irregular heart rhythms, called arrhythmias. In some cases, when there are symptoms present, a pacemaker can be implanted, but in most of these cases, the symptoms are mild and often go unnoticed, so don't go blaming yourself, dear."

Now, as Tova walked around the cramped quarters, she could recall every word of her talk with Laurie, and she was grateful that the nurse had taken the time to answer her questions and allay some of her fears.

Because she *had* been blaming herself.

All of a sudden, Tova recalled a girl from Baltimore, Chana Feinbach, who had attended Machon Chana with her. She hadn't been in most of her classes and she hadn't known her all that well, but she now remembered that Shari had once mentioned that Chana's father was a renowned heart surgeon who had created an implantable cardiac defibrillator, or something like that. For some reason, she even recalled his name—Dr. Hershy Feinbach. Shari had seemed to think he was pretty famous.

She wondered if she would have learned more about these things if she had been better friends with Chana Feinbach. Then she would've known the signs to look for ….

It was futile thinking, she knew.

At that very moment, Tova spied her father walking toward her. It was so good to see him—she hadn't seen him in ages. Still, she couldn't help but notice that he looked much older than when she'd seen him last. His shoulders looked rounded and stooped, as if he was carrying the weight of the world on them. Seeing his daughter, he rushed down the hallway, his scarf thrown haphazardly around his neck.

"Ta, where's your coat?" she asked.

He looked down, his once dark hair flecked with a lot of grey.

"I guess I forgot it in the car." He smiled wanly. "So how is she? The same?"

Tova nodded.

"Thanks, Tova, for holding the fort and all that. But I'm here now, so you can go home, relax …"

"I'm not going anywhere."

He checked his watch. "It's almost nine. Don't you have to go to work?"

"I'm taking the day off."

Isaac Miller looked at his daughter, a quiet understanding between them. She saw the lines etched around his eyes in deep grooves that didn't used to be there. He just seemed so much older than when she'd seen him last, she found herself thinking again.

"Where's Perri? Is she here?"

"No, no," he mumbled. "She had to stay with the kids."

Tova felt a stab of sympathy for her father. It couldn't have been easy for him all of those years. First he'd been alone, then he'd married and built a family with his new wife, while his daughter had kept her distance ….

His children must've been getting older. The oldest one, a boy, was probably in his upper teens already, but he was Perri's son from her first marriage. His name was Ephraim, that much she knew. There was a brood of them, and she couldn't keep them all straight, not that she'd put much effort into keeping track of her father's other family. It was slightly embarrassing that she didn't even know their ages, but it was too awkward to ask about them at this point.

Life just hadn't been easy, for either of them.

"Tova," her father said quietly. "You don't have to—"

"I know. I want to."

He shrugged. "Fair enough. I won't argue with you."

He sat down on the chair opposite her, as Laurie had done the night before. It occurred to Tova that her father had never argued with her. She'd often surmised that his desire to keep the peace stemmed from a place of well-meaning pity. He felt sorry for her, his only daughter from his first disastrous marriage, and no doubt he partly blamed himself for her solitary existence these past years. Still, she'd had his own mother to live with ... *Now* what would she do?

As if reading his daughter's mind, he murmured, "You know, you're more than welcome to come live with us in Chicago, in case ..."

"She could get better, Ta."

He looked at her gravely.

"I just spoke to one of the doctors on the floor. At her age, I think we have to be realistic, Tova'le."

He used to call her that as a little girl, before so much had happened to upset their lives. She'd nearly forgotten all about that nickname, but now it warmed her to hear it again.

Tova sighed a deep, anguished sigh. She, too, had been carrying a heavy burden. It was almost as if carrying the weight of her mother and grandmother, alone, for such a long time had become a burden that she could no longer carry.

"I have my job," she murmured.

She wasn't being entirely truthful, and from the look on her father's face, he knew it just as well as she did. As much as she enjoyed her accounting job and the people she worked with, it was just a job. With her impressive resume, sterling reputation, and spotless work record, she could easily find a job in the Chicago area.

She just didn't want to.

She was an adult. She could live on her own if it came to that. In essence, that's what she'd been doing, anyway. Her grandmother didn't take care of her; it was she who took care of her grandmother. Still, the thought of coming home to an empty apartment after work wasn't appealing to her at all. On the other hand, coming home to her father and Perri's children didn't seem any better.

There was plenty of time to think about it. Right now, she just needed to get through the day, which seemed never-ending although it was still the morning.

"Have you had anything to eat, Ta?"

He looked at her. "Me? Uh, no. I'm fine. How about you, Tova? Did you eat anything?"

"I don't remember."

They sat in silence for several more moments, enmeshed in their own thoughts. But their thoughts came to a screeching halt when they saw two nurses walking quickly, accompanied by a doctor. They were carrying what looked like a very large, blue plastic sheet into the room. It almost looked like an inflatable raft. One nurse disappeared with the doctor into the ICU and one remained behind to explain to them what was happening.

"Therapeutic hypothermia," the nurse said quietly.

"I'm sorry, what's that?" Isaac asked.

"We're trying to bring her body temperature down."

"Wait, is she running a fever?" he asked, alarmed.

"Oh, no, nothing like that ... We do this to cool down patients, to make the body less stressed. There's ice water in the plastic sheets. Sometimes that does the trick."

"And what happens after?" Tova asked.

"Well, sometimes they wake up."

And, with that, she joined the others in the room.

Tova got up and walked around, her muscles tense and tight from sitting for so long. She remembered studying for the grueling CPA exams, sitting hunched over her laptop for hours each day until she thought she couldn't bear it any longer. And then, one day, it was over. She'd gotten through it and moved on.

Surely she'd get through today as well, as difficult as it seemed—but whether her grandmother would make it through remained to be seen.

Her father still sat in his chair, deep in thought. But Tova was restless, and she paced the corridor first one way, then the other. She was on her fourth round of pacing when her father said quietly, "Tova."

"Yes, Ta?"

"Pacing isn't going to help matters. Why don't you sit down?"

She sat down once more.

He cleared his throat. "Ah, I know that the timing isn't that great, but there's something I want to tell you."

She waited expectantly.

Her father rubbed his hands together, looking as if he wasn't sure how to proceed.

"It's like this," he began. "Ephraim thought of someone for you. I know it's crazy to even mention it at a time like this, but we're both here …."

"Isn't Ephraim, like, seventeen or eighteen?"

"He's almost twenty, actually. It's his *chavrusa*, who's twenty-two. He learns in the Mir."

While it was nice of Ephraim to think of someone for her, the question still needed to be asked.

"What's his story?"

"Story?"

"Yes, I mean … why would he go out with me?"

Her father looked genuinely puzzled. "Why not?"

Tova blushed. "Ta, I don't know if you realize this, but I'm not exactly … well, inundated with offers. I've only gone out once in three years."

Understanding began to dawn on her father's face, and his eyes looked sad.

"I see."

"It's no one's fault, Ta," she said. "But you have to admit that I just don't sound that great on paper."

He frowned. "You're so much more than a piece of paper, it's just ridiculous."

She shrugged. "That's the system, Ta."

"Well, the system is broken." He looked at her seriously. "Tova, I never want you to feel like you have to settle. You're a wonderful girl. I know it's been tough on you … you deserve everything that you're looking for. Really, I mean that."

Tova didn't consider herself to be an emotional type of girl. With all that she'd endured, she just couldn't afford the luxury. But her father had never said anything like that to her before, and with her emotions running high and her current state of exhaustion, she felt a lump form in her throat and tears well in her eyes. She didn't trust herself to speak, so she just nodded.

Of course, her father cared a great deal about her. She'd always known that. Still, when she was younger, there had been times when she had to make Kiddush for her mother on Friday night, all the while imagining her own father making Kiddush at a different table. For his other children. It was a deep pain that she'd never shared with anyone. She didn't dwell on it most of the time, but when he said those words, they touched her deeply. Just hearing him say that acted like a balm to her weary, battered soul.

"Thanks, Ta."

He nodded.

After several moments, a thought occurred to her.

"Ta, wait, what's this boy's name?" she asked.

She never got a chance to hear the answer, because at that moment the nurse rushed out.

They looked up expectantly. The nurse was smiling and looked hopeful.

"Her eyes are open," she said brightly.

They stood up quickly.

"You mean she's awake?" Isaac asked.

The nurse hesitated. "I wouldn't call it exactly 'awake,' but it might be a sign of a return to consciousness. We'll know more over the next twenty-four hours."

"Do patients ever open their eyes but then never regain consciousness?" Tova asked.

"I'm afraid so, yes," she responded. "Mr. Miller, come with me.

You can see her for a few minutes, if you'd like."

He followed the nurse into the ICU and Tova sat back down on the chair to wait, her mind swirling. It was only then that a new, disturbing thought occurred to her.

She couldn't possibly go out with the boy Ephraim had thought of for her.

Unless …

Unless he'd previously been married.

CHAPTER TEN

EVA

IT WAS SEVEN-THIRTY IN the evening, and Eva was running late. She was usually fastidious about being on time, just as she was fastidious about everything else. But the day thus far had been an unmitigated disaster, with everything going wrong.

Though she'd felt groggy and jetlagged when awakened promptly at 6 a.m., she resisted the urge to turn off her alarm and sleep in. Instead, she'd forced herself to get dressed and have her freshly squeezed morning orange juice exactly on time. Her housekeeper, Jeannette, was an expert juicer. Each night, Eva would leave her instructions on which juice she'd like the following morning, along with other instructions for the day. Mondays were usually a kale blend, but since Eva had just returned from such an exhausting trip, she knew she'd need the extra shot of Vitamin C. It had become a routine of sorts for her and Jeannette. Routine for Eva wasn't just something she enjoyed; it was a necessity. Anything that deviated from her routine made her irritable and threw her off her game, which would never do. Jeannette seemed to understand this, and she was capable and followed orders efficiently. She was quite unlike her new intern at the office, Sophie, who was a complete catastrophe.

As she rushed about that morning, she made a mental note to tell Shmiel that he'd have to learn and adapt quickly to her routine. There were no two ways about that.

And so she'd arrived at her office early, and had just taken off her camel-colored cashmere coat and Hermes scarf when her secretary came in, a pensive look on her usually placid face.

"We have a problem with the Crane deal," she said bluntly.

Eva appreciated her directness. Edith Berman had been her secretary forever, and they got along precisely because Eva worked steadily and detested frivolous chitchat, and Edith was much the same way.

When she had something to say, she said it. Like now.

"What problem?" Eva asked. "We already have an inspector. Everything is good to go …."

"Zoning issues."

Eva blanched. "Zoning issues? How is that possible? There were no zoning issues with the building."

"Not with the building. With the air space."

"You have got to be kidding me," she whispered.

Her secretary wasn't joking, that much was certain. Edith never joked.

Eva sat down on the leather chair behind her polished mahogany desk.

"Start talking."

"The building next door bought the air rights to this building six years ago, apparently," Edith said matter-of-factly. "They're already at thirty-five stories high, and they want the option of going horizontal one day, if they want to expand. So they own the air rights. That's it. So the buyer backed out."

Eva had worked on this deal, day and night, for over four months. The building in question was an older, pre-war building, seven stories high, in the middle of Midtown Manhattan. The buyer was looking to raze it and build in its stead a thirty-five-story skyscraper. They'd been completely unaware that the building next door owned the air rights to the building.

Air rights were a thorny problem, especially in Manhattan, where every inch of space was coveted. It was as if the very air cost money to breathe, polluted or not.

"When did this happen?" Eva asked stonily.

"You were on the plane."

Eva swiveled on her chair and stared at the large gold plaque on the wall behind her. Air rights went back to early English common law, with its basis in the legal maxim that was etched on her wall.

"*Cujus est solum, ejus est usque ad coelem et ad inferos ....*"

"To whomsoever the soil belongs, he also owns to the sky and to the depths."

It was basic Real Estate 101, especially in New York. If someone owned the property, he also owned up to thirty-five stories of air space above it, which was why there were fewer and fewer low-rise buildings left in the city's landscape. Building never stopped, it seemed. Smaller properties were bought and torn down, and skyscrapers rebuilt on the site, maximizing usage for today's world.

This maxim also happened to make Eva a very rich woman.

She just wasn't expecting this.

And she wasn't about to go down without a fight.

The whole grueling day was spent with Eva on the phone,

skyping, teleconferencing, trying her best to minimize the damage, and most of all, spare her company's reputation and integrity.

After hours had elapsed, Eva, in most probability, had accomplished that goal, but the deal that had gone south was, in fact, irredeemable. Not every deal was able to be salvaged, Eva knew, but it was hard not to take it as a personal blow. Especially after the entire debacle with her son in Israel, which had left her touchy and combative.

Rather, even *more* touchy and combative than usual.

Simcha still hadn't called her to apologize for his wife's rude behavior.

And she wasn't about to do anything of the sort, either.

It was a stalemate, in essence.

Throughout that hectic day, Eva constantly checked her cell phone for a message from her son. She was secretly hoping he'd leave her a text, just to find out how her flight to the States had been.

But there was nothing.

The irony was not lost on Eva. Here she was, a powerful woman in Midtown Manhattan, who'd built a real estate empire from the ground up. She was a force to be reckoned with—she'd earned a reputation for getting winning results along with her enviable career. Her son's quiet wife, on the other hand, was an accountant. A CPA, to be sure, but she worked in a *bakery.*

A bakery.

Here she was, managing million-dollar deals, and that girl worked in a bakery. It was simply staggering. *Why couldn't Simcha realize how very different they were? Why did he blame her for their lack of relationship, and think his wife was blameless?*

A new thought occurred to her. Maybe her son *did* realize.

Perhaps he expected her to be the one to make amends because she, after all, was infinitely better at communication, and had so much more experience dealing with people. Some of the reasons for her success, she thought, were her brilliant marketing strategies … she'd employed every method she'd known in order to close a deal.

That had to be it.

Simcha obviously wanted her to use her myriad talents to win over his meek, mousy wife. The more she thought about it, the more appealing it sounded.

But when four o'clock had come and gone without a word from him, Eva knew that she was fooling herself. He didn't want her to use her talents to win over his wife. In all probability, he just wanted her to apologize.

Which was something that she'd never do.

Which brought her back to exactly where she'd started that day—on the phone, trying to galvanize other deals to make up for the one deal she'd lost. Accepting defeat was not something she could tolerate.

Simply put, Eva hated losing.

The very thought of losing her own son to that … that bakery girl was something that weighed heavily on her mind the whole day.

And there was not a thing that she could do about it.

She was supposed to meet Shmiel at a restaurant in Midtown Manhattan for dinner at eight. She had so much to do, she didn't know how she'd ever be able to get there on time.

There were three more important calls to make before she

could even think of leaving the office. There was a stack of papers that needed her signature, and then there was Sophie, the intern, who was just a disaster, spilling coffee on some very important papers and misplacing the Rhine account file.

She needed to be dealt with.

"Sophie," she called. "Come in here, please."

A few moments later, an anxious young woman entered her office. She wore dark rimmed glasses and was dressed conservatively, and her hands kept fidgeting nervously. Unfortunately, she reminded Eva of Simcha's wife, not so much in looks but in demeanor. The girl looked positively afraid of her own shadow.

"Yes, Ms. Adler? You wanted to see me?"

"Sophie, sit down." She gestured to a chair.

Sophie sat down, her face pale with apprehension.

"Look, I'm sorry about the coffee—"

"Sophie, this is the third time this week that you've messed up," Eva said bluntly. "And those are only the times I know about ... I was away, let's not forget. I'm a patient woman, but really, this is bordering on ridiculous. What seems to be the problem?"

Sophie turned red with embarrassment.

"I'm sorry, Ms. Adler, it's just that I got a little nervous—"

"Let's get something straight, shall we?" Eva said brightly. "There's nothing to be nervous about. You're not handling million dollar deals—I am. You are a paid intern. You're here to help things run smoothly and make my life easier, not harder. Now where is the Rhine account file? Did you find it?"

"It's around here somewhere," Sophie said, flustered. "I'll keep looking."

"You do that."

Then, with a wave of her hand, she was summarily dismissed.

The poor woman had not walked two feet when she suddenly turned around.

"Um ... Ms. Adler?"

"What now, Sophie?" Eva answered brusquely. "I thought we were finished here."

"Yes, ma'am. Um ... I just wanted to say, that is—"

Eva glared at her. She simply could not abide people who took forever to get their point across.

Sophie's face was bright red, and she looked more miserable than ever.

"It's just that, well ... I'm handing in my two weeks' notice, Ms. Adler. I won't be working here anymore."

Eva gaped at her. "How is that possible? I hired you for a ten-month internship. You've been here—what? Two months?"

Sophie shook her head miserably.

"One month."

"It seems like much longer," Eva commented in a clipped tone. "Someone offered you a different job, I take it?"

"No, ma'am. It's just that ... that ..."

Eva waited, eyebrows raised.

"In the whole time I've been here, I can't seem to do anything right. You've never said I was doing a good job, or anything. I just don't think this is the right environment for me." A tear slowly coursed down her cheek.

Eva bristled. When she finally spoke, her tone was icy. "Sophie, forgive me, but I thought that you wanted to work at my prestigious company for the job training ... the resume building. Not the compliments."

"Yes, but—"

"This is a tough business, Sophie, not for the faint of heart. Just today I saw a seventeen-million dollar deal fall through the cracks. Am I falling apart? Hardly. It just makes me want to try harder. In this business, the strong succeed. The weak fail."

Sophie was silent, tears coursing down her face. But then she looked up and said proudly, "Yes, that may be true, Ms. Adler. But you could still be a little nicer."

And, with that, she turned and left the office, not looking back.

Eva was flabbergasted.

Of all the nerve!

As if she didn't have enough problems of her own, Eva silently raged.

Really, a paid intern telling her to change her personality ...! What utter nonsense. To be nicer ... why, if she'd be *nice,* there was no way she'd survive in this business, much less thrive. What did Sophie know, besides nothing? The poor, ineffectual woman could hardly hold herself together. For a fleeting moment, she remembered that smug therapist, Dr. Don Fischer, who thought he had all the answers. She wondered what he'd think of Sophie. Though Eva wasn't a psychologist, it was clear that the woman was simply afraid of success.

She'd be happy to see her gone. The office would certainly get on better without her there, misplacing everything within her reach. Still, she couldn't help but feel a bit affronted. Here she was, trying to give this poor creature a chance at life, and to have her largesse thrown back in her face ... It was all a bit too much. And though Eva considered herself positively stoic under the most trying of circumstances, this new grievance, however minor, coupled with her daughter-in-law's blatant rudeness, just seemed too much to bear.

And so Eva was in well-checked hysteria mode for the rest of that afternoon and early evening, which was why she was running late for her appointment with Shmiel. Funny that she couldn't bring herself to call it a *date.*

"Appointment" sounded much safer in her estimation, and so that's what she chose to consider it.

Eva got to the restaurant, La Cherie, at eight-twenty, which was a minor miracle. It had just started snowing … ugh. Nothing about this day was going right, it seemed. When she entered the restaurant, she quickly removed her wet scarf and checked her reflection in the mirror in the small entranceway.

She was no beauty, she knew. Her dark eyes were small and close together, her nose was rather large and pointed, and her chin was pointed, as well. Still, she tried to look as attractive as possible, and there she believed she'd succeeded. Her black *sheitel*, though a trifle wet at the moment, was cut in the latest bob, her makeup was flawlessly applied and continuously retouched throughout the day, and her figure was still quite slim as a result of her constant dieting and exercise regimen. And, of course, the occasional liposuction, though no one needed to be apprised of that. Least of all, one Shmiel Goodman.

She knew that her cashmere coat was stunning. For the staggering amount she had paid for it, it had better be. Her high-heeled boots were impractical but gorgeous, and she knew that she made a more than decent impression. It wasn't as if Shmiel Goodman would notice the difference … but still, she always liked to look her best.

She took a calming breath before entering the restaurant. It was a lovely place. The dining area was large and dimly lit, with wood floors that were polished to a high gleam and beveled mirrors around each cozy table banquette. She had been there before on important business meetings and knew that they served very high-end food and employed a meticulous wait staff.

The maître d' came over.

"Can I help you, Ma'am?"

"Yes, my name is Eva Adler. I'm supposed to join Samuel Goodman—I believe he might be here already."

"Very good, yes, he's here. Come right this way, Ma'am."

A chair had been removed from the table to make room for Shmiel's wheelchair. His grey hair and beard were neatly trimmed, and his small, wire-framed glasses perched on the tip of his nose as he perused the menu. He seemed a bit pensive.

"Sorry I'm late, Shmiel," she said, as she slid into the chair.

"No problem at all." He waved his hand. "I just got here myself. Boris just went to park the car after he dropped me off."

"Boris?"

"He's my right-hand man—my driver and aide. I don't know where I'd be without him."

"Oh, I see," she said. She hadn't realized that he employed an aide, and wasn't at all sure that she liked the sound of it. She didn't like an outsider interfering with personal matters … perhaps Jeanette could help out, if need be.

Well, no matter discussing all of that now. There would be plenty of time for that later. After the day she'd had, she just wanted to enjoy her evening, and Shmiel was usually an amiable companion.

"So, how was your trip?" Shmiel asked.

"Not as smooth as I would have liked," Eva answered. "My son was ... difficult."

Shmiel considered this for a moment. After clearing his throat, he said, "You know, Eva, I'm a little relieved to hear that."

Her eyebrows lifted. Now what did *that* mean?

"I think we need to consider the ramifications of this ... joint venture," he said. "My children, too, were less than pleased. I think we should take a step back and rethink things, for the time being, in any case."

Eva thought fast. He'd misinterpreted what she'd said, of course. Simcha hadn't been upset about her news at all. He'd just been touchy because of that wife of his, but of course Shmiel couldn't possibly know that. On the other hand, *his* children had been less than pleased about her, which stung. It was, in all probability, his sons who were against the idea, since they'd lost their mother a mere two years earlier. Surely it couldn't have been that angel, Devora, who was opposed.

"What did your daughter-in-law, Devora, think about it?" she asked directly.

"Actually—" He cleared his throat again. "— she was the most opposed to the idea. My sons weren't enthusiastic, maybe, but Devora was very vocal about it. No offense, of course."

"Of course," she murmured. "None taken."

Well.

It wasn't enough that she'd lost a seventeen-million dollar deal that day, apparently. She also had to be brutally rejected by Shmiel Goodman ... a *cripple*! Rejecting *her*!

And all because of that daughter-in-law of his, who seemed so angelic, but obviously had her talons out when no one was looking … Of all the unmitigated gall …

She massaged her temples. Really, there was a limit to what one person could endure in one day.

"Are you okay?" Shmiel asked with concern.

"Yes, yes … just a headache," she responded. "It's been a very long day."

"Why don't you order something?" he asked. "You probably need to eat a good dinner. That ought to help."

Don't be nice to me, she thought. It would just make things all the more difficult. But she was suddenly ravenous, and the menu did sound appealing. The waiter came by and asked, "Would you like to hear the specials for this evening?" and Eva found herself answering *yes.*

It was a relief to concentrate on whether to choose steak tartare salad or chicken eggroll in plum jam for an appetizer. She chose the former while Shmiel chose the latter, and they said they would order the main dishes a bit later.

Oddly enough, Eva was at a loss for words. Her head still throbbed, painfully.

"So," Shmiel said. It was more of a statement than a beginning.

"So," she answered.

"Are we in agreement that the best thing to do is to take a step back and think things through?"

Eva thought about what she wanted to say, the message she wanted to convey. In her mind, she thought of an emotional response, something along the lines of how cowardly it was to back out of a marriage proposal just because of adult children, how hurtful it was to have him discuss this calmly as if he were discussing the weather, and so on.

But something held her back. She knew that it would be the wrong approach with someone like Shmiel, who, like herself, had suffered a loss and was no doubt still in pain. And so she was simply businesslike in her response, and didn't allow her emotions to rise to the surface.

"I'm willing to wait, Shmiel," she said calmly. "But I'd like to inform you that I have no intention of waiting forever. And I would further like to inform you that I plan to fully employ all of my resources and talent, if need be, to try to win your adult children over to my way of thinking. And be forewarned … I'm good at what I do."

Shmiel's mouth turned up at the corners. "Yes, I'm sure you are."

"I don't enjoy defeat, you know."

"Of course not."

"I also believe that this … joint venture, as you call it, would benefit both of us. So I'm not giving up on anything just yet."

Shmiel nodded. "Well, that's what I figured you'd say."

And then Eva proceeded to tell him about the deal that had fallen through in the eleventh hour, and he asked many questions about it. It was nice to have someone who genuinely seemed interested in her day—very nice, in fact, since she could hardly recall the last time that had been. Or if it had ever been.

So engrossed were they in their conversation that they didn't even notice when the appetizers arrived. The waiter discreetly placed them on the table and withdrew, and Eva realized how very hungry she was.

It wasn't just the food, of course, and Eva knew it. She was hungry for companionship, for camaraderie, though she'd fought against that very idea for so long. She'd been a lone warrior for most of her adult life, but for once, it actually felt good to put down her battle gear and just stop fighting.

She enjoyed her appetizer very much, and Shmiel also commented that his dish was quite good. They had just ordered their main dishes when Shmiel leaned forward and quietly said, "Don't look now, but do you see who just sat down at the next table?"

From her vantage point, it wasn't easy to spot anyone, since there was a riotous vase of flowers blocking her view.

"No, who is it?" she asked.

"Aaron Bergstein, the real estate developer. He's an old friend of mine from yeshiva days. He owns half of Manhattan, you know."

Of course she knew that. She just hadn't realized that Shmiel was acquainted with him. She further knew that Simcha was currently living in one of the Bergstein properties in Yerushalayim. Maybe that could be a way of introducing herself, she surmised. She'd secretly been hoping to have a business meeting with him for the last few years, but it hadn't ever come to fruition, as of yet.

All of these thoughts were swirling in her head when the unexpected happened.

Aaron Bergstein himself, formidably tall and broad, sauntered over to their table, his hand outstretched to shake Shmiel's hand.

"Sam, good to see you," he boomed. "It's been ages."

"Yes, it sure has been a long time, Aaron," Shmiel said.

"What are you doing in that wheelchair?" Aaron asked bluntly.

"I had a little accident years ago."

"Oh, I'm sorry to hear that, Sam," he said sincerely. "Me and my big mouth."

"Let me introduce you to Eva Adler, of the Adler Prestige Group."

"Pleased to meet you," Aaron said. "I've heard of you—you've made quite a name for yourself in this business."

"Thank you."

Hearing those words from a mogul like Aaron Bergstein was like soothing honey on her fractured soul. And to think that an introduction had been so easily made because of Shmiel Goodman further enforced the idea in her mind that they'd make a good team, her and Shmiel, as unlikely a match as it seemed.

And when Eva made her mind up, there was no stopping her.

"I understand that my son and his wife are currently your tenants in Jerusalem, Mr. Bergstein," she said.

"Really?" he replied, pulling up a chair. "What a small world …"

CHAPTER ELEVEN

SHARI

"JUST A MINUTE, COMING!" she called.

Her neighbor had come by at least twice to introduce herself, and it was embarrassing that she still hadn't met her, as of yet. The first unannounced visit had come at the worst possible time, when she'd been having a meltdown over her mother-in-law's behavior. The second time, she hadn't been at home, and she was fully prepared to apologize when she went to answer the door.

She was surprised to see, though, that it wasn't her neighbor. It was a girl who looked quite familiar, but she couldn't quite place from where she knew her.

"Yes?" she asked tentatively.

She was astonished when the girl looked genuinely hurt.

"You don't remember me, right?" she said softly. "Well, I'm not even surprised."

There was something so defeated, so disappointed in her tone that Shari couldn't even begin to fathom ... and all at once, she knew who this girl was. Shari couldn't recall her name, but she'd attended Machon Chana the same year as she did. She hadn't been in any of her classes, and their paths hadn't crossed all that much, but this girl had known Gali and Tova from camp, or something like that. She was a quiet, introverted type, never saying much, and Shari had barely noticed her that year.

"Oh, I'm so sorry," Shari said, flustered. "Of course I remember you. Please come in."

The girl quietly entered the apartment, still cluttered with a tower of boxes piled high in the corner. They'd definitely made progress unpacking, however. The furniture was in, and thank heavens, her mother-in-law was out, so each night she and Simcha stayed up late unpacking, box after box. The final remaining tower of boxes in the corner was thankfully the last of it.

Shari gestured to the leather sofa. "Won't you sit down?"

The girl sat down on the edge of the couch, looking uncomfortable. She was a mere wisp of a girl and looked much younger than her age, with freckles and a ponytail to tame her unruly, auburn hair. She was single, but other than that, Shari couldn't recall anything else about her. Shari found herself wishing that she could recall her name, but her mind was a complete blank.

"It's so nice you came over," Shari said graciously. "Are you in Yerushalayim for a visit?"

The girl stared at her. "I live in the apartment right next door, right on the same landing. I'm living with my brother and sister-in-law. My sister-in-law, Rachel, came over to welcome you, but you weren't home."

Understanding began to dawn on her, and Shari felt mortified at her own lack of awareness. It all made sense now. This girl's name was Pearl Marcus, and her sister-in-law, Rachel Marcus, had been the one who had stopped by several times.

Between her trips to the doctor, moving apartments, her mother-in-law's disastrous visit, the Marcianos' return from France—

well, she'd been more than a little preoccupied. Still, it was jarring to realize how insulated she'd been, how she'd been so caught up in her own little world that she hadn't noticed the goings-on in the world around her. *When had she become so self-absorbed?* It just seemed so wrong.

Mentally chiding herself for her lack of manners, she said apologetically, "You know, I'm sorry I didn't realize that you're living next door. A lot has been going on in my life, and I'm just trying to—"

"Oh, I understand," Pearl said quickly. "I'm the type who no one notices. Don't worry about it."

Shari felt her cheeks flame, so ashamed was she at this admission. It was true, of course, but how callous of her not to notice ... not to care. Here she was, bemoaning her fate to herself each day, wishing for a child, wishing for a mother-in-law who was more tolerable ....

It was a reality check for her to see this struggling girl, completely alone and forgotten, sitting on her couch, desperate for a friend.

"I'm really sorry," she said again. "It's just that I've had so much going on, I guess I just haven't—"

"You mean you never saw me?" the girl persisted. "I've seen you lots of times. You and your husband. I see you go to work in the mornings, and your husband goes to learn ...."

And then, in a stunning flash of clarity, Shari remembered that first day, over a month earlier, when Simcha had surprised her by taking her to see the apartment. She'd had an eerie feeling then that someone was watching her, but she'd convinced herself that it had just been a curtain fluttering in the window.

Could it be that Pearl Marcus had been watching them,

waiting for the right moment to come over? How very odd.

"Uh, do you work?" Shari asked. "Or are you in school?"

"No," Pearl said. "I babysit for my niece every day so Rachel can go to work."

"Oh, that's very nice of you."

Silence. Shari couldn't think of anything to say. The whole impromptu visit was just so awkward.

"Well, I guess you're wondering why I came here," Pearl continued. "I just wanted to tell you that I don't hold any grudges."

If Shari had been expecting her to say anything, it was not that.

"Grudges?" Shari repeated. To the best of her knowledge, they'd never had any interaction of any kind ....

Why on earth would there be any grudges?

"Yeah. When we were in seminary, you and Gali were going to Petach Tikvah for Shabbos and I wanted to go, too, and you kind of made plans without me. So I had to stay in the dorm for Shabbos. All by myself. But, like I said, I'm completely over it and I don't hold anything against you."

Well.

Shari felt her face turning pink. She was genuinely shocked. Not only couldn't she remember anything like that ever happening, it was obvious that the episode *did* bother Pearl a lot, and probably had bothered her for the last three years. It certainly didn't seem as if she had many friends, or had much going on in her life, in any case. She couldn't recall even going with Gali to Petach Tikvah, and certainly not excluding this girl. Still, it must've happened—or at least, Pearl Marcus thought it did.

Shari found herself apologizing for the third time in a row.

"I'm so sorry, Pearl," she said earnestly. "I don't even remember that happening, but I'm sorry if I hurt your feelings. I never meant to do that."

"I know you never meant it," Pearl replied. "That's why I don't hold anything against you. Or Gali, either. You know, I've thought about it a lot. Popular people have no idea what it's like for the rest of us."

"Popular?" Shari echoed weakly.

"You know, everyone likes you and wants to be your friend, so it's easy for you."

Shari could hardly believe what she was hearing. It was almost as if this girl was still in high school, the way she was talking. Shari felt many, many years older than her. She'd married young, had her own personal struggles to contend with ...

Easy?

Nothing was easy.

But, truth be told, she hadn't had to struggle alone. Putting it into perspective, she'd had Simcha by her side for the last three years, and this girl had not had anyone, from the sound of things. It was natural for her to recall details from their year in seminary more vividly, since she'd had nothing else on which to focus.

Shari had more than a sneaking suspicion that Pearl had thought about her quite often over these past few years, while she hadn't even been aware of Pearl's existence. The knowledge was more than a little jarring ... She just didn't know what to do about it.

Wait ... she did know, actually. Here was a *chessed* just waiting to happen, and she couldn't ignore it. She couldn't ignore Pearl Marcus this time around, and she felt like this was an opportunity that had just fallen into her lap. She wasn't about to make the same mistake twice.

"Uh, Pearl," she began, carefully avoiding all topics of friendship and popularity. "Do you ever go out on Shabbos? Would you like to come for a meal?"

"You don't have to invite me over because you're feeling guilty, you know," Pearl said. "I told you that I'm completely over the whole Petach Tikvah thing."

It certainly didn't seem that way to Shari, but instead of visiting that topic again, she merely said, "Not at all, Pearl, we'd love to have you. And it's not like you have a far walk. What do you say?"

Conflicting emotions seemed to struggle in Pearl's face. Though there was most definitely a part of her that seemed unsure, the part of her that really wanted to eat a meal with Shari and her husband won out.

"Okay, I guess," she said. "Tomorrow night?"

Shari thought fast. *Was today already Thursday?*

She supposed it was. Well, okay.

An opportunity had come her way and she'd accepted the challenge willingly. Perhaps it wouldn't be a challenge, after all. Maybe they'd have a nice time together.

Somehow, she didn't think so, but maybe …

"Sure, tomorrow night is great," she said.

"Can I make something?"

Shari swallowed. "Sure."

"How about a salad? I make really good salads."

"You know what? I'd really appreciate that. Lately, I think my salads have been getting a little boring."

"Okay, fine. So I'll come by tomorrow night, then." She got up off the couch, and Shari walked her to the door.

"Thanks so much for stopping in, Pearl," she said.

"Sure, well … see you tomorrow night."

Shari closed the door behind her and locked it. She then placed her hands over her eyes.

What had just happened?

What would Simcha say?

She wasn't at all sure. On the other hand, if this was a test of some sort, she was determined to pass it, somehow.

THE NEXT MORNING, SHARI'S phone on the nightstand rang early. She was still in bed since on Friday she allowed herself the luxury of sleeping a bit later than usual. She leaned over to see who it was, and answered the phone with a smile. It was her Aunt Efrat, her father's oldest sister. She had lived in Yerushalayim her entire life, though she'd married an American doctor thirty-five years earlier. The irony wasn't lost on her that her aunt, who was an Israeli through and through, had married an American while living her entire life in Israel, while her parents, who were both Israeli, had lived most of their adult lives in Brooklyn.

"Shari, my darling," she began in heavily accented English, which she always insisted on speaking when conversing with Shari. "I'm so sorry to call at such an inconvenient hour, but I need from you to ask something."

"Of course, Aunt Efrat."

"I need from you to ask a huge, huge favor."

"Okay, sure, what do you need?" Shari yawned.

"Well, the favor, like I say, is huge, very huge. You can always say no, yes?"

Shari sat up. "Oh, I'm sure it'll be no problem."

"Well, I only ask you if you gua-RAN-tee, I mean gua-RAN-tee, that you say no if it's not good for you, yes?"

"Okay, fine."

"Yes?"

"Yes."

"Okay, here it is, my darling. Uncle David's flight was delay, he got stuck b'New York l'Shabbat ... and I was supposed to go to my friend Livnat for the meal tonight. You know how I don't like to eat Shabbat alone, yes? You remember my neighbor and good friend Livnat, yes?"

"Yes, I do. She lives next door to you, right?"

"Yes, my darling. Poor David, stuck in New York."

Her Uncle David worked approximately half of the year in New York, at Mount Sinai Medical Center, commuting back and forth, and this wasn't the first time this had happened.

"Well, my darling," her aunt continued. "You won't believe this, but Livnat has the flu. Sick to a dog."

"Sick like a dog," Shari corrected. Aunt Efrat always insisted on being corrected when she used an idiom incorrectly. Oddly enough, she conversed with her husband in Ivrit, and she seemingly only spoke to Shari and her friend Livnat in English.

"Yes, my darling, thank you. Sick like a dog."

"So what's the huge favor?"

"Oh, here it is ... if I may eat at your apartment with you tonight?"

Shari grinned. "Is that the huge favor? Of course, we'd love to have you!"

"You are gua-RAN-tee that it's not too much for you? I don't like to be, how you say, a third wheelbarrow."

"A third wheel, and no, it'll be just perfect. We're actually having a guest, someone who was with me in seminary. It'll be wonderful. Come over when Simcha is in shul, okay?"

"*B'seder*, my darling. You are the most bestest girl in the entire Yerushalayim, yes?"

"Yes," Shari giggled.

"You know, I can say that because my daughter lives in Beitar, right, my darling?"

"Right."

"I went to them last Shabbat, and I don't want to be a third wheelbarrow, like I say."

"Third wheel."

"Oh, what have you. My English is getting worser every second, yes? Bye, my darling. See you tonight, *b'ezrat Hashem*."

Grinning to herself, Shari got up and started her day, appreciatively saying under her breath, *Hashem, thank You for sending us Aunt Efrat tonight.*

She felt sorry for her Uncle David who was stuck in New York for an extra weekend, but she felt so relieved that Hashem had orchestrated that her aunt would be with them for Shabbos. Surely, even an awkward meal could be livened up by her exuberant, lively personality.

She wasn't sure why she'd felt so worried the entire evening before about hosting Pearl Marcus. There was just something about Pearl that made her a bit wary—the way she'd said that she watched Shari and her husband leave every morning, the way she'd acted when she came over. It would have been rather awkward.

No matter, it would surely be better with Aunt Efrat there.

AS SHARI LIT THE candles that Friday night, she felt a calmness of spirit that had eluded her for weeks. As she said the *brachah* on the candles, she didn't think of her mother-in-law, or the fact that Pearl Marcus would likely be knocking on her door at any moment, or the small tower of boxes that still remained in the corner of the living room. Mercifully, she felt an inner peace that stole over her as she gazed at the candles, and her mind felt clear and unencumbered.

All would be well, she knew. How everything would work out remained to be seen, but it was out of her control, in any case. With the candles shining brightly, she felt a serenity that she hadn't felt in a long time, and she silently thanked Hashem for granting her that special moment of inner peace and calm. When she was done with her special *tefillos*, she looked around the room and felt so grateful.

The leather couch fit perfectly in the spacious room, and the area rug looked brand new, since it had been sitting in storage until now. The kitchen was spotless and lovely, and the boxes in the living room notwithstanding, it already felt like a real home.

There was a knock on the front door and Shari went to open it, wondering which of her guests would be there first.

It was Pearl Marcus, holding a large glass bowl filled with salad.

"Good Shabbos, Pearl!" she exclaimed. "Please, come in. Thanks so much for the salad."

Pearl walked into the room and sat down on the couch a bit self-consciously. Shari brought the salad to the kitchen. "It looks incredible, Pearl."

"Thanks. I make really good salads."

"You sure do."

Not knowing what else to say, Shari said brightly, "My aunt is going to join us tonight. My father's sister, my Aunt Efrat."

"Does she live here?" Pearl asked.

"Yes, right here in Ramat Eshkol, on Ramat Hagolan."

"That's a really nice street," Pearl commented. "Is she married?"

"Yes, yes, she is," Shari replied. "My Uncle David is a doctor who commutes back and forth to New York for work. He got stuck there for Shabbos because his flight was delayed, so she's coming here instead."

"My father is a doctor. An endocrinologist."

"Oh, that's nice." Shari realized that she knew virtually nothing about her guest. "Where are you from?"

"Montreal, remember?"

"Oh, that's right," Shari said, though she hadn't any idea. Somehow, this girl was under the impression that they knew each other much better than they really did. Shari wondered if they'd had a conversation in seminary that she'd forgotten about, and supposed it was possible.

"Shari, remember when Miriam Newman fainted in seminary?"

Shari looked at her blankly.

"I was so scared," Pearl said. "She fainted nearly on top of me. I was the one who called Hatzalah, remember?"

Shari knew Miriam Newman, the girl in question, and vaguely remembered that she'd heard about her fainting on a fast day, but she couldn't recall it clearly. What did that have to do with anything?

"Uh, I don't really remember that well," she said slowly.

"Well, she just called me today," Pearl said proudly. "We've kept in touch."

"That's so nice," Shari said, secretly wishing that her aunt would come already, if just to keep the stilted conversation flowing.

"She has two kids already," Pearl remarked.

Shari swallowed. "That's so nice."

Pearl continued on, oblivious to Shari's discomfort. "She just had her second baby, a girl, two weeks ago. She said it was only fifteen minutes of labor, can you imagine? She wasn't even in a room yet—the baby was born in the hallway of the hospital ...."

Mercifully, there was a blessed knock at the door, and Shari jumped up to answer it.

"Aunt Efrat!" she exclaimed. "Oh, my goodness, you're soaking wet!"

"It just started raining on my way here, my darling," she said with a smile. She took off her scarf and handed her wet coat to Shari. "*Gishmei brachah*—it's only the end of February, we could use the rain."

"Of course, of course," Shari agreed, leading her aunt into the living room and hanging up her coat in the hallway. "Aunt Efrat, this is Pearl Marcus, a friend from seminary." She used the word "friend" purposely, knowing that it would please Pearl. She wasn't sure how many friends Pearl had, besides Miriam Newman.

"How lovely," Aunt Efrat said, sitting down on the couch. "From where are you?"

"Montreal."

"Ahh ... Canada, yes? My husband, David, has family in Montreal ... the Skolnik family, yes? You know them?"

"No." Pearl shook her head.

"How can that be? Skolnik? You aren't acquainted? Is Montreal a big town?"

"Yes, very big," Pearl replied, her eyes wide. It was obvious that she didn't quite know what to make of Aunt Efrat, with her hearty voice and ready laugh.

"Ahh, well ... he has other cousins, too. The Goldstein family, yes? You know them?"

"No."

Aunt Efrat continued to play Jewish geography until Simcha returned from shul and they all went into the dining room.

Simcha seemed much calmer and more relaxed since his mother had left. The night she left, he'd come back from her hotel more than a bit upset, but Shari hadn't pressed him for details that were obviously distressing to him.

Now, mere days later, his spirits seemed somewhat restored, and for that, she was grateful.

Shari had made quite a lovely meal. First there was gefilte fish, followed by chicken soup. It had come out more rich and flavorful than usual, earning rave reviews from Aunt Efrat, who consumed two bowls. Then she served a variety of homemade dips with Israeli salads, which Pearl seemed to enjoy. That was followed by roasted chicken with vegetables, a steaming potato kugel, and Pearl's salad, which was tossed with dried mangos and pomegranate seeds.

No one had any room left for the chocolate cake she'd baked, so they all sat around the table with glasses of hot tea after the meal ended.

"So, tell me, Pearl," Aunt Efrat said. "You date, yes? In a husband, for what are you looking?"

Pearl smiled. "Why, do you have someone for me?"

Aunt Efrat grinned coyly. "Perhaps I do."

"Well, I'm not sure—"

Aunt Efrat waved her hand. "Of course you're not sure! You're very young, yes? But you have some idea, yes?"

"Well, I want someone who has a plan to work, or someone in school. I'm not the career type of girl, I guess."

Aunt Efrat nodded enthusiastically. "That's just what I thought! You know, it's not easy, always being right, my darlings. Ahhh, well ... but that's just how I am."

Shari laughed. "You're always right, Aunt Efrat, that's for sure."

"I know, not easy, yes? Anyway, I have the perfect one for you. My neighbors, they have a son, yes? He's in school to be a dentist, yes? This sounds good to you, yes?"

Pearl looked from Shari to Aunt Efrat, confused. "Do you mean he's Israeli? Because I really think I'm looking for an American—"

Aunt Efrat smiled. "Of course, my darling! They are Americans—they moved here ten years ago. He goes to school in New Jersey, yes? But the parents live here, and they are my neighbors. He'll be here for Pesach, yes?"

"Sounds good to me," Simcha said cheerily. "I could use a good dentist."

Shari looked at him, laughing. If Aunt Efrat, of all people, could make a *shidduch* for Pearl Marcus, that would just be ... well, amazing. Pearl was a little unusual when it came to social pleasantries, though, and she wondered if her aunt had picked up on that.

"So how you Americans do?" Aunt Efrat said. "I call up my neighbor and ask her? How it goes by you?"

"Oh, it's a crazy system, Aunt Efrat," Shari answered. "Everyone has a resume nowadays."

"What is this?"

"A piece of paper, with my information on it," Pearl said.

"Information? What information?"

"You know, like where I went for summer camp, where I went to school, the names of my parents, our family *rav*, that sort of thing."

Aunt Efrat's eyebrows rose. "*Oy vavoy*, such *shtuyot*, I never hear of this. I'm so happy my daughter is married, yes? Okay, but you Americans do things your own way—"

"I'm Canadian," Pearl stated.

"Yes, but Canada is much closer to America than Eretz Yisrael, yes?" she continued. "No matter, I do this your way, yes? I call up my neighbor and ask if I can give her your information?"

"My resume, yes," Pearl clarified. "I can email it to you."

"Uh, Aunt Efrat, what's the boy's name?" Shari said.

"Lovely people, the Perlmans. I can't remember his first name, but nice boy, very nice boy."

Shari looked at Pearl doubtfully. "Pearl Perlman?"

Aunt Efrat nodded enthusiastically. "Of course, my darling! Why do you think I thought of it? And also, my Pearl darling, just think how clean your teeth will be!"

They all burst out laughing. Leave it to Aunt Efrat to know just how to liven everyone's spirits. Instead of the meal being uncomfortable, as Shari had feared, it was a merry party, and it had lasted much longer than she'd expected. It seemed like everyone was loath to leave.

But after the candles had burned down and the meal had truly come to an end, Pearl and Aunt Efrat left the apartment, each thanking Shari and Simcha for a wonderful time. The rain had stopped and Aunt Efrat refused their offer to walk her back to her home on Ramat Hagolan.

Shari and Simcha finally sat down on the couch and relaxed for the first time in weeks. The evening had been a complete success, to Shari's tremendous relief. She was so grateful it had all worked out.

"Everything was delicious, Shari," Simcha said, sleepily closing his eyes.

"Thanks."

"It seems like Aunt Efrat and this girl really got along."

"Yeah, you know what I was thinking?"

"What?"

"I was thinking that my aunt has a knack for getting along with everyone."

He agreed as he said, "It's a real talent. I should ask her for a few tips."

Shari knew that his mother's visit was still very much on his mind, but she didn't press him about it. She knew that his mother had said some hurtful remarks, but she didn't know any details. In fact, she found that she didn't want to know more. In all likelihood, the cutting remarks had been about herself.

It was better to leave it alone, at least for the time being. Perhaps one day, time and distance would heal the chasm between mother and son. As for herself, she didn't have any illusions about having a relationship with Simcha's mother. It was best not to dwell upon it, she knew.

She preferred instead to think about what had transpired at the Shabbos table. Who knew … maybe her vivacious Aunt Efrat had a *shidduch* idea that could actually work.

Only time would tell.

CHAPTER TWELVE

GALI

THE DAY OF THE anniversary party arrived, and Gali was up with the dawn to prepare for it. Truth be told, she hadn't slept the entire night. She also hadn't slept the night before that ....

She doubted if she'd ever be able to sleep again.

She just had the most awful feeling that her suspicions were true, however outrageous. She had no proof, of course, so she didn't tell her parents about it. At first, she thought it would be easy to find a picture of Leah Nes Or from a yearbook or camp picture, but that was much easier said than done. There was nothing online, it was as if she didn't even exist. And since she didn't want to divulge this information to anyone, she couldn't exactly ask her friends to find her a picture. That would be stooping to a lower level, somehow, and Gali was uncomfortable with it. As of yet, she hadn't told Yigal, since her rational side was secretly wishing that she was just being creative and fanciful, and things like this just didn't happen.

So her awful fears had been brewing inside her for the last few days, at times threatening to overwhelm her. She'd passed the time by staying very busy, throwing herself into her work, knowing that the food she'd prepared for this party was truly exceptional. She didn't think her clients were likely to forget this meal for a long, long time.

Additionally, what had also helped her through these last few grueling days was the knowledge that she'd be getting married in Yerushalayim, Ir Hakodesh. The very thought of it made her feel heady with excitement. She could hardly believe that it had been so easy, in retrospect.

On that Wednesday evening, her parents had been talking in the large family room, adjacent to the kitchen. She'd gotten up her courage and walked into the room, and her parents had looked up at her expectantly.

"It's the *kallah*," her father beamed proudly. "What's new, sweetheart?"

"Um … actually, there *is* something new, Daddy. Something I'd like to discuss with both of you."

The expression on her face must have been pensive, because she had an awful lot on her mind that day. Her parents looked alarmed.

"Is everything okay?" her mother had asked, concerned.

"Yes, everything is fine," she'd answered. "It's just that … that …"

Her parents looked at her, waiting. It wasn't like her to stammer.

"It's just that Yigal's aunt happens to be the wedding coordinator at the Waldorf Astoria," she said, in a rush. "In Yerushalayim. She handles everything—the band, the flowers, the centerpieces … You name it, it's done. She's the very best there is, and Yigal thought it would be so amazing if we could get married in Yerushalayim." The words tumbled out fast and furious, and her parents just stared at her.

"It's really what I want," she continued. "I mean, who even has that opportunity? I know that most of your friends wouldn't be there, and I feel bad about that, but the *vort* was almost like a wedding, right? And a smaller, more intimate wedding in Yerushalayim ... A *chuppah* on the roof at sunset—can you imagine the view? A stone's throw from the Kosel ... I never thought that I'd be given such an opportunity. It's like my dream come true ...."

Her parents had remained very quiet, looking stunned.

"Please let us get married there," she begged. "It's what we both want. It'll be much easier for you, Ma. Everything will be taken care of to the highest of standards. Besides, Yerushalayim has a *kedushah* that you can't find in L.A. You can't disagree with that. It'll be the wedding of my dreams ...."

Hot, salty tears had cascaded down her face at these last words, so sincere and heartfelt, and when her parents finally spoke, there was only one thing they could say.

"Well, if you both feel so strongly about it, who are we to object? We only want you be happy, Avigail," said her father, coming over to her for a hug. "There's nothing to cry about, honey."

"As long as his aunt takes care of everything just the way I want it," her mother said wistfully. "I'll need to be in touch with her, of course."

"Of course," Gali agreed. "Do you really mean it? We can really have a wedding in Yerushalayim? Are you sure you don't mind?"

Her mother smiled. "Well, we made all the boys' weddings right here in L.A.—but you know what? I'm getting tired of it."

Gali's mouth had flung open at that. Here was her mother, selflessly reassuring her that she'd hand over the reins to someone else—and she was giving her blessing.

"Ma, are you really sure?"

Her mother had smiled. "Of course, Gali. This will be something new, and I'll see to it that it'll be spectacular. No worries!"

Gali once again felt a fleeting sympathy for Yigal's aunt, but hadn't Yigal said that she could hold her own?

"Thank you, thank you, thank you!" she squealed before running over to hug her parents. Then she'd run upstairs to call Yigal with the news.

Now was Sunday, the day of the anniversary party. She was in the kitchen early in the morning, putting the finishing touches on her parmesan crisps, which had come out perfect. She was just taking the sweet potato mousses out of the oven when the doorbell rang. Gali didn't pay much attention to it, and Elizabeth went to answer the door.

She soon came back into the kitchen with a large, oblong box.

"Present for you, Miss Gali," Elizabeth chirped.

Gali dried her hands on her apron and opened the large, white box, exclaiming, "Oh, how beautiful!"

Inside the box were a dozen red, long-stemmed roses. The attached card simply said, *Thinking of you.*

"How sweet!" Gali said. "I guess Yigal sent these in honor of the party tonight."

"You sure be working hard, Miss Gali," Elizabeth remarked. "I think the party will be a success for sure."

"I hope so," Gali said fervently. "Oh! The pasta!"

She raced back to the kitchen to cover the homemade pasta dough with plastic wrap to keep it from drying out, and so it was Elizabeth who placed the magnificent roses in a large vase in the foyer. There was still the ravioli to shape and fill, and she quickly placed the hot filling into piping bags, which she rested atop a bowl of ice water to prevent further cooking. Then she had to roll out her dough into smooth, elastic sheets before placing a scoop of filling onto each square. She would then assemble each ravioli and refrigerate them, dropping them into boiling water just before serving to prevent the pasta from getting too soft.

The day passed by in a blur of activity for Gali, and before she knew it, it was already four o'clock in the afternoon. After loading all of the food into her SUV in specially insulated containers, she ran upstairs to shower and change for the dinner service that evening.

She always wore her hair up in a messy bun when she was working, which made serving the food easier. She topped her outfit with a brand-new white chef's coat, personalized with *Chef Gali* on the pocket, a charming gift from her future mother-in-law that she really appreciated.

She then flew down the stairs and out the kitchen door to her car, ready to go.

But once she was out of the house, she stopped dead in her tracks.

The security gate was once again open.

And this time, there was a message scrawled on the rear windshield of her SUV.

The three words looked like a child's scrawl in red crayon, but the sinister message they conveyed obviously wasn't written by a child.

I'M WATCHING YOU

Gali's heart was beating so rapidly, she began to feel faint. She sat down on the steps outside the French patio doors and tried to breathe.

Stay calm, she told herself. *It's just a prank. A prank from someone who is clearly not well …*

But then she thought her heart would stop.

The food.

She quickly ran to the doors of the car, which were, thankfully, locked. Peering inside, she saw that the coolers and food containers were still there, exactly as she'd left them.

It seemed as if the perpetrator had hastily scribbled the message and then left quickly, out of fear, perhaps.

Gali caught sight of herself in the side mirror of her car. Her face looked positively ashen.

Taking deep breaths, she looked around the grounds of her house, but she already knew that there would be no one there. The person responsible for this had left, that much was certain. The question remaining was … *would that person be back*?

She walked back into the house and tried to collect herself.

Elizabeth caught sight of Gali's face and dragged her over to a chair, exclaiming, "Oh, my goodness, you do too much. Look at you. You be falling apart, Miss Gali, and that be the truth. Sit here awhile and relax."

It did feel good to sit there on the kitchen stool with Elizabeth, where she felt cared for and safe. Thankfully, her mother was still out shopping. She wanted very badly to erase the evidence before she'd return, knowing how her mother would react.

The last thing she wanted was the police getting involved, and that would certainly be her mother's initial reaction. No, this had to be dealt with in a different, more discreet manner.

Meanwhile, Elizabeth, who couldn't begin to fathom what had really happened, got her a bottle of iced tea. She sipped it gratefully, her mind furiously churning in all directions. *Who ... why ... what to do ...*

Miserably, she thought she knew the *who* and the *why*.

But what was she going to do about it?

It was a riddle inside of an enigma, a terrible problem that seemed to have no end in sight ... she felt as if she was a victim of a deranged stalker.

She clearly *was* the victim of a deranged stalker, though she'd never heard of anyone being followed by a *chassan*'s ex-*kallah*. It was just too outrageous.

If her suspicions were correct. It was a big *if*. There must be some way she could find out for sure. She just wouldn't have any peace of mind until she knew the truth. Gali looked at the large clock on the wall and realized that precious minutes were ticking by, minutes she couldn't afford to lose. She allowed herself the luxury of ten minutes to rest, but then she determinedly got up, feeling a bit restored. She thanked Elizabeth on her way out and discreetly grabbed a bottle of Windex and a roll of paper towels. She knew she should keep some sort of evidence as proof, but she also wanted to protect her mother from having to deal with this. So she swiftly took a picture of the back of her SUV on her phone. Then working quickly, she managed to remove almost all of the frightening evidence.

It was only when she was behind the driver's seat, turning out of the driveway, when she had an epiphany. All at once, she realized that her house had a very sophisticated alarm system, complete with outdoor cameras discreetly placed nearly everywhere. Of course.

She would finally know for sure.

Tonight, after the party, when her parents were asleep, she'd go downstairs to the main computer and replay the video that showed a clear view of the driveway and front yard. She secretly dreaded what she'd see, already believing in her heart who was responsible … but she still needed to be absolutely certain.

Maybe it was a mere coincidence.

Maybe her overactive imagination was playing tricks on her.

But she spied the paper towels on the floor of her car, smeared with red crayon or lipstick—she wasn't sure which. Her imagination hadn't manufactured *that.*

Gali, the consummate professional, made a quick decision. She could fall apart and ruin the upcoming party, and with it her solid reputation, or she could cater this party to the very best of her ability and not dwell on what had just happened.

She chose the latter. It just wouldn't be fair to her clients, after all, or to herself. There was too much at stake. Besides, she felt a little more at ease knowing that she had a plan for later that evening that would give her the information she desperately needed to know. Then she'd have a better idea of what she was dealing with, which of course was scary but somehow seemed infinitely better than not knowing.

The drive to Beverly Hills wasn't that long, but with traffic it seemed to take much longer than usual. Gali clenched her teeth and clutched the steering wheel tightly the whole ride there. Before long, she was driving into the graveled, circular driveway of the Frank home.

"Showtime," she murmured under her breath as she let herself out of the car.

TWO HOURS LATER FOUND Gali in the Franks' enormous kitchen as the family's guests arrived at the front of the house. She was more than ready for them. No one would have ever guessed what had occurred to her only hours earlier, for Gali was the model of composed efficiency. A housekeeper, Marla, had helped Gali carry all of the food into the house, and she had hired two waiters who were waiting for her signal in the small hallway off the kitchen.

Everything was running smoothly so far. The table was beautifully set in a gold theme in honor of the golden anniversary. There were candles everywhere, ensconced in large gold candelabras, and Gali had swathed the table in gold silk brocade. China and crystal sparkled in the light, and joy was reflected in the faces of the elderly Mr. and Mrs. Frank, knowing that their children had orchestrated this intimate dinner in their honor with just a few close friends. The scene was truly heartwarming, and it was what Gali loved most about her job—knowing that this meal would be remembered for a long, long time.

She could almost forget about the terrifying incident. Almost.

The gazpacho was ready to be served, and Gali signaled to her waiters. They efficiently began bringing the appetizers into the large dining room. Gali could hear the *ooh*s and *aah*s of the guests, and inwardly it gave her a small measure of satisfaction.

She had this timed like a well-oiled machine, and fifteen minutes after the empty dishes were brought back into the kitchen, the arancini balls were plated and on their way out to the guests. She'd learned enough to let some time elapse between each course for conversation. Otherwise the meal would seem too rushed, and from the sound of things, the guests were having a marvelous time.

It was time to drop the ravioli into the huge pot of boiling water. When they began to float to the surface, she scooped them up with a large, slotted spoon and tossed them into the basil cream sauce. She then plated them with the ramps and sweet potato mousse, finishing the plate with a swirl of chive oil for color. It was a sensational plate, she knew. She privately thought that this dish was one of her best.

After the last plate was brought out to the guests, Gali was able to breathe for a bit. She adjusted her bun, which had only gotten messier.

She knew that there would be a much longer time lapse before dessert. Besides enjoying the main course, the adult children had created a special video in their parents' honor, and it would take some time to view it.

Still, she decided to plate the blueberries and lime curd, so she'd only have to add the ice cream and churros right before serving. She went to the portable cooler to remove the lime curd and blueberries, and discovered to her horror that the blueberries were missing.

They just ... weren't there.

Her blood froze.

Thankfully, the churros batter was there, all ready in piping bags, but the blueberries were, in fact, missing. All sorts of sinister imaginings began to flood her mind, and her cool, calm resolve threatened to crumble. *Could that girl have done it? But how? The doors to the car had been locked.*

Unless ... unless ...

Unless, in fact, they hadn't been locked, and the girl had taken the blueberries and locked the doors behind her. If that were the case, Gali knew how fortunate she was that only the blueberries had been taken. Although they were a nice accompaniment, they weren't absolutely necessary to the overall dish.

A new thought occurred to her. Maybe, in her haste, she herself had accidentally left the blueberries in her kitchen. It wasn't very likely, but it was still possible.

Thinking furiously, she quickly called her mother, who answered on the first ring—which was, in itself, a rarity.

"Ma?" she whispered. "Are you home?"

"Yes, Gali," her mother answered, sounding concerned. "Is everything okay? How's the party?"

"It's good, everything's fine," she answered quickly. "But can you check on something for me? Did I leave the macerated blueberries in the kitchen?"

"Oh, my … I'll check."

The seconds ticked by agonizingly slowly, and Gali found herself hoping that her mother would come back and say, *Yes, I found them right here on the counter.* It would allay some of her fears, at least, knowing that no one had taken them.

But unfortunately, that's not what her mother said. In fact, when she answered, she sounded puzzled. "Gali, they're not here. I can't find them anywhere, and Elizabeth says she saw you packing them up."

Beads of perspiration formed on Gali's brow, and she hastily wiped them away. It just didn't make sense.

It meant that the girl had rummaged through the cooler and taken the blueberries, while leaving everything else.

Who would do such a thing?

Wait.

Wait just a minute ….

Gali suddenly remembered that when she'd packed up the car, she had actually taken the container of blueberries and placed it on top of the other containers to make space for everything. She hadn't been paying too much attention at the time, but now she was almost sure of it.

That meant that the girl hadn't had to rummage through everything. The blueberries had been easy to spot, right on top.

So it made sense, after all.

Gali's breath returned to normal, and after hastily thanking her mother, she had an idea. Maybe the Franks happened to have some blueberries in their fridge. She would take it off the bill, if need be.

Miraculously, there were two large containers of blueberries in the fridge that appeared to be of high quality. She only needed fifteen minutes to macerate them. She quickly went to work, grabbing lemon liqueur and sugar from the cabinet. Under her breath, she thanked Hashem for giving her the time to save the dessert.

While the family and guests watched the video in the dining room, blissfully unaware, Gali was hard at work in the kitchen, trying to salvage her dish.

At long last the video came to an end, and from the sound of things it had been a huge success, with loads of laughter mixed with many tears. Gali was more than ready to serve her dessert, which she knew was a crowning achievement.

Twenty plates were beautifully plated with a scoop of ice cream next to hot churros, a piping of lime curd, and a smattering of macerated blueberries. It was an absolutely gorgeous plate, and the perfect way to end the magnificent meal.

While the guests *ooh*ed and *aah*ed and enjoyed the beautifully presented dishes, Gali finally had a chance to sit down in the kitchen and savor the satisfaction of having done her very best and succeeded. In her innermost heart, she knew that the impetus that drove her was more than just her reputation and her career. She genuinely wanted her clients to be thrilled with the results. Not everyone had the chance to celebrate a fiftieth wedding anniversary, and she wanted the evening to be special for the Franks.

She secretly wished that one day, she and Yigal would also celebrate a fiftieth wedding anniversary, yet she was very much aware that she had an extra hurdle to pass that most *kallah*s did not have.

It was a test. Not so much from the girl, since she knew there was little she could do to help her. But it was a test, nonetheless, and how she handled herself from that moment on would determine if she received a passing grade, if not in this world, then in the next.

Now that the party was over, she knew what was in store for her. After packing everything up and cleaning the kitchen, she had to go home and investigate the evidence on the security cameras. If there was anything she'd rather not do, she couldn't think of it.

But it would have to be done, like it or not.

Soon Mrs. Frank, accompanied by her eldest daughter, Puah Levy, entered the kitchen.

"Chef Gali," Puah said, "this is my mother."

"Pleased to meet you, Mrs. Frank," said Gali, stretching out her hand. "I really hope you enjoyed your anniversary dinner. *Mazel tov.*"

Mrs. Frank dabbed her glistening eyes with a handkerchief. "It was the best night of my life, my dear. You created the most magnificent meal I could possibly have imagined, better than any restaurant … and to see our grown children around the table, and the wonderful video … Sorry, I guess I'm just a little emotional."

Gali smiled and patted her hand. "I'm so glad."

"Chef Gali, that meal was truly inspirational, above anything I was expecting," Puah said. "I'd like to give you a bonus, if I may. To show our appreciation."

She pressed four crisp one hundred dollar bills into Gali's hand.

"Thank you," Gali said, surprised. No one had ever done that before, and she was touched. "But I have to tell you that the blueberries—I, well, misplaced the blueberries, and so I had to improvise with blueberries I found in your fridge, Mrs. Frank. I hope that's okay. I can take it off the bill if you'd like."

Mrs. Frank and her daughter laughed.

"Oh, don't be silly," Mrs. Frank said graciously. "I wouldn't hear of it. They were—what? A few dollars at the most. I'm so happy I had them here!"

"Me, too," Gali agreed. "All's well that ends well, I guess."

"We'll know who to call the next time we have a party, Chef Gali," Puah said, beaming. "Thank you for everything."

Mother and daughter left the kitchen to see their last remaining guests to the door, and Gali let herself out the back entrance, through the kitchen, after stowing the containers carefully in her SUV once more.

After thanking Marla once again for her help, Gali got behind the wheel and backed out of the driveway. She was exhausted but triumphant, knowing that she'd done her very best. But then she glanced over at the paper towels on the floor near the passenger's seat … They were still there, red lipstick and all.

She was driving down Pico Boulevard when her phone rang. It was Yigal.

Smiling, she answered it.

"Hello?"

"So, how did it go?" Yigal's voice was so warm, so comforting, that for one mortifying nanosecond her voice got choked up and an avalanche of unshed tears threatened to overwhelm her. It was just too much, keeping this terrifying secret from him, but she had to gain more information first. She forced herself not to crumble into pieces as she replied, "It was good. It went well."

He paused. "Uh-oh. Something's wrong … what is it? Something didn't come out right?"

"No, no," she said. "It was really great, Yigal. They loved everything. It was a huge success … they even gave me a bonus."

"That's so nice!" he exclaimed. "So why do you sound so down?"

"I guess I'm just a little worn out, that's all. It was a lot of work."

"Oh, of course," Yigal said, sounding relieved. "I'm just so happy it went well."

"Thanks," Gali said. "Oh, and Yigal … Thanks so much for the flowers — they're just beautiful. It was really thoughtful of you."

"Flowers?" He sounded confused. "What flowers?"

Gali's heart started to race. Oh, no. Did that mean … ?

"Roses, red roses, a dozen of them, long-stemmed."

"Uh …" Yigal sounded mystified, which could only mean one thing. He hadn't sent them.

"They were delivered this afternoon with a card that said, 'Thinking of you.' You had them delivered, right? On account of the party tonight?" Her voice sounded unnaturally high to her own ears, verging on hysteria.

Yigal sounded contrite as he said, "No, Gali, I wish I had thought of it, but I didn't send them. The card wasn't signed?"

Gali's heart was beating so thunderously that she thought for sure Yigal could hear it on the line.

"No," Gali whispered.

"You're not upset, Gali, are you?" he asked. "I'll try to remember next time."

He was so wonderful … It was just too much to hold it in.

She came precariously close to telling him the truth about what was going on, but the time was still not quite right. She still didn't know what the truth even was.

"Yigal, it's fine," she managed. "I'm sure I'll figure it out."

"Maybe you have a secret admirer," he teased.

Her heart sank when she thought of who her secret admirer was, in all probability.

What if that girl would try to harm her in some way? She clearly wasn't at all balanced.

Yigal then said that he had to daven Maariv, and so she was spared from more conversation for the time being, at least.

At last she was home, and after she threw the soiled paper towels into the garbage bins outside the driveway, she raced into the house, her heart beating a rapid staccato.

It was now or never.

She knew she couldn't wait any longer. Miraculously, her parents were already upstairs, and the main level was quiet. Elizabeth had ostensibly gone to bed. She made a beeline for the vase of roses in the darkened foyer and carried them gingerly into the kitchen, which had better lighting. She didn't know what she was looking for, as they appeared to be regular, long-stemmed roses.

She was puzzled. Her brow furrowed, she wondered if she was imagining everything. She'd always had a vivid imagination, and she wondered if all of her pent-up anxiety was somehow spiraling into a ridiculous paranoia.

But then she saw it.

A tiny, black plastic piece was attached to one of the rose's stems. She would never have noticed it if she hadn't been searching ....

What was it?

She knew. It was a minuscule camera. Hadn't the message said, "I'm watching you"? Surely, whoever had sent these flowers thought that she'd place them in her own room, where she could be watched.

Her heart was pounding and her skin felt clammy.

Why was she being followed?

She thought she knew why ... It was because she was engaged to Yigal, and jealousy was a monster that did strange things to people.

She placed the camera into her pocket and went into the family room, over to the main computer system, and sat down. It took her a while to locate the footage she needed, but she managed to set it to replay that afternoon. She needed sometime between four and five o'clock. She settled down to watch, her heart beating thunderously.

For the first fifteen minutes, nothing happened at all. She sat there watching her SUV in the driveway, her uneasiness growing. More agonizing minutes ticked by ....

Then, at 4:23 p.m., she saw a hooded figure walk up the driveway slowly, tentatively.

A blurry, hooded figure.

"Come closer," Gali whispered under her breath, her eyes practically resting on the screen.

The figure did come closer.

And Gali thought her heart would stop.

A girl in a long, black skirt and cotton hoodie approached the car. She looked around, and not realizing that she was being filmed, she opened the driver's door. It opened easily, obviously unlocked.

She got behind the wheel of the car.

Gali couldn't breathe.

What was she doing in her car?

Then, after a minute or two, she got out and walked around the car. She opened the trunk and withdrew from it a medium-sized plastic container.

"The blueberries," Gali whispered.

The girl furtively looked around and closed the trunk. Taking something from her pocket, which Gali supposed was lipstick, she wrote the sinister words on the back windshield, before walking quickly away, back down the driveway. But before she walked away, she turned around once more to look at the house.

Gali froze the picture on the screen and zoomed in, magnifying the picture to a much bigger size.

There was no mistake about it.

Leah Rosen stared right back at her.

Or, as her name really was … Leah Nes Or.

With shaking fingers, Gali kept her picture on the screen and saved it in a special folder. Her heart was galloping … She thought her parents would hear it upstairs, it was so loud. She then saved the video from 4:23 until 4:30 in the same folder, should she ever need proof of what had happened.

Her lips felt bloodless and her mouth felt dry. Her hands were still trembling, but at least now she knew, and with the knowledge came a level of clarity. Oddly enough, most of the initial panic was beginning to subside. What remained was a wave of sheer pity for the unbalanced girl, who obviously had much deeper issues than Gali could've ever imagined. She'd thought that there was something a bit peculiar about her that day in Santa Monica, but she'd had no idea as to the depths of her disturbing behavior.

It was then that Gali had a thought.

It was almost ironic that Leah had written, *I'M WATCHING YOU.*

Under her breath, Gali murmured, "Well, Leah, now I'm watching *you*."

CHAPTER THIRTEEN

TOVA

ON WEDNESDAY MORNING, TOVA sat down in Dan Davis's office, wondering what this was all about. That morning, her boss had told her that he'd like to speak with her, which in itself wasn't unusual, but his tone had seemed … well, different. She was hoping it had nothing to do with the fact that she'd taken off three days of work in a row.

It had been a difficult week. Her grandmother's condition hadn't improved all that much, but she'd stabilized enough that the doctors felt that her situation wasn't critical. She was still in a twilight, though. Her eyes occasionally fluttered open but there was no cognizance, no recognition of any kind. Tova had spoken to the nice nurse, Laurie, about it the day before.

"How long can patients stay this way?" she'd asked.

"It's hard to predict," Laurie had replied. "There are patients who can stay this way for weeks, or months, even. But at her age, well, it's hard to say …"

"It's so hard to be in limbo like this," Tova murmured, knowing that it was true on many levels. In fact, her whole life seemed to be in an indeterminate state. She wasn't moving forward, going to the next step, and she couldn't afford to look backward, so she was acutely aware of the precariousness of her unusual situation. With her grandmother around, she'd still been alone. But without her grandmother, she was even more alone.

Her father had left after two days. He couldn't take off more time from work, and there wasn't much to do, in any case. If her grandmother had been awake or aware, he would have stayed, but there was little he could do for her.

And so Tova had sat by her grandmother's bedside for the better part of three days before returning to a mountain of work on her desk. She had been in the middle of tackling that mountain and getting herself organized when she was interrupted by Dan Davis's knock on her office door.

"Tova," he'd said. "When you have a minute, come to my office. I'd like a word with you."

There was something in his *tone.* It was an indefinable something, but it was enough to make her clench her teeth together while she waited for his return.

What was this all about?

It couldn't have been her work, since she knew that it was nearly flawless—when she was there, that is. She'd missed three whole days *during tax season.*

She didn't think he'd fire her, of course. But she didn't know it with absolute certainty.

As she sat waiting, she kicked her foot back and forth in an agitated, jittery manner, which was unlike her. After five minutes, Dan Davis still hadn't returned to his office, so she impatiently looked around the room. There were pictures of his wife and family on his desk, along with assorted trinkets, a calendar, and piles of papers. On the wall were many diplomas and numerous awards.

He'd been honored by nearly every Jewish institution and organization in the Detroit area, as well as many others in the Midwest.

Tova was just wondering if she should go back to her own office and talk to him a different time, when he returned, looking a bit sheepish.

"Sorry," he said. "I was on an important call."

He wearily sat down on the brown leather chair behind his desk, and swiveled to face her.

"So, we have a little situation," he stated.

Tova's thoughts raced. His tone sounded ominous. *He wouldn't fire her for missing three days, would he?*

"I'm really sorry, Mr. Davis," she said. "It's just that my grandmother, I mean, I couldn't just leave her—"

He waved his hand. "No need to explain. I totally understand."

Relief flooded her, but then he said something that caught her completely off-guard.

"Tova, this has nothing to do with that."

"Oh."

"Yes, well, you know that I started another office in Israel last year," he began. "In Yerushalayim, in a business park."

"Yes, I know the place," she said. "Tax services for Americans who still have most of their assets here in the States."

"Right," he said. "But it's not just taxes—it's investments, too. We're offering all sorts of financial services, and most of our clientele are Americans."

"Um, okay ...," she said, not knowing where this was headed.

He reached into his desk drawer and pulled out what looked like an airline ticket.

"Please tell me that your passport is up to date."

She looked at him, wide-eyed.

What in the world?

"I'm afraid that I have to ask you to go to Israel for me. I was supposed to go tomorrow, but my daughter-in-law just gave birth in Toronto a few days ago. My wife is there already and the bris is on Friday morning …."

"Me?" she said, more than a little surprised.

He continued as if he hadn't heard her. "There's no one more competent, and that's the truth. I know it's short notice, and your grandmother is in the hospital, but it's a dire situation. My office manager got married last week and the new associate is drowning from the workload, since the new girl we hired doesn't seem to be working out. You have to see what's going on, that's all. Maybe you could train the new girl, at least for the time being."

"Thursday?" she said, feeling overwhelmed. "But that's tomorrow, and my grandmother, I mean, my father is coming for Shabbos, but—"

"It's only until Tuesday evening. I thought you could rest up over Shabbos, then work all day Sunday, Monday, and Tuesday, and get things in order … If anyone can restore order in that office in three days' time, it's you."

"Thank you, but traveling on a Thursday … That would mean—"

"You'll be fine," he said. "You'll arrive Friday morning, and the days are longer now. You'll have plenty of time. Besides, I can't change the tickets, since they were originally mine. It's a miracle that my travel agent was able to transfer them to you. I'm not even sure how he was able to do it, to be perfectly frank. And I hope you don't mind sitting in business class, either."

"No, I don't mind—"

She looked up at him and saw that he was grinning. She'd been so rattled that she hadn't even realized that he was making a joke.

"Look, I know it's a lot to ask ... but someone really needs to get things in order, and I can't be there. So do we have a deal?"

Tova thought of what the grueling past week had been like, and now her boss was holding a ticket in his hand to Israel ... for her? It just seemed almost too good to be true. She wasn't an impulsive person, but all of a sudden, throwing some clothes into a bag and flying halfway across the world the very next day seemed very appealing.

"I'll do it," she said. "And thank you, Mr. Davis, for believing in me."

He smiled and nodded, handing her the ticket.

"Just be on that plane," he said.

"I will."

TRUE TO HER WORD, the next morning found Tova racing through the airport. She sailed through security and had just reached the gate when she heard the announcement.

Flight 357, nonstop service to JFK, has been delayed by thirty minutes. We'll begin our regular boarding schedule, but due to our flight attendants' late arrival, we'll have to wait for them to board before takeoff.

She checked her watch. It would be close, but still manageable. The plane was there, the pilots were there ... they were just waiting for two flight attendants. Her flight to Israel, leaving from JFK, was in the afternoon, but since it was an international flight she hoped she'd get there with enough time to spare. She was anxious and jittery, and she paced the floor at the gate, wondering when they'd begin to board.

She noticed that there was a young family there, waiting with her. The mother was probably not much older than she was herself. She had a toddler in a stroller.

Tova, of course, was traveling alone, and she was acutely aware of the fact. Interesting how her solitary existence hadn't mattered much to her for a long while, but recently, all that had changed. After her recent dating experience, her sense of loneliness had only heightened. And her dream about her grandfather, while being comforting, also seemed to pose troubling questions that seemed unanswerable.

She walked over to the family.

"Hi," she said. "I guess we're on the same flight—are you also going to Israel?"

"No," said the young woman, with a heavy British accent. "We're actually going to England, after a stopover in JFK."

"Oh, I see," Tova said. "Thank you."

She walked away and continued pacing, which she knew was futile and wouldn't get her to New York any faster, but she was so restless she couldn't help herself.

The clock on the wall ticked slowly. She took out her *Tehillim* and started to say the well-known paragraphs almost by heart, when her phone rang.

It was her father, and her heart skipped a beat. She hadn't had the time to tell him about her plans, so it wasn't as if he knew where she was. Why was he calling her in the middle of the workday?

What if . . . ?

"Hello?" she said quickly.

"Hi, Tova," her father answered. "Is everything okay?"

"Yes, why—"

"Oh, it's nothing to worry about," he quickly said. "Everything is fine. I just got a little nervous when I couldn't reach you at your office."

"You called my office?"

"Yes, we're actually coming to visit Bubby this afternoon, so we'll stay over tonight. Is that okay with you?"

"Oh, of course," she replied, flustered. "It's just that ... well, I'm not home. I'm actually at the airport, Ta."

"At the airport?" He sounded confused. "Where are you going?"

"I'm actually flying to Israel tonight," she said. "It's for work ... My boss wanted me to go last minute to help clear up some problems in the new office in Yerushalayim. I was going to call you but didn't have a chance. And I thought that since you'll be there this weekend—"

"Oh, of course, Tova, no need to explain. You have to—"

"It's not like I was given much choice—"

"No need to explain," he reiterated. "Bubby is my responsibility, not yours. I want you to go and try to relax a little, Tova."

If there was anything that Tova wasn't used to, it was relaxing. And this trip was going to be mostly work. Still, she hoped that she'd be able to take a little time for herself, to daven at the Kosel, to reconnect ... to breathe ....

"Thanks, Ta."

"It's actually perfect timing. You're leaving for a few days, but we'll be there instead. We'll just let ourselves in, don't worry."

"The guest room has clean linens, and you'll find towels in

the closet," she said. Just then, she saw the tardy flight attendants walking briskly toward the gate, and she felt relieved that they'd be on their way soon.

"Ta, I think they're going to board soon."

Her father wished her a safe flight and she got into line with her boarding pass, thanking Hashem that they hadn't been delayed further.

Sure enough, before long she was walking down the long corridor that led to the plane. She could hardly believe that she was on her way to New York, and from there, to Israel. She was humbled by the fact that for thousands of years the thought of traveling to that special land had been nearly impossible, and nowadays it was so easy.

Why she had merited that right, she didn't know, but she felt grateful beyond measure. She found her aisle seat, placed her small bag into the overhead bin, and sat down, eager to get this leg of her journey completed so she could board the plane to Israel.

She hadn't realized how exhausted she was. The last few days had been a maelstrom of motion. She'd been with her grandmother in the hospital for days on end, and then she'd returned to work only the day before. She'd worked practically nonstop the entire day, and then she had to do laundry and pack, surviving on adrenaline and very little sleep.

She awoke with a start when the wheels touched the ground in New York. She couldn't remember anything about the flight at all, and thankfully, no one had sat down next to her. She could hardly believe that two hours had elapsed, but checking her watch, she realized that they had.

She stretched her weary muscles, wanting to stand up when

the plane would at last roll to a stop. She then noticed an elderly woman with dark, wrinkled, leathery skin, sitting across the aisle from her. The woman was watching her with keen eyes under an enormous kerchief, a siddur in her hand. A shawl was draped over her shoulders, and in her free hand, she clutched a cane.

"It was a smooth flight, no?" Tova asked, in what she hoped was a friendly tone.

The diminutive woman nodded and smiled.

"Are you going on to Israel?" Tova asked.

"*Non, non*," the woman replied with a heavy French accent. "I go to Paris, to my daughter."

"Oh, how nice. Do you live in Detroit?"

"*Non*, I was in Los Angeles, by my son. I stopped in Michigan for a few days, to see my friend ... But now, *baruch Hashem*, I'm going back home to my daughter. She is the Rabbanit Sara Beneviste. Her husband is Rav Yosef Beneviste—perhaps you've heard of them?"

"No, no, I haven't," Tova said apologetically.

The older woman smiled proudly. "Ah, they are world-renowned for their *hachnasat orchim*. Rav Yosef, my son-in-law, is the Rav of the Jewish community in Paris."

"How wonderful," Tova said. "You must be very proud of them."

The woman nodded and smiled. At that moment, the plane came to a complete stop and the doors were flung open. Tova reached out to help the woman get to her feet, and reached up to take her small suitcase from the overhead bin.

"*Merci,*" said the woman.

"Have a safe trip back to France," Tova replied with a smile.

She followed the throng of people hurriedly leaving the plane. When she entered the gate area, she checked the screens to see where she should go. Sure enough, she needed to be on the other side of the airport, in a completely different building. Checking her watch, she saw that she only had thirty minutes to get there. She fervently hoped that her luggage would find its way there, too.

She rushed through the airport, her passport in hand, scanning the crowds. There were so many people, and in a sea of unfamiliar faces, Tova once again felt very much alone.

After asking directions and getting lost several times, Tova finally reached the El-Al terminal. She stood in line and tried to relax. She'd made it.

It was bedlam at the gate. Toddlers were crying in their strollers and flight attendants managed to look stern and harassed at the same time. Tova smiled to herself, remembering when she'd flown to Israel for seminary for what had been the best year of her life.

So far, she told herself. *So far.*

It was hard to believe that one day her complicated circumstances would change. After all, her life had been difficult for as long as she could remember. But still, she truly believed that one day her life would be normal, and even ... joyous.

She believed.

Soon it was her turn in line, and she handed her passport to the woman at the counter. The woman stamped it and lifted her heavy suitcase onto the conveyor belt.

"You'll be in business class," she said in a clipped Israeli accent. "Seat 8A. Enjoy your flight."

"Thank you," Tova replied. Almost as an afterthought, she said,

"Sorry, but what time does the flight arrive in Tel Aviv tomorrow?"

"Eleven o'clock, Friday morning."

"Okay, thanks."

It was almost the end of March, and she surmised that Shabbos would start at around six o'clock. She'd have plenty of time to get her luggage and take a taxi to Yerushalayim.

Checking her itinerary, she saw that Dan Davis had booked a suite in the Waldorf Astoria Hotel.

Nice. Not that she'd be there all that much. She knew that this was a business trip, but still, maybe Shari would walk over to the hotel on Shabbos. It was quite a walk from Ramat Eshkol to Rechavia, at least forty-five minutes, but knowing Shari, she'd be there.

She walked to the gate, sat down on an uncomfortable chair, and called Shari.

The phone rang but no one answered.

Hoping Shari wasn't already asleep, Tova left a voicemail message explaining the situation and how she'd love to see her, and then sat back and tried to relax a bit.

Before long, they began to board. The best part was that she'd never been in business class before, and as she boarded the plane, she saw how roomy and spacious the seats were. She was so *tired.* She looked forward to sleeping for much of the ride.

And she looked forward to seeing the blue sky of Yerushalayim the following day with every breath of her being. Her excitement mounting, she stowed her carry-on into the bin above her seat and sat down on the extremely comfortable, large reclining chair. Such luxury …

Thank You, Hashem, she murmured under her breath.

A steady stream of people were boarding the plane. She knew it would take a while, so she nestled into the comfort of her pillow, and before she knew it she was asleep.

Two hours later, she awoke. It was much quieter on the plane now than it had been during the boarding process, and business class was especially quiet. She wondered what country they were flying over, and she turned to the window next to her to look out.

She couldn't believe what she saw.

They were still on the ground in JFK.

They hadn't moved an inch. She frantically looked at her watch. Two full hours had elapsed, which meant that they'd be landing at one o'clock on Friday afternoon. Just then, a voice on the loudspeaker thanked everyone for their patience. The problem was resolved, the voice said, and they'd soon be on their way.

What problem?

She must've been more tired than she'd realized. She was a little uneasy, but she tried to calm herself. It was cutting things a bit close, but surely, she'd still be able to get to Yerushalayim with time to spare.

Sure enough, the plane soon revved its engines and raced down the runway before lifting majestically into the air. Houses, cars, and buildings grew smaller and smaller from her vantage point in the sky. All of the worldly problems that enveloped her on a daily basis seemed to shrink into the distance, as well. She thought of Hashem looking down on everyone from His lofty place up on high, their problems reaching Him in the glorious heavens.

Everything that happened to her, He knew about. He was pulling the strings all along, guiding her in His Master Plan. Comforted, she sat back and took out her *Tehillim.*

And that's how she spent most of the next several hours, alternating between saying *Tehillim* and dozing.

She didn't know how much time had elapsed when she heard an unnerving announcement over the speaker.

"Is there a doctor on board? If there's a doctor, please go to Row 24."

There seemed to be a commotion in the coach cabin, but the curtains were drawn in business class, so she had no way of knowing what was going on.

After several minutes, a flight attendant walked through the aisle. Tova leaned over and asked, "Is everything all right? Does someone need help?"

"Don't worry, a passenger is not feeling well. We may need to make an unscheduled landing."

An unscheduled landing?

Tova's heart began to pound. How would they have time for an unscheduled landing and still arrive in Israel before Shabbos? Maybe it wouldn't come to that, she told herself. Maybe the passenger would begin to feel better. Maybe they wouldn't have to stop, after all.

She wasn't sure what propelled her—curiosity, mostly—but she soon found herself walking down the aisle into the economy cabin. She could see that in the aisle seat of Row 24, an overhead oxygen mask had been pulled down, and a man was bending over an elderly woman who looked positively ashen.

A few flight attendants formed a small circle around them.

Tova supposed that the man was a doctor who'd volunteered his services.

It's probably nothing, she told herself. *She's in good hands … It's probably just some chest pain. She'll certainly feel better with the oxygen. Maybe they'll give her something to drink. We'll continue on our way with no stopping. We'll get to Israel before Shabbos … I'll see Shari—it'll be great.*

She walked back to her seat, feeling foolish. She wasn't usually nosy, and she felt like she'd somehow eavesdropped on a private matter. Still, if she hadn't been so worried about Shabbos, she doubted that she would've gone to look.

She felt so restless. She said some more *Tehillim* but found that she wasn't focusing on the words.

She soon heard thc crackling of the loudspeaker.

"… This is your captain speaking. I'm afraid that I've had to radio ahead to Charles de Gaulle Airport in Paris, where we are making an unscheduled landing due to a passenger's health concerns. This is not an emergency, ladies and gentlemen. I repeat, this is not an emergency. We are just taking every precaution necessary. We should be on the ground in approximately fifteen minutes. From there, we'll continue on to Tel Aviv."

Tova could hardly believe the drastic turn of events. She'd heard of such stories, of course, but nothing like this had ever happened to her before.

She checked her watch.

They'd drop the woman off at the airport in Paris and then be on their way, no doubt. It couldn't take that much time … Surely they'd land in Tel Aviv by two o'clock in the afternoon, or thereabouts ….

There was nothing to worry about.

Tova sat back in her chair, tense, her eyes never leaving her watch. Fifteen minutes passed … then twenty ….

They were descending from a high altitude, first turning one way, then another. A wave of nausea gripped Tova.

She leaned her head back as the plane dropped even lower.

Breathe ... breathe ...

The wheels touched down. Tova could hardly believe that here she was, in Paris, France, when she really wanted to be in Israel.

Why was it that nothing ever seemed to go easy for her?

Several moments passed, and then a flight attendant opened the door to the plane. Four paramedics quickly boarded the plane, pushing a stretcher down the aisle right past her seat.

Tova opened her *Tehillim* once more and began to recite the passages.

Hashem, please watch over that woman.

Hashem, please let me get to Yerushalayim in time for Shabbos.

Precious minutes ticked by ... After about fifteen minutes, Tova turned her head to see what was happening, but she couldn't see anything from her vantage point. After twenty-three minutes had elapsed, she could see the paramedics once again wheeling the stretcher, this time with the elderly woman on it, a portable oxygen mask on her face.

Tova breathed a sigh of relief.

Surely, any moment now they'd seal the door to the airplane and once again be on their way.

More minutes ticked by ....

After another twenty minutes had elapsed, with Tova's heart doing somersaults in her chest, there was another announcement on the loudspeaker.

"This is your captain speaking, once again. Ladies and gentlemen, I apologize for the delay. We're just filling out paperwork. Making emergency landings requires a certain protocol. We should get clearance for takeoff in about an hour ... Thank you for your patience. We'll try to get you back in the air as soon as we can."

Another hour?

By her own estimation, even if they were back in the air in another hour, that would mean an estimated arrival time of around four o'clock in the afternoon. In Tel Aviv. On Friday afternoon.

And Shabbos was at six.

It was so risky ... She supposed that she could always go to Bnei Brak for Shabbos, which was much closer to the airport.

And stay where?

She began to realize that she wasn't the only one who was worried. A small group of passengers was talking to the flight attendant, who was nodding her head in assent.

After ten minutes or so, there was another announcement over the loudspeaker.

"Uh, this is your captain. Thank you for your patience, ladies and gentlemen. It's come to my attention that some of you on the flight are concerned about arriving in Tel Aviv too close to the Sabbath. If that's the case, you're welcome to disembark here in Paris, and we'll give you a voucher for a flight to Tel Aviv on Sunday morning. Please speak to the flight attendant at the gate."

Tova didn't know what to do, and she felt panicked. *Why* did everything in her life have to have so much drama? *Why* couldn't she just fly to Israel smoothly like other people?

She knew it was futile to ask *why*. This was what Hashem wanted to happen, obviously. But if she was in France for Shabbos, where would she stay? In the airport? By herself?

It was then that she suddenly remembered the elderly French woman, wrapped in a shawl, who had been on her flight from

Detroit to JFK. She'd been flying to France, to her daughter's house, hadn't she?

What was her daughter's name?

Rabbanit Sara Beneviste … and she and her husband were world-renowned for their hachnasat orchim.

Could she really just show up unannounced in the Rebbetzin's house? No, of course not. She'd have to call her first. Just how she would contact the Rebbetzin and arrive at her home without her suitcase, in a strange city, remained to be seen. And what would be with her luggage? Would it fly on to Israel without her?

She was impossibly torn. On the one hand, everything could ostensibly still work out. They could be on their way soon, she'd get to Yerushalayim like she'd originally planned, and all would be well.

Or not.

They could stay here on the tarmac with the flight delayed indefinitely, mired in red tape and bureaucracy. One hour could very well drag into two hours …

What should she do?

"Hashem, tell me what to do," she murmured under her breath. "Please."

She turned and suddenly saw a young, chassidish couple come forward with their carry-on bags.

"Excuse me," Tova said to the young wife. "Are you leaving the plane?"

"Yes," she replied. "Arriving at four or four-thirty is just too risky, and my husband has cousins here. Our luggage will be waiting for us on Sunday."

Tova knew that arriving so late on a Friday afternoon, when

Shabbos was at six, was just cutting things way too close. She had no choice.

She reached up and shakily gathered her carry-on bag and her purse, and before she could change her mind, she followed the young couple off the plane on rubbery legs.

She was going to be in Paris for Shabbos.

CHAPTER FOURTEEN

EVA

EVA GOT TO WORK earlier than usual. She was so wired, it wasn't as if she could sleep anyway. The Fischer deal was closing on that very day, Thursday, and she was restless and jittery. She arrived at her office, pleased to see that Edith Berman was already there. She felt like a hypocrite, actually holding a steaming cup of coffee, which she usually never touched, but she needed the caffeine. She hadn't slept in days. To her credit, the loyal Edith saw the cup in her hand and said not a word.

She walked to her office and left the door open.

"Edith?" she called.

Edith appeared at the door.

"Has the money come through yet?"

"Adam Fischer said the deposit should be wired to the account any moment now. I'll let you know as soon as it is."

"Very good."

There was nothing to do now but wait. How she hated that she had time to think. Thinking about recent events just made her feel more anxious and confused, and she wished that she had mountains of work to distract her. As soon as the money was wired into the escrow account, she could begin to tackle the paperwork, but not before.

She was just so … on edge.

It had nothing to do with the deal that was about to go through, of course. She was used to closing deals. No, this was something different, something much more personal. After so many years of being alone, and actually thriving on her independence, Eva had no idea how she'd found herself in such an unusual predicament. Nothing in her life had ever been typical, that much was certain. But now she was faced with a dilemma that she wouldn't have dreamed of just a few weeks earlier.

Even one week earlier.

Plain and simple, the fact was that she no longer had a suitor who was interested in marriage.

She now had two suitors.

Shmiel Goodman, of course, had apparently recognized the folly of his ways and had begun a quiet campaign to win her back into his good graces. He'd been calling her incessantly for the past two days and leaving messages. But she hadn't called him back.

Let him wait it out. He'd only called after Aaron Bergstein had begun to take her out the past three evenings in a row.

It had started as a series of business meetings, at least at first. He was a real estate developer, so he had the properties and she had the clients. The correlation was obvious.

But it was only after they'd met several times that Eva had realized there was much more to the famous Aaron Bergstein than met the eye. He had two adult children, both married, who were the pride of his life. His ex-wife had remarried years earlier and had a new family of her own.

She'd wondered why he'd never remarried, and she'd wanted to casually ask him about it, but the timing had never been quite right. And then, the past evening, before she'd even had a chance to verbalize it aloud, he'd readily volunteered the information.

Just like that.

And that meant ... ?

She wasn't sure, and that's what had kept her up the entire night, tossing and turning fitfully. Wondering.

They'd been seated in the most elegant new restaurant in the city. It was a brand-new, five-star eating establishment that had a two-month waiting list. She'd casually mentioned to Aaron that she was interested in dining there, and he'd made a phone call.

One phone call from Aaron Bergstein was all it took, and a table miraculously became available for that very day. Eva had been impressed, and for her that took some doing. She enjoyed being able to snap her fingers, so to speak, and have the red carpet unrolled for her, like royalty.

I could get used to this, she found herself thinking.

He'd called to apprise her of the situation and they'd agreed to meet at eight. They hadn't gone there together, of course, since the fledgling relationship was still so new and tenuous. At that point, they'd both been dancing around any serious topics. Still, she'd taken the rest of the afternoon off, something she hadn't done in ... well, ever, and headed to Bergdorf Goodman, where she employed a personal shopper, Robyn Friedman.

"Something special for dinner tonight," Eva told Robyn.

Robyn looked at her and beamed.

"I have something perfect, Ms. Adler. Just came in yesterday."

She disappeared, returning moments later holding a dress

that was, in fact, just about perfect.

"Prada," Robyn gushed.

It was a simple, elegant dress in a very beautiful wool, which was good for the chilly, early March weather. The top of it was white and the rest was entirely black, but it was the fullness of the bell sleeves that really made an impression.

She rushed to the dressing room, and sure enough it fit her like a glove.

She gazed at her reflection in the mirror, somewhat disappointedly, knowing in her heart that she hadn't been blessed with beauty. Still, she told herself that this dress was very flattering, her tenacity had gotten her thus far, and she was meeting the famous Aaron Bergstein for dinner that evening at the most posh new eatery in the city. That was something that not everyone could claim. And the best news of all was that her precious son had called her a few days earlier to check in, so apparently, all was forgiven.

Well, perhaps not *entirely* forgiven. His voice had sounded a bit subdued, but it was clearly a start.

She hadn't apologized, of course, for she'd done nothing wrong.

Still, it felt wonderful to be on speaking terms again. She made a private vow never to bring up his wife's long list of shortcomings to him ever again, which made her feel positively benevolent. In any case, these days found her in such a good mood, she was willing to let bygones be bygones.

Exiting the dressing room, she said to Robyn, "I'll take it."

Robyn smiled. "That'll be twenty-six hundred dollars."

Eva handed over her credit card.

So that's where they'd been, at dinner. They'd just ordered the appetizers when Aaron leaned forward and said, "So you're probably wondering why I never married again."

"The thought had crossed my mind," she said, surprised. "But I figured that you were too busy, like me."

"Oh, absolutely," he agreed. "Especially at first, after the divorce … work was what I did best. So I just worked, and worked, and then I worked some more."

"I get it."

"Then, a few years ago, I realized that here I am, all alone."

"So you've dated these last few years?" she asked, spearing an olive with her small fork. "I somehow was under the impression that you hadn't."

He looked sheepish as he said, "Well, very little, actually. No one had the temerity to bring it up."

"And you're not the type to while away your time in the library?" she teased. "Or the grocery store?"

"No. Not at all."

"I see," she said.

"But that's all changed," he commented, drawing her in even further.

"Really?" she said, eyebrows raised. "In what way?"

"Well, I've never met anyone quite like you before," he stated honestly. "We have so much in common. We're both driven, forces to be reckoned with, if you gather my meaning."

At that moment, the waiter came by with their appetizers. She looked down at her plate of salad. It was a beautifully presented plate, with edible flowers and seeds and who knew what else ….

She found that her appetite had fled, though, probably from

sheer nerves. This was no ordinary man, Aaron Bergstein, and deep down, Eva felt a little intimidated, a sensation that she wasn't at all accustomed to feeling. It was true that they had much in common. The man was almost like her alter-ego, in a way. He was inordinately successful. He was powerful. He was commanding and larger than life, and when she looked at him, it was hard not to see herself.

She just didn't know if she truly wanted to tie herself to him for the rest of her life, since quite honestly, she wasn't sure that she liked herself all that much. Not that he'd mentioned or even hinted at a future together ... *but still, what had he been trying to say?*

They'd gotten through the appetizer, which she was certain was delicious, but she couldn't recall how it tasted. Her mind was completely muddled when it was time to order the main course, so it was a relief when he ordered for her.

"Two filet mignons, medium rare, and a bottle of the Bordeaux, 2009."

She'd never had anyone order for her before, and though her brain was a bit addled by his candid admission, she realized that he hadn't asked her how she liked her steak cooked. Truth be told, she would've ordered it exactly the same way, but how on earth could he possibly know that?

She'd let it go, of course, since the waiter had been asking her something.

"Excuse me?"

"I was just asking what you'd like as a side dish. I recommend the haricots verts—they're excellent."

"Oh, that's fine," she murmured.

Aaron turned toward the waiter and added, "She'll also have bone marrow in tamarind sauce."

Eva noticed that he hadn't asked her if she liked marrow bones. It so happened that she did—but still. He hadn't asked her. She didn't suppose that he was the type to ask, as he was used to telling others what to do, much as she was.

Still, it was a little unnerving to do that on a date. If that's, in fact, what this was.

Was it?

She was so confused. She decided to discuss work—namely, the deal that was about to be closed, which seemed a safer topic.

"Four million for that apartment is a steal," he said. "You could've squeezed out a little more, in my opinion. It's only twenty-one hundred a square foot in a pre-war building, which is a joke. The same square footage literally a block away is commanding twenty-nine hundred a square foot."

She didn't recall asking him for his opinion, but in all fairness, she would've said the same thing in his shoes.

"I represented the buyer, not the seller," she reminded him.

"Oh, right, well … in that case, you did a good job negotiating," he commented dryly.

"Thanks," she said, reveling in the praise, however terse it had been. "It was on the market for twelve weeks."

"What was wrong with it? Those apartments are usually snapped up in a day. I've had bidding wars before these co-ops even hit the market."

She shrugged. "Cosmetic, mostly. It was renovated in 2008, and not to everyone's taste. Marble everywhere … a very certain look."

"And you found the buyer," he said, sitting back in his chair. "Congratulations."

"Thanks," she said again. "We're closing tomorrow."

"Look, Eva … May I call you that?"

"Of course."

"I don't know where this will go, but I'd like to see you again."

Eva smiled uncertainly. "You're seeing me right now."

"Well, we have a lot in common."

"You already said that."

"I guess I'm not so great with words," Aaron said. "That's what my ex used to say … maybe she was right."

Eva looked at him directly. "Are you trying to ask me something?"

Aaron twisted his napkin. "Well, where does Sam Goodman fit in all this?"

Oh. So that's what he'd meant … He wanted to keep seeing her, but only if she was single and unattached. Obviously.

She didn't know what to say. To a casual onlooker, there was no question. Aaron Bergstein had it all—money and prestige, and while he wasn't handsome, he was certainly imposing. The two of them would be a power couple. Shmiel Goodman was a simple accountant who lived an unassuming life, and he required an aide to help him with everyday chores.

Eva wanted to tell that to Aaron, how he had nothing to worry about. But instead, she found herself saying, "Well, I'm not exactly sure."

Aaron's eyebrows rose. "Meaning what?"

Eva swallowed. "Meaning just that. I'm not exactly sure."

Aaron looked mystified. Clearly, in his estimation he had

nothing in common with Shmiel Goodman, and so could not understand the hesitation on her part.

For what it was worth, neither could she. *Why had she said that?*

They'd been spared further conversation at that point, for their main courses had arrived. Eva cut into her steak. Though it must have been perfectly cooked, she couldn't remember how it tasted. They switched to other topics after that, which left Eva with the uneasy feeling that Aaron had somehow gotten the answer he'd been looking for, and would now let the matter drop.

Aaron Bergstein was used to getting his way. He wasn't the type to compete with someone else, at least not in this arena. *And what was there to compete with, in any case?*

Between Shmiel Goodman and Aaron Bergstein, Aaron was the clear winner.

Wasn't he?

And so she couldn't sleep that evening, playing and replaying their conversation in her mind until she thought she'd go mad.

She still hadn't returned Shmiel's calls, either. She found herself at an impasse and wasn't sure how she wanted to proceed. Here she was, an adult, and a successful one at that, and she couldn't wrap her head around this predicament.

There was no one to whom she could turn for advice. Her so-called friends were worthless, and she didn't value their opinions, in any case. She had no family to speak of, and it wasn't as if Simcha would be helpful, either. Speaking to his wife was out of the question, and it wasn't as if she would have any pearls of wisdom to share, in any case ....

She'd never needed anyone before, but now she felt that she wanted to speak to someone about this situation. She wanted clarity, but it was so elusive … with whom could she speak?

Eva got up from her desk and paced around her office. She'd had it done in chic taupes and greys. The dark wood floor was a gorgeous contrast, and the modish white furniture was inviting and serene. But she didn't see any of it at that moment. All she could see in her mind's eye was Shmiel Goodman. And Aaron Bergstein.

Had she ruined her chances with Aaron Bergstein? And what about Shmiel? He would surely come around to her way of thinking; he was practically putty in her hands. But Aaron Bergstein, now that was a different matter altogether.

What did she want?

Or, more importantly, *who* was it that she wanted? She just didn't know.

Edith came once more to her doorway.

"The deposit came through," she said. "It was wired into the account two minutes ago."

"Oh, good," she said. "I'll handle the paperwork."

She went back to her desk, eager for the respite. The paperwork alone would keep her occupied for the next several hours, and that was exactly what she wanted.

After ten minutes, though, she stopped, unable to continue.

The deal she'd been working on, the Fischer deal, involved two brothers who'd recently purchased a building together in Manhattan. The transaction had gone through effortlessly, thus far. Adam and Joel Fischer were easy to deal with, but she now saw with dismay that there was another brother, ostensibly a silent partner in this venture, who hadn't yet signed his share of the paperwork.

His name now leapt off the page at her.

Dr. Don Fischer.

Oh, no.

Instinctively, she knew who it was. She leaned over and grabbed her pocketbook from the edge of her desk. Withdrawing her wallet, she thumbed through various credit cards until she found what she was looking for. A faded, wrinkled card from five years earlier stared back at her.

Dr. Don Fischer.

He'd told her that she'd be back. It had been almost a taunt, almost a dare ....

How she hated being wrong. *Of all the ridiculous ...*

She had no choice. The paperwork needed his signature, and the sooner she got this deal done, the better.

She made the call.

AT FOUR O'CLOCK THAT same afternoon, Eva found herself in the waiting room of Dr. Fischer's office, to her own disbelief. She only needed ten minutes of his time, she told herself. It was a different office than the last time, much more upscale and on Park Avenue, no less. She couldn't sit still, so she paced the floor of the posh waiting room. It was empty, save for the receptionist behind a sleek, curved glass desk.

So he'd done well for himself, fool that he was. She really had no idea what had possessed her to call his office five years earlier. She must've been having some sort of out-of-body experience. Desperation, she supposed. She now looked at some of his awards that were prominently displayed in a glass case near the waiting area.

Dr. Don Fischer, Winner of the Award for Research in Geriatric Psychiatry ... APA Award, from the American Psychiatric Association ...

Wait a minute. The man was a *psychiatrist*?

She'd been under the impression that he was a therapist, not a real medical doctor. She begrudgingly admitted to herself that he couldn't have been as great a fool as she'd previously thought. Still, why had her friend even recommended him in the first place, five years earlier? *Of all the nerve ... it's not like she was crazy.* She was as sane as anyone, probably even more so.

She was seething with indignation and outrage, and she tapped her high heel against the floor impatiently, her blood boiling.

The clock on the wall ticked slowly, and Eva's thoughts rioted through her mind.

There are seventeen pages for him to initial and sign ... It should only take thirty to forty minutes, and then I'll never have to look at his smug face ever again ... Should I date Aaron Bergstein? Or should I date Shmiel Goodman? One is wealthy and powerful, and basically everything I could ever want in a spouse. And the other is practically an invalid who needs care and has nothing in common with me or my lifestyle. So which should it be?

No one would believe her predicament, since it seemed ludicrous. She didn't even understand why she was so conflicted. Aaron Bergstein was everything she was looking for ... *wasn't he*? And now here she was, in Dr. Don Fischer's office yet again, not as a client this time but as his real estate broker, which gave her a small measure of satisfaction. The tables were turned.

Now, *he* was *her* client, and it suited her, being in the proverbial driver's seat. She further knew that there was zero likelihood that he'd remember her from five years earlier, which was the only reason she'd even ventured to his office.

Still, her heart was palpitating so violently, she could feel its thrumming in her ears. She hadn't slept, she couldn't focus … really, this was all a bit much for her. The thought occurred to her to just end everything with both Aaron and Shmiel and just be done with it. She wasn't a starry-eyed teenager anymore, and all that was left was exhaustion.

The receptionist looked up.

"Ms. Adler? Dr. Fischer will see you now."

She walked into his office. He sat behind a large mahogany desk, looking much the same as he had five years earlier. He looked up and saw her, his tortoise-shell glasses still askew, and grinned.

"Told you that you'd be back," he remarked.

She was dumbstruck.

Never in all of her years had she ever felt her cheeks flame with embarrassment like they did at that very moment.

"I'm sure you didn't expect me to remember you, but I actually have a very good memory," he said.

What was the man, some sort of mind reader?

"Why don't you sit down?" He gestured toward the chair that faced him. Seemingly of their own volition, her legs traitorously carried her to the chair, where she sat down.

She was so *tired.*

"I understand that there are papers for me to sign?" he inquired.

"Your brothers already signed," she answered him in a clipped tone, like she was talking to an unruly child, and began to leaf through the stack of papers.

"Oh, they're much more organized than I am," he said cheerfully.

"Well, I can see that," she snapped. "If you'd have been more responsible, you wouldn't have wasted my entire afternoon."

"Sorry about that."

She looked up, chagrined to discover that not only did he not look sorry, he actually had the nerve to look amused.

She turned back to the stack of papers on the desk.

"Initial here," she instructed. "Then again on page 2 …"

He signed his initials on each document and asked several questions that she answered automatically, with fincssc and skill. She'd done this for more years than she cared to remember. But then he asked her a question that caught her off-guard.

"So, how have you been? What's been going on with your life?"

"That's a personal question that doesn't pertain to the task at hand," she answered hurriedly.

"True."

"Furthermore, I am not your client."

"No, you're not."

"In fact, you are *my* client … Sign over here on page 8. Initial the bottom of page 9."

He signed his name with a flourish.

"Actually …," she said.

"Yes?"

"Well, as a matter of fact …" She hardly knew where to begin, and for several moments she just sat there, unable to articulate what she wanted to say. But then … but then …

She started to speak, and to her complete surprise it all came out in a torrent of words … She spoke for twenty minutes straight, the words streaming out of her mouth of their own volition, first about Shmiel Goodman and his accident, then of her son, Simcha, and where he was living, which brought her to Aaron Bergstein ....

"As in *the* Aaron Bergstein?" he interrupted. "The billionaire?"

"Yes, that's the one."

"I see."

"So what do you think I should do?"

She was shocked that the words had flung, unbidden, out of her mouth. *Why was she asking him, of all people? It wasn't as if he had anything useful to say. The man was an insufferable fool.*

"You mean, you'd like me to tell you which man is more suitable, I take it?" He smiled.

"Oh, never mind," she said.

He leaned back in his chair and chuckled.

"You know I can't do that. Only you can make that decision."

Eva's temper flared. "How typical ... I have to ask you, how do you make any money doing this? I just don't get it. People have to make their own decisions, you tell them nothing, and then you expect to be paid?"

He grinned broadly.

"That's pretty much it, Eva. You've figured me out."

"You're a fraud."

"Is that it? I've been called worse."

"And a charlatan," she added.

"*Ooh*, that's a good one," he said cheerfully, not looking at all wounded.

She folded her arms and glared at him.

"Look, what do you want me to say?" he said. "You chose two

very disparate men. In layman's terms, one is someone who will boss you around. And the other is someone that *you'll* boss around. It all comes down to which you'd prefer, really."

"*Excuse me?*"

"Instead of focusing on all of that, why don't we focus on the real issue?" he continued calmly.

"Oh? And which issue would that be?" she asked icily.

"All right," he said. "It's like this ... why do you dislike your daughter-in-law?"

She hadn't been expecting that. She hadn't even mentioned her name. *How could he possibly have known?*

"Who said anything about her? *I* never did. Sign the bottom of paragraph 3, page 14."

"Precisely," he agreed. "So why do you resent her?"

"I don't resent her," Eva lied. "I just don't exactly get along with her."

"Because you resent her," he reiterated. "Tell me this, is she cruel? Is she an evil person?"

She thought it over. "No."

"Is she rude or indifferent to your son?"

"No, I don't think so."

"Does he seem happy?"

"Well, yes, but—"

"But what?"

She hesitated. "It's just that, well ... he doesn't know any better. Sign here."

He nodded. "I see. So your son is simple-minded, is that it?"

Her voice was sharp. "I'll have you know that my son was the smartest boy in his yeshiva. Ask anyone."

"Oh, I believe you," he said. "He's just simple when it comes to picking wives, eh?"

Once again, Eva's cheeks flamed vermilion. Her silence spoke volumes.

"So I'll ask you again. Why do you dislike her? What's her name, by the way?"

"Shari, but I fail to see what difference that makes—"

"Oh, it makes all the difference in the world. When you have a relationship with someone, it's beneficial to speak his or her name. You asked me for my opinion, right?"

"I don't know why," she snapped. "It's not like you have any useful advice."

"You want advice?" he asked. "Well, I'll give it to you. You resent Shari because you're human, Eva. You don't like believing that you're human, but you are. And it terrifies you."

"Oh, of all the nonsensical—"

He reclined back in his chair and watched her intently.

"Of course I'm human. Why are you saying I don't believe that?"

The man was clearly a bigger imbecile than she'd previously thought.

"Being human terrifies you, Eva. That's why you've thrown yourself into your work, never allowing yourself the luxury of relaxing for even a second, right? Never letting your guard down … working through pure adrenaline, right? Sound familiar?"

"Well, maybe, but I fail to see—"

"The thrill of the chase … the art of the deal … keeping yourself so busy every second of every day, you've become almost robotic. You don't have time to think, you don't have time to feel—"

"Of course I do."

"Do you? How about your friends?"

"What about them?"

"Would you say you have many friends, or are they few and far between?"

She stared at him.

"Working around the clock doesn't lend itself to keeping friendships, does it?"

"Friends are stupid." She shrugged.

"Friends are human, Eva. They have feelings, too. It's all part of the human experience. People like you, who are afraid of the human experience, will find every way to distance themselves from all of it."

"That's the most insane argument I've ever heard. Why am I supposedly afraid of being human, as you call it?"

"Because humans get hurt," he answered gently. "Part of the human experience is pain. You've been hurt, Eva. You lost your husband at a very young age, you've been terribly hurt, and by being a warrior, impervious to pain, you've been able to avoid having to endure any more suffering."

She was silent.

He waited several moments before adding, "Your son's marriage, his happiness with your young daughter-in-law, is all a painful reminder of what you've lost. It's not Shari who you hate, it's what she represents. She's the young wife that you never had the chance to be. I'll say it again … *she's the young wife that you never had the chance to be.*"

Eva paled.

"That isn't true," she whispered.

He walked around to the front of his desk and sat in the chair across from her. His gaze was intense, but there was a wealth of understanding in his eyes.

"You know that it is," he said quietly.

And then Eva did something that she hadn't done in twenty years.

To her utter mortification, hot tears welled up in her eyes and then spilled over and ran down her cheeks.

"It's just not fair," she choked, crying in earnest.

"I know." He reached over to his desk and handed her a wad of tissues, which only made her feel more pathetic.

Neither of them spoke. There was only the sound of her shuddering sobs as she buried her face in the tissues.

"I'll bet you haven't done much crying over the years," he said softly. "Feels good to let it out, doesn't it?"

"Crying is just a waste of time," she sputtered.

He got up and sat back down behind his desk, all the while looking at her sympathetically.

"I know. Friends are stupid, crying is a waste of time … being real isn't all that easy. But being real, living in reality—well, it's infinitely better than the alternative, isn't it?"

She looked at him, her face blotchy and stained with tears. She had never looked worse, in all probability, and she'd never felt more vulnerable.

It was more than a little disconcerting to realize that this man was somehow able to peer into her very soul. Her imperious outer veneer, of which she was so proud, had just crumbled before him like dust in the wind.

"Okay, so maybe you have a valid point," she murmured.

"Good," he responded. "You're a smart woman, Eva. If you

want a modicum of normalcy in your life, of happiness, you'll have to start by doing something that won't be so easy. You have to start by apologizing to your daughter-in-law."

She shook her head. "No."

"Fine," he replied. "Then apologize to your son. Really, you can do it. He's your son, right? Tell him what happened here … ask him for another chance. Tell him you'll prove to him that you're willing to change."

"And what do I get in return?" she challenged.

"Fair enough," he said. "In return, I promise you that you'll have a wonderful relationship with your son, and with your daughter-in-law as well. You'll get paid dividends, trust me."

She sat there, staring at him.

Could she do it?

She wasn't quite sure. But she had to admit that this man, Dr. Don Fischer … he was actually more intelligent than she'd originally thought. She would at least give him credit for that.

She suddenly realized that their work was done. The stack of papers was signed, and there was no further reason for her to be there. She awkwardly got up from her chair, feeling different, somehow. It was strange to think that she'd unburdened herself to a total stranger and the world was still spinning on its axis.

Gathering her pocketbook, she turned to him.

"You know, you still haven't told me what to do about Shmiel Goodman and Aaron Bergstein," she said, challengingly.

He grinned. "I'm not running a dating service, Eva. You'll have to decide that on your own."

She nodded, knowing that he spoke the truth.

"We're done signing papers, right?"

"Yes, that's it for now," she mumbled. "I'll finish up everything tonight."

He thanked her and stood up.

Dazedly, she gathered the papers and left his office, pulling on her cashmere coat as she went outside, bracing herself against the cold wind. Yet, oddly enough, as she walked outside, she didn't even feel the frigid air that blew about her mercilessly. She was also oblivious to the traffic noises that blared around her in every direction.

Clarity was a sensation that had eluded her for some time but now jolted within her like a bolt of lightning. Dr. Fischer hadn't answered the question, but it no longer mattered. Her breathing had returned to normal, her anxiety had eased, and she felt the lightness of spirit that comes with newfound insight. What she had to do seemed perfectly obvious and crystal clear. Her mind was made up.

She knew in her heart which man she would choose.

CHAPTER FIFTEEN

GALI

IT WAS SUNDAY MORNING, and Gali had spent another sleepless night. She knew that their alarm system was the best around, but she was on edge, tired, and anxious. All night long, every little sound had caused her to tense. The predicament in which she found herself was becoming unbearable.

She dragged herself out of bed and looked at her reflection in the mirror. She hadn't been able to eat too much lately, and her face was sallow and drawn. There were puffy bags under her eyes. Even her blonde-streaked hair looked limp and lifeless.

She was a mess.

As if on cue, her phone rang. It was Yigal.

"Hi, Gali," he said. "How are you?"

It was no use. She simply had to tell him. She realized that he truly was her other half, and keeping this from him was ripping her apart and causing her tremendous anxiety.

"Yigal, I have something important I need to tell you …," she whispered, not wanting anyone to overhear. She knew that the walls of her room were thick and sturdy, but she was becoming paranoid.

"Oh, good." He sounded relieved. "I had a feeling that

something was up, but I didn't want to pressure you. I figured you'd tell me whatever it was when you were ready."

Her eyes misted over. That was her Yigal … he was a prince. *How long had he known?*

"I'm so relieved to hear you say that," she said. "It's nothing to do with you, with us … I just want you to know that. We're fine, and we'll always be fine."

"Good," he said again, sounding concerned. "It's nothing medical, right? You're feeling okay?"

"Yes, it's nothing like that. Just a little sleep deprived. I haven't slept in a while."

"Why not?"

"Look, I can't tell you in the house, over the phone … Are you busy today?"

"I don't have to be at the hospital until four this afternoon. Why don't we go for a hike, up in Los Feliz? Maybe we'll go to the Griffith Observatory? It's a clear day—we'll be able to see for miles."

It sounded perfect. She needed to get away from this house and from jumping out of her skin every time a floorboard creaked.

He said he'd pick her up within the hour, so Gali ran about, trying to salvage her appearance as best as she could. She chose a casual, lightweight outfit and pulled her hair into a ponytail. She then put on her sneakers for the hike and ran down the stairs, energized at the thought of spending a few hours with Yigal, whom she hadn't seen in days.

Her mother was in the kitchen, drinking an iced coffee at the island and perusing a magazine of bridal gowns.

"Gali," her mother said. "What about this one?"

The gown was spectacular, with a three-foot train, but it was a bit much.

"It's nice," she replied. "But I wanted something a little simpler, you know?"

"Hmm … where are you going?"

"Yigal is picking me up."

Her mother stared at her. "You're not going out with your *chassan* dressed like *that*, are you?"

"What's wrong with the way I'm dressed?" she asked.

"You're wearing a ponytail."

She shrugged. "It's hot, and we're going for a hike."

"A *hike*?" Her mother's mouth was a perfect circle.

Just then the doorbell rang and Gali sprinted to get it, while her mother muttered under her breath about kids nowadays, and how hiking was not at all the thing to do in her day.

Gali opened the door and saw Yigal, all at once feeling infinitely better than she'd felt in days. He stood there, smiling at her.

"Ready?"

"Yes, I'm ready."

As they left together, she realized that it was true on every level. She was ready to tell him what had recently transpired, she was ready to tackle whatever would come their way, and she was ready to spend the rest of her life with him.

THEY WERE AT THE Griffith Observatory, high above Los Angeles. It was an unusually clear day, like Yigal had said, and the view stretched endlessly for miles. It was the most perfect spot, and they were far away and almost higher than the clouds. She didn't feel threatened there, and didn't find herself looking over her shoulder.

There was a bench in the shade, and they strolled over to it and sat down.

"Okay." Yigal turned to her. "I think you need to tell me what's going on."

And so she began.

She told him about that day in the bookstore, how she'd wanted to order him a *sefer* that he'd wanted, how she'd met a girl there, how she'd felt sorry for her and invited her to join her at the farmer's market in Santa Monica, how she'd felt that the girl's behavior had been odd, to say the least.

"Then I was sitting in the kitchen with my notebook, planning the menu ... you know, for the anniversary dinner last week."

"Right," he said.

"And I'd written in the notebook, at the very top of the page ... the name of this girl, Leah Rosen." She swallowed.

Telling him this part would be the hardest, she knew.

"Go on," he said encouragingly.

"And no one was home, the house was quiet ... and for some reason, my eyes kept returning to that name written in my notebook. And I realized ..."

She looked at him, not knowing how to say it.

He waited, his gaze intent upon her, listening.

"I realized that the name Rosen, if you write it backwards, is really Nes Or."

His face turned white.

"Yigal, I'm so sorry to have to tell you this. There's so much more ... I've been keeping this inside for days, not wanting to tell you, but I'm going to have a nervous breakdown ... I just can't take it anymore."

Yigal was thunderstruck. He'd had no idea what she would say, but never in his wildest nightmares had he thought it would be this. Poor Gali … his heart went out to her. Here she was, his *kallah*, and instead of this being the best time of her life, she'd been burdened with an awful reality that he couldn't begin to fathom.

There was more to come, he knew.

"Just tell me," he managed, looking ill.

She told him. She told him every detail, keeping nothing from him. She told him about the lipstick on her car … about the dirty paper towels she'd thrown into the trash bins outside her house that night … the missing blueberries at the dinner … the roses that had been delivered … the tiny camera that was attached to the stems … how she'd checked the footage of their surveillance camera … how she'd seen Leah Nes Or right there, on the computer screen in her very own family room … how she'd saved the file …

Gali had tears running down her cheeks and she didn't even realize it. So much turmoil had been brewing inside her, and it felt so good, so *right*, to finally be unburdening herself to Yigal. She'd carried the weight around for days and it had become too heavy for her to bear it alone.

Together, they would manage it.

Yigal looked positively ashen, his own eyes filled with tears, but he was silent, trying to take it all in.

It was unthinkable what Gali had been dealing with, all alone.

What if Leah Nes Or had tried to harm her in some way?

Hadn't she threatened to make him pay for what he'd done? He'd never forgive himself if anything happened to Gali. As she talked, she'd never looked lovelier. She was his future wife, the future mother of his children ....

"This is all my fault," he whispered finally.

Gali wiped her eyes. "Yigal, this isn't your fault. She's ... she's not well. She needs help. I actually feel sorry for her."

Yigal was inarticulate, marveling at her response. Any other girl would be in full-blown hysteria, but not his Gali. She was so special. She looked at things through such a mature, grounded prism.

He felt like the luckiest guy in the world.

"Besides," Gali continued, "I was the one who invited her to the farmer's market ...."

That was easy for him to understand.

"Gali, don't you see?" he asked. "Of course you did, that's the way you are. You fell right into her trap. You think she just happened to be in that store at the same time? I don't believe it for a second."

And there it was. He was right, of course.

Gali looked down at the sparkling ring on her finger, wondering where Leah Nes Or was at that moment, what she was thinking, what she was plotting ....

"Gali, I know you won't like this, but I'm going to have to tell my father," he said softly.

"Oh, no! Why?"

"He's a lawyer, right? He has connections. I'll get a temporary restraining order ... She won't be allowed to come anywhere near you."

She hadn't thought of that.

"I'll definitely sleep better," she murmured.

"So will I, believe me."

She knew in her heart that her safety and well-being were uppermost in his mind, and she felt cherished and cared for. She wondered if Leah Nes Or had felt cherished and cared for by her parents when she was growing up, or if she'd felt insecure and lonely. *Did she have any friends? What caused her to be this way?* She supposed she'd never know the answer.

They stayed there on the bench for a long time, Yigal's mind working furiously. Gali felt so much relief at having this problem aired that her heart felt lighter than it had in days.

"So what's next?" she asked.

"I'll go home and tell my father what's been happening. I'd call him now, but I want to tell him in person. Don't worry, he won't tell my mother ... she'd be hysterical."

"Mine, too. I really don't want my parents to know about this. They would be absolutely frantic."

He nodded. "With my father's connections, we'll probably be able to get this done quickly. It's all going to be taken care of, Gali. It'll be over soon, and you won't need to worry about it anymore."

A thought occurred to her. "How will she even know that we have a restraining order? How does it work?"

His brow furrowed. "I don't know much about law, but I think that defendants are served with restraining orders. So she'll know. And to get a restraining order, I'm pretty sure that you'll have to go to court and tell your story to a judge."

"What? Oh, no!"

"I'll be there with you, don't worry. It's good that you saved the file on your computer. Is it on a USB?"

"Yes."

Gali saw other *frum* couples walking around the observatory.

She was sure that none of them were discussing courts and restraining orders.

It was unbelievable. Here they were, the day was beautiful and warm, the view was endless and breathtaking, but she and Yigal were sitting on this bench, loath to move an inch. They were that terrified, not knowing what was in store for them.

They knew that they weren't dealing with someone rational, which made things all the more frightening.

"Yigal, what if we're overreacting?" Gali asked. "What if I'm exaggerating the whole thing? Maybe she's ... unbalanced, but maybe she doesn't mean any harm."

He shook his head. "We can't take that chance, can we? By the way, where is that tiny camera? You might want to bring it to court to show the judge. It's evidence, too."

Gali reached into her purse and pulled it out, keeping it covered with her hand.

"I didn't want to leave it around. I was afraid that Elizabeth would throw it out."

"Smart girl," he said, staring at it.

A new, awful thought came to Gali. "You don't think there's a microphone on it, do you? That would mean that she—"

"Heard us?"

Gali felt faint. He grabbed the tiny camera, which was no bigger than a nickel. It had tiny teeth on it, which allowed it to hold onto the rose's stem. It almost looked like a mini hair clip, like she'd worn in grade school.

He held it in his palm, poking and prodding it with his thumb, but of course, there was no way to know.

"It could be a listening device, I guess," he said doubtfully.

She was silent.

"We're on to you," he spoke into it in a menacing tone. "We're going to the police."

Gali looked at him and couldn't help but smile. He was so earnest, so sincere … making threats into the tiny clip, not knowing if anyone was even listening in on the other end.

"That should scare off anyone, am I right?" He grinned at her.

"I know I feel much safer."

She put it back into the inner pocket of her purse.

"This is all so crazy … I don't think anyone else has ever had to deal with this."

"I'm so, so sorry, Gali. I really am."

"It's not your fault," she said again. "We'll see this through together."

They finally got up from the bench and stretched before walking back down the steep driveway toward their car. Knowing that she had Yigal next to her did a lot to calm her nerves. They'd go back home and face the music … whatever would come their way.

THEY WERE DRIVING UP Gali's street when they realized that something was very, very wrong. There were police cars everywhere … someone was screaming … neighbors were coming out of their houses to see what all the commotion was about ….

The neighborhood, which was usually ultra-quiet, had turned into bedlam.

What was going on?

Their car couldn't get through, so Yigal quickly parked. They walked down the street together, their panic growing with each passing step. They soon saw Gali's neighbor, Judy Rubin, in a frenzied state, talking to two policemen.

"Uh-oh," Gali whispered. "You don't think ... ?"

"I don't know what to think," he said quietly.

At first, Gali thought that there had been a break-in at the Rubins' house. But then she saw two more policemen talking to someone else near her own gated lawn, and the person was shrieking. She couldn't hear what was being said, but judging from the number of people who were milling around, watching, it wasn't good. There were many policemen standing there, blocking her view so she couldn't see who was shouting, but she instinctively knew.

What had that girl done now?

She glanced over at Yigal, who looked ill with fright.

Just then, Judy Rubin saw Gali and said something to the cops, who nodded their assent. She motioned Gali and Yigal over to where she was standing.

"Mrs. Rubin, what happened?"

"Gali, thank goodness you're all right," was all she said. "Yigal, watch over her like a hawk."

"Believe me, I will," he said gravely.

"We've had some trouble here. Is that your house, miss?" a cop asked Gali, gesturing to the grand home next door.

Gali nodded, unable to speak.

"Do you live with your parents?"

"Yes. Are they okay?" she asked, her voice wavering.

"They aren't at home," the other cop said quickly. "Do you know where they are?"

"No," she answered, flooded with relief. For a second, she'd thought that they were somehow involved in this, this … she still didn't know what had occurred.

Just then, an ambulance made its way down the street.

What was going on? Was someone hurt?

"Please tell me what's going on," she begged the cop, who was looking at her with concern.

He pointed to her house again, and this time, the policeman standing on her lawn had moved over a bit, and she saw.

Her blood grew cold as she surveyed the scene.

The gate was wide open and Leah Nes Or was right there, on her front lawn, being held down by two harried-looking policemen.

"Let me go!" she shouted. "I didn't do anything! Get off me!"

It was if the entire universe had turned upside down.

This was her house, her street, Yigal was standing right beside her … She couldn't take it all in. She saw the cops were largely ignoring Leah's protests as they held her down. They tried to talk to her reasonably, saying things like, "Calm down, now. We're trying to help you. Miss, you need to calm down."

Across Gali's large dining room windows were big letters sprayed in red paint.

The words *I'M WATCHING YOU* were scrawled there, for all the world to see.

The red paint looked so sinister, almost like blood.

And there was Elizabeth, her housekeeper, being put on a stretcher, a packet of ice on her head. She was moaning.

Gali ran over to the stretcher on wobbly legs.

"Elizabeth, what happened?'

"Oh, Miss Gali," she said. "No worry, I tripped and hit my head on the granite counter … My head be splitting, but I was so scared. I saw this girl right through the dining room, spraying the windows ... I called the cops, but then I tripped right over. Fell down, so clumsy ..."

"Oh, Elizabeth!"

For one quaking moment, Gali thought that Leah Nes Or had harmed her in some way. On the other hand, if she hadn't been there, scaring the poor housekeeper out of her wits, this wouldn't have happened.

"We're just taking her in to make sure she doesn't have a concussion," one of the paramedics told Gali.

Just then, Gali saw her mother's car driving down the street toward the scene. It couldn't be—it was almost surreal. She suddenly felt like she was detached from it all. The sun was hot on her back ... a crowd of people were gathered, watching ... the ambulance was there ... policemen were swarming everywhere ... Leah Nes Or was still shouting ... it was just too much.

Gali fainted.

MUCH LATER THAT NIGHT, when the ambulance had left, and the police had escorted Leah Nes Or down to the police station, and the crowds had dispersed, Gali sat on a cushioned chair in the family room. A cashmere shawl was draped around her shoulders. Every so often, she shivered involuntarily, though the room was warm. She felt cold from within, no doubt from sheer worry and sleeplessness. She was surrounded by Yigal, who had called in a different resident to cover his rounds that evening, as well as her parents and Yigal's parents. Physically, Gali had recuperated. All they needed now was to discuss how to proceed.

"I still can't believe you didn't tell us." Gali's mother looked wounded. "You've been shouldering all of that agony on your own."

"I didn't want to worry you," Gali repeated for what must've been the hundredth time.

"Well, what if she'd harmed you in some way? What then?" she insisted. "Next time, you have to tell us something like this."

"There won't be a next time," Yigal said, looking at Gali. "Not if I can help it."

"Yigal," her father said. "We'll always be indebted to you for taking Gali out today. I shudder to think what could've happened had she been here."

Yigal nodded. "I know, but Gali didn't want to worry you. Or me, for that matter. I just found out this morning."

His mother nodded. "I'm just grateful to Hashem that you didn't end up with such a monster, Yigal. Can you imagine?"

He held up his hand. "Ima, please … no name-calling. Please."

Ronit Ben Ezri shrugged. "I just say things like I see it."

Gali's mother nodded in agreement.

Gali and Yigal's eyes met. They both wanted more than anything to be away from the family room to talk together in private. But alas, it wasn't meant to be.

Reuven Ben Ezri's cell phone rang. "Jake?" His voice boomed into the receiver. "What did you find out?"

They couldn't understand much of the one-sided conversation. They were quiet, waiting.

Before long, he hung up.

"All right," he told them. "My man, Jake, has information. Apparently, her parents are headed to LAX right now. They're flying in tonight … they're apologetic. They claim they had no idea that she was capable of this behavior, and they're asking us not to press charges or push for a restraining order. It might be a moot point, anyway, since they're going to take her back with them on a plane tomorrow."

"If she goes," Ronit said. "Who said she'll go with them?"

"Oh, I think spending half the night in a police station will be an incentive," Reuven responded dryly.

"Are we supposed to just snap our fingers and forget everything?" Gali's mother said sarcastically, snapping her fingers for emphasis. "Does that mean Gali can't ever go to New York? She'll always be looking over her shoulder!"

"I never liked New York that much, anyway," Gali interjected. "I'm definitely more West Coast."

Yigal looked at her and grinned.

Her mother gave her a *look.*

"Why don't we cross that bridge when we come to it?" Reuven suggested. "New York is a large city … I can always get an ex parte restraining order if need be. Who knows? Maybe this girl needs medication. After she gets the help she needs, then we'll see …."

"It makes sense to me," Gali's father said. "I don't think we need to jump in too hastily. Let's not forget, the girl is leaving tomorrow."

"I'll just feel better when she gets on that plane," Gali's mother said.

Ronit nodded in agreement.

Yigal handed over the minuscule camera that had been attached to the roses to his father.

"For safekeeping," he said.

His father looked at it, nodded, and put it in his pocket. "I'll put it in the safe. I'd also like the USB with the surveillance footage.

I'll save it for evidence, in case we need it one day."

Gali handed it over and asked, her voice higher-pitched than usual, "You don't think she'll come back, do you? I'd hate to be looking over my shoulder my whole life, like my mother said."

Yigal turned to his father. "Abba, maybe you could persuade a judge to give an ex parte restraining order anyway? Even though she's leaving tomorrow? She could come back, you know. I think Gali and I would feel better—"

"I guess I could," his father mused. "She wouldn't be at the second hearing, though, so the case against her could be dismissed. Still, this girl couldn't possibly understand the legal ramifications—"

"Exactly," Yigal said. "As the defendant, wouldn't she be served with papers?"

Gali gazed at him with admiration. *He was so brilliant ... How did he know so much?*

"I could have my man in New York serve her with the papers, no problem," his father said. "She'd have no way of knowing if those papers would or wouldn't be expiring, in any case ... It would certainly be a deterrent."

"You mean, she'd think twice before following me again," Gali clarified.

"Oh, most definitely," Reuven said. "She wouldn't want to risk coming near you again."

Gali's mother let out a huge sigh. "That would make me sleep better at night, Reuven. Thank you."

She then asked aloud the question that had been plaguing Gali the entire day.

"What I don't understand is why the girl was following our

daughter, who never did anything to her. I would think that she'd come after you, Yigal."

Yigal was quiet, thinking.

"Yigal, she never tried to do anything to you, did she?" his mother asked tremulously.

"She did today," he replied softly. "Ima, don't you understand? She knew that the worst thing that could possibly happen to me would be to lose Gali. Any other girl would be scared off …."

The room got quiet after that, and Gali smiled wanly for the first time that day.

"Don't worry, I'm not that easily scared off, Yigal," she said in a small voice.

"I'm glad to hear it." He grinned at her.

And he meant it.

CHAPTER SIXTEEN

TOVA

TOVA BOARDED THE PLANE that Sunday morning as if in a dream. She was finally on her way to Israel after spending Shabbos in Paris. She stood on line in Charles de Gaulle Airport with her passport in hand, like all of the other passengers, but her mind was elsewhere. It wasn't on the fact that her luggage was waiting for her in Ben Gurion Airport in Tel Aviv, and she only was traveling with her small carry-on bag. She also barely noticed that she was wearing the exact same outfit that she'd been wearing on that fateful Friday.

Had that been only two days ago?

So much had happened to her in the span of two days.

Oddly enough, she could recall everything that had occurred in crystalline detail, from landing on that harried Friday afternoon up until that very moment. She boarded the plane, got herself settled in her seat, and leaned back, her *Tehillim* on her lap, and thought back to Friday afternoon, reliving every moment ….

SHE'D WALKED OFF THE plane two days earlier, following closely behind the young couple ahead of her.

"Excuse me," she'd panted, hurriedly catching up to them.

"Oh, I'm sorry," said the young woman, turning around. "I didn't see you behind us."

"Oh, that's okay," Tova said. "I'm just wondering what to do ...."

"Would you like to share a taxi? We're headed to the Ninth arrondissement for Shabbos."

"I think so," she replied, relieved. "You wouldn't happen to have the phone number of a Rebbetzin in town named Sarah Beneviste, would you?"

The woman shook her head kindly. "No, I don't, but my husband's cousin might. Before we do anything, though, we're just hurrying to the customer service desk to iron things out. You can come with us if you'd like."

"Oh, of course. Thanks."

Tova continued trailing the couple, who walked remarkably fast with many pieces of carry-on luggage and a toddler in a stroller, to boot. They also seemed so calm, while Tova felt positively frazzled.

Here she was, in Paris of all places, without her luggage. She didn't know a soul, Shabbos was in a few short hours ... She had thought she'd be able to rest over Shabbos in Israel and get to work early Sunday morning, but instead she'd be boarding yet another plane. She'd never imagined such a strange set of circumstances, and she felt completely overwhelmed.

Forcing herself to remain calm, she waited on line with the couple, who introduced themselves as Rabbi and Mrs. Fried. To Tova's immense relief, when it was their turn Rabbi Fried started speaking in rapid-fire French to the ticket agent. After a manager came forward to intervene and the whole situation was straightened out, Tova had a brand-new ticket in her hand for Sunday morning along with the assurance that her bags would be waiting for her in Tel Aviv.

It was easier to breathe after that. At least she wouldn't be stranded in this place forever, she thought. She tried to think of it as an adventure, even though there was no place she'd rather not be. Mrs. Fried murmured something to her husband, and within several minutes he called his relative and got Tova a phone number for the Rebbetzin in Paris.

As they walked toward the long corridor that would lead them to the exit, Tova made the call.

After several rings, a woman answered, with a lovely, lilting voice.

"Allo?"

"Um, hi, yes," Tova stammered. "You don't know me, but my name is Tova Miller, and I'm calling from the airport. I was on the way to Israel … A woman on our plane was having chest pains, so I had to deplane here in Paris."

"*Vous etes Americain?*"

"Yes, yes … I'm an American, and I actually met your mother in the airport in Detroit—"

"*Maman?*"

Oh, dear. It was such a strange request, she knew, and her French was rusty, but she tried it.

"*Vous etes mere, vous avez de nombreux invites* …." She hoped that meant that her mother had mentioned that she hosted guests.

The woman sounded a bit confused at first, which was understandable, but soon she seemed to understand her predicament.

"*Tu peux parler Anglais*," the woman replied soothingly. "You can speak English. I understand eet a leedle bit."

"Okay, thank you," Tova replied nervously. "I couldn't continue on the plane. It would be cutting it too close to Shabbos, and I didn't want to risk it … and I figured that since your mother mentioned that you have guests—"

"*Merci*, thank you for calling," the Rebbetzin said in a heavily accented English. "We eez love to host you for Shabbat. The apartment eez 9 Rue de Maubeuge, in zee Ninth arrondissement. You eez our welcome guest. My *maman* eez here, as well. You eez get, how you say … reacquainted."

Tova was horrified to discover that she was on the verge of tears. This saintly woman didn't know her, yet she was willing to open her home to a complete stranger.

"Thank you," Tova whispered.

"No eez thank," the woman insisted. "We eez with other guests as well … eez most wonderful. See you soon, safe travel to you."

Tova hung up feeling much better. She'd be safe for Shabbos and her luggage would be safe, as well.

Everything was for the best, she knew.

She shared a taxi with the Frieds, and they zoomed through the winding streets, studded with old, picturesque buildings and shops and throngs of passersby, occasionally stranded in traffic.

This was Paris … the City of Lights ….

Only she didn't want to be there. She wanted to be in Yerushalayim, and she didn't understand why her plans always seemed to go awry. Feeling dejected and out of place, she stared out of the window, noticing that it had started to drizzle. People were scurrying under their umbrellas. Many outdoor cafes were bringing chairs and tables indoors. Traffic had slowed to a crawl in one of the arrondissements, though she didn't know which ….

Her melancholy mood matched the dismal weather.

Why did everything have to be so hard? Why did nothing ever seem to go right for her?

Before long, the traffic eased up, and they were once again flying through the streets of Paris at an exhilarating pace. Looking at the architecture, the looming buildings and small shops with awnings and flowers that lined either side of the street, she had to admit to herself that the city did have a certain allure, and if she had to be stranded somewhere for Shabbos, it could've been much worse. She could practically hear Gali say something like, "*Stranded in Paris for Shabbos? Are you kidding? What fun!*"... or something along those lines.

After several more minutes ticked by, they pulled up to 9 Rue de Maubeuge, a corner building, flanked on each side by a wide intersection. It was a large, imposing stone structure, with long windows and wrought iron balustrades framing small terraces. On the ground floor of the building was a small restaurant, a shoe store, and a hair salon.

Tova thanked the Frieds profusely for all of their help and exited the taxi, carrying with her the only possession she had, her carry-on bag. The cab didn't wait to see her safely to her destination, but rather took off on the cobbled streets at a fast pace.

Tova looked at the building, hoping that she'd heard the address correctly. If she hadn't, and the kindly Rabbanit Sara Beneviste lived somewhere else, *then what would she do*?

She needn't have worried, though. She saw their name on a mailbox in the building's small foyer. It wasn't much of a foyer, really. Inside the double oak doors was a narrow inner corridor that led to a steep stairwell. The lighting inside was dim, and the hallway was shadowy and dark, which only increased her anxiety. Still, she didn't have much of a choice.

She was here for Shabbos and she decided that she might as well make the best of it. She trudged up the stairs, carrying her bulky carry-on over her shoulder. She checked all of the doors on the first landing. None of them said the name Beneviste, so she kept climbing the old, steep stairs.

On the fourth floor, the highest floor … the last door on the landing said *Mishpachat Beneviste.*

Thank You, Hashem, Tova whispered. She was infinitely relieved. At last.

She knocked tentatively on the door, hearing strains of music in the apartment.

The door was opened by a lovely woman, seemingly in her mid-50's, with a brightly colored turban on her head and a flowered apron.

Tova extended her hand. "Hi, I'm Tova Miller—"

She needn't have bothered, for the Rebbetzin rushed forward, giving her such a sincere, warm hug that she was left inarticulate and near tears.

"Meez Tova, *Je suis si desole pour toi*! I feel so bad for all you've been through! Come een, come een!"

When Tova was ushered into the spacious apartment, a feeling of warmth and camaraderie pervaded her senses. The delectable smell of Shabbos wafted through the apartment, a teenaged girl was practicing a piece of music on the console piano in the corner of the living room, and everything seemed so … so normal. So right. The saintly Rebbetzin brought her into a small galley kitchen, which was framed with large windows on each side, making it at once cozy and bright.

"Rabbanit Beneviste, thank you so much—"

The Rebbetzin waved her hand. "No eez need to thank! Our greatest pleasure! Ahh … here is Maman now …."

The elderly lady, her silken kerchief still draped over her head and leaning on her cane, came forward with her hand outstretched.

"*Bonjour*, *ma cher*. So we meet again." She smiled.

"So nice to see you again," Tova said warmly. "Did you have a nice flight back?"

"*Baruch Hashem*," she replied, pointing above. "At my age, traveling is a special *zechut*. You have difficult journey, I understand?"

The elderly woman seemed to know English better than her daughter, and so Tova unburdened herself to the two women in the warm kitchen, over freshly baked cinnamon rolls. They listened, fascinated by the bizarre story.

"… and so I had to deplane, because it was cutting it too close," she explained.

Rabbanit Beneviste nodded. "Too close to Shabbat."

The elderly woman sat back in her chair and gazed upward, toward the ceiling. Her dark skin was leathery but her eyes still twinkled with youthful brightness.

"*Hashgachah pratit*," she intoned. "You were meant to be here for Shabbat, *ma cher*, that much I know."

"I can't thank you enough," Tova said again.

They again reiterated what a pleasure it was for them to host her, and then the benevolent Rabbanit Beneviste showed her to her room, which was located off the kitchen. It was small and narrow, no bigger than a closet, with just a bed and small nightstand, but it looked warm and inviting. In fact, that was Tova's impression of the entire apartment and the Beneviste family—warm and inviting.

It just felt so *homey.* And Tova hadn't had a home in … well, for most of her life.

Yet here she was, in Paris for Shabbos, by the home of strangers, and for some inexplicable reason she felt cared for and safe, with all the comforts of home. She appreciated their kindness beyond measure. Closing the door behind her, ostensibly to get ready before Shabbos, she gazed longingly at the bed. She was so *tired.* She would've loved the luxury of taking a nap before Shabbos, but there wasn't any time. Shabbos was rapidly approaching, and she suddenly realized that she had nothing to wear except for the clothing on her back. She was wearing an olive green sweater and a long black skirt. It would simply have to do.

At that moment, there was a small, tentative knock on her door.

Tova opened it. It was Rabbanit Beneviste's daughter, the one who'd been playing the piano earlier. She looked about fourteen or fifteen years old.

"*Pardon,*" she said. "For you?"

She held out a lovely black dress, her own in all probability, for Tova to wear on Shabbos. The simple act of kindness made Tova's eyes well up with tears.

"Is this dress yours?" Tova asked.

The girl nodded. "Please … for Shabbat."

Tova was touched, murmuring, "*Merci*, and what is your name?"

"Miriam," the girl said.

"You play the piano very well, Miriam," Tova offered.

The girl smiled and withdrew silently, leaving Tova to get ready for Shabbos. She tried to brush her unruly hair and finally gave up, putting it into a twisted, messy bun. She had her makeup bag with her, so she was able to put on some fresh lipstick. The dress fit her perfectly, and it was very becoming. She felt better wearing it, and more ready for Shabbos. The sky was getting darker and she left her room, leaving the door slightly ajar.

Shabbos was coming, and sure enough, she saw Rabbanit Beneviste already at the table, lighting the candles. Her daughter, Miriam, sat on the couch with her grandmother, who had already lit. There was a cherubic little girl between them, all blonde curls and chubby cheeks, with enormous brown eyes taking up much of her adorable face.

"Shabbat Shalom," the elderly woman said, smiling.

"Shabbat Shalom," Tova answered. Turning to the little girl, she asked, "And what is your name?"

The girl looked at her in confusion.

Miriam said to her, "*Comment tu t'appelles*?"

The little girl smiled shyly. "Naomie."

Tova decided to try out her rather poor French skills on the little girl, who couldn't have been more than three years old, by telling her the story of how she'd been on a plane in the sky and how she'd had to leave the plane to get there for Shabbos.

The girl sat, enthralled, listening to her tale. Tova wasn't sure how many mistakes she'd made, but when she was done, the girl looked at her very seriously and asked in a sweet voice, "*As-tu vu ma mere*?"

Confused, Tova asked Miriam, "Is she asking me if I saw her mother?"

Miriam nodded and said softly, her lovely French accent lilting, "Yes. This is our good friend. Her young mother passed away only before two months."

Tova felt stabbed upon hearing this. Her heart went out to the child, who in her innocence had thought that Tova had seen her mother in the sky. Instinctively, she held out her arms, and to her surprise and delight, the girl slid off the couch and ran to her.

Enveloping her in a hug, Tova sat with little Naomie on her lap, who gave her a gaze of pure worship. Tova knew what it was like not to have a mother, and the empathy she had for the child was piercingly real. And so they sat that way until the men returned from shul.

IT WAS A BEAUTIFUL meal. Tova couldn't recall what they'd eaten, but the food had been plentiful and delicious, of that there was no doubt. Rav Beneviste sat at the head of the table, a tall man, his beard streaked with grey. He spoke Torah throughout the meal and still made sure to compliment his wife on every dish served. He was joined by his wife and daughter, and a son who appeared to be around eighteen or nineteen. Two other jovial men from the shul also ate at their table, and a third man, much younger than the rest. He had fine features and a stoic smile on his face, and a sadness in his eyes that came from a broken heart.

His name was Moshe Marciano, and he was the father of little Naomie. He'd been more than a little surprised to arrive home from shul to see his daughter comfortably ensconced in the arms of a young American woman whom he'd never before seen. Introductions were rapidly made in both English and French, and before long he'd been apprised of the harrowing situation in which she'd found herself, and the chain of bizarre events that led her, Tova Miller from Detroit, to be in Paris for Shabbos.

Throughout the meal he kept glancing at his daughter, who'd

insisted on sitting next to Tova, gazing adoringly at her throughout the meal. She only ate the food that Tova offered her, refusing food from anyone else. Tova made sure to cut the food into small, bite-size pieces for her.

"*Maman a coupe mon poulet*," she whispered softly to Tova.

Her mother had cut up her chicken for her.

Not knowing what to say to that, Tova said softly, "*N'est-ce pas delicieux*? Is it delicious?"

"Oui."

And she ate the chicken happily.

"Thank you very much," Moshe Marciano said apologetically. "I never seem to cut it quite right. She's very particular, my daughter." He looked fondly at Naomie.

He knew English very well, and Tova found herself wondering how he'd learned it so well.

She noticed the shadow that crossed his face, and she wondered if he was remembering the meals his wife had prepared for him. Her heart constricted.

The meal lasted quite a while, but the Benevistes were such a pleasant family that it never felt awkward in the least. They tried their best to make everyone feel included, and Tova truly enjoyed herself more than she ever thought possible. They even teased Moshe Marciano for his expert knowledge of English.

"I went to yeshiva in America … I went to camp each summer in America, too," he explained. Tova wanted to ask where he'd gone to camp, but was more than a little self-conscious. It was none of her business, after all.

So she was surprised when he volunteered the information. "I went to camp in the Midwest, in South Haven, Michigan."

"Maybe you hear of it?" Rabbanit Beneviste asked Tova.

"Of course," she said warmly. "I'm actually from Detroit. That's in Michigan."

Rabbanit Beneviste's mother commented on what a small world it was, and Rabbanit Beneviste's tinkly laughter made them all feel comfortable and relaxed. It was like a party, with Tova helping to serve each course with Miriam. When the meal was finally over, when the candles had burned down low and little Naomie had fallen asleep on the couch, she helped clear the table.

"Sit," Rabbanit Beneviste chided. "You eez guest. Please ... go in living room, eez my greatest pleasure ... No help, please."

She shooed Tova out of the kitchen and into the living room.

Rabbanit Beneviste's mother was on the couch, speaking with Moshe Marciano. Feeling a bit out of place, Tova was about to leave the room when the elderly woman motioned to her to join them.

"Come," she said. "I am very sleepy and must go rest, but allow me to make a more formal introduction, you say? This is Moshe Marciano, our dear neighbor. And this is Tova Miller, from Michigan, *non*? Please ... stay and perhaps get acquainted, if you will. I will now excuse myself. Shabbat Shalom ..."

She exited the room quietly. Rav Beneviste was walking his two guests home, and Moshe Marciano looked helplessly at Tova, unable to leave himself since his angelic daughter was curled up fast asleep on the couch.

Tova stood awkwardly in the entranceway of the room.

"Thank you for taking such good care of Naomie tonight," he said, his English perfect save for a slight French accent.

"Oh, my pleasure," she replied, flustered. "I really didn't do anything."

He shook his head. "No, you did, more than you realize. She felt very comfortable with you, and she doesn't feel comfortable with everyone — not since her mother, well ..."

Without thinking, she blurted out, "I heard ... I'm so sorry. Truly."

He nodded gravely.

She continued in a rush, her voice thick with emotion, "I know it's not the same situation, and forgive me if I'm speaking too freely, but I know what's it's like not to have a mother."

He looked at her puzzledly and gestured to the chair, offering her a seat.

"Please ..."

So she sat.

And she told him the story of her life, of how she'd been left without a mother at a tender young age, and how she'd also been bereft of a father. She hadn't told her story in such detail to her best friends in the world, Shari and Gali, but for some inexplicable reason she felt the need to share her story with him, for she saw the sadness in his eyes and the brokenness of his heart. She wanted to give him *chizuk* by showing him that she was whole, that she'd made something of herself and was leading a fine life, and that his daughter would one day undoubtedly do the same.

He told her of the early days of his marriage, how happy they'd been, and how the days had seemed so fleeting because before they knew it, they'd been mired in a dark, lonely world of hospitals and needles and doctors.

They were so engrossed in their conversation that neither of them heard Rav Beneviste quietly return. Neither of them were aware that everyone else had gone off to bed, and they were further unaware of the lateness of the hour.

The apartment grew very quiet but they still talked and talked, and on occasion a tear would course down Moshe's cheek as he spoke of his wife, and seeing his pain and feeling her own caused Tova's own eyes to fill with tears as well.

They talked like this until late into the night. Tova forgot how very tired she was, and she forgot how she came to be there in the most unlikeliest of places, and she forgot about Dan Davis and her job and everything that awaited her in Eretz Yisrael after Shabbos.

Talking was somehow cathartic, and the longer they talked, the more at ease they both became. Occasionally there was some laughter mingled with the tears, and still they talked while Naomie slept blissfully unaware, snuggled into the pillows of the sofa.

Finally, Tova glanced at her watch and was shocked to discover that it was after three o'clock in the morning. They had talked for over four hours straight. Realizing the lateness of the hour, Moshe apologized to her, saying, "I'm sorry for keeping you up so late. You must be exhausted."

"No, I'm fine, really," she said.

"I'd better get back and put Naomie into bed."

"Do you have a far walk?"

"No, I'm actually right around the corner, two buildings away …."

He leaned down, gently scooped up his daughter in his arms, thanked her, and quietly left the apartment, saying that they'd be back for lunch tomorrow.

Only, Tova realized when she was getting ready for bed as quietly as she could, it already *was* tomorrow.

There were so many thoughts swirling in her mind, but she was asleep literally as soon as her head touched the pillow.

THE SEUDAH ON SHABBOS day was just as pleasant and amiable as the evening before, or perhaps even more so, since all the people dining were better acquainted than the previous evening. Little Naomie was thrilled to see Tova again and insisted on sitting on her lap. There she sat contentedly, occasionally glancing back adoringly at Tova with huge brown eyes.

"It looks like you have a fan," Naomie's father commented dryly.

"It goes both ways," she reassured him. "I'm a big fan of hers, too."

He smiled. It was the first time Tova had seen him truly smile, and she realized how much younger he looked with a genuine smile on his face.

All of the food was delicious, but the challah was by far Tova's favorite. She'd never tasted anything quite like it, and she had at least three slices.

"This challah is amazing, Rabbanit Beneviste," she said sincerely. "I think it's the best I've ever tasted."

"*Merci, ma cher* ... it's a secret recipe!" she responded, with a wink at Moshe.

Everyone laughed, though Tova didn't understand the joke.

"I'm a baker," Moshe told her. "The challah was made at my family's *patisserie*."

"Oh." Tova blushed. "I can't believe it's not homemade—it's so delicious."

He looked pleased and amused by this. There were many conversations going on at the table at once, with smatterings of English for her benefit, of course, but mostly in French. At times Tova felt a bit out of her element, but overall she felt content to just be there and enjoy the easy camaraderie of the Beneviste family. She hadn't realized how very much she'd missed the warmth of a large family Shabbos meal ... She hadn't been a part of one for so long.

She silently vowed that one day, when she was married with a home of her own, she'd always host Shabbos meals where everyone would be welcome at her table.

"Meez Tova, is that true?" Rabbanit Beneviste was motioning to her.

"Oh, I'm sorry?"

"It eez true that you are accountant, yes?" she inquired.

"A CPA, yes," she answered.

At this, Moshe said, "That's impressive. I have two friends back in the States who tried for the CPA exams ...."

"Did they pass?"

"No, I'm afraid not. They make it almost impossible to pass."

Tova nodded. "They don't make it easy, that's for sure."

She knew how fortunate she was to have passed all four grueling exams in such a relatively short amount of time, and that others weren't as lucky.

After the meal, after the others had washed and bentched, the same scenario played out. Rav Beneviste walked his two guests home, Rabbanit Beneviste disappeared, ostensibly to take a nap, and her elderly mother insisted that Tova join her and Moshe in the living room. So once again Tova found herself speaking with Moshe Marciano, with his young daughter once again asleep on the living room sofa, only this time, she was joined by the elderly woman, who soon fell asleep in the large wing chair near the window.

Their conversation flowed just as freely as it had the night before, but it was lighter in tone. They talked. And talked.

And it felt natural.

The afternoon wore on and the sun started to sink lower in the sky. Moshe Marciano went to shul, leaving Tova to watch over little Naomie, who had awakened from her nap and was playing with the dollhouse in the corner of the room. A sudden memory jolted within her like lightning.

She remembered her dream.

Oddly enough, she hadn't thought about it the evening before. But suddenly, she remembered it and wondered at its meaning. She stood up and paced around the living room.

It was too soon, of course … much too soon.

And she had her job … She had to take care of the office in Yerushalayim. Dan Davis was counting on her. She'd given her word.

And it wasn't as if they had anything in common, really.

He was French … he was Sefardi.

She was American … she was Ashkenazi.

She was an accountant … he was a baker.

She was all alone, but he'd been married and had a child.

She looked at Naomie, who had rushed over to her, showing her the little family of dolls she'd been playing with, and her heart expanded with a tenderness that she'd never known she possessed.

Naomie held out her arms and Tova lifted her up, asking her if she liked to dance.

"*Aimes-tu danser?*"

Naomie smiled. "*Oui.*"

The two of them danced together in the apartment as the sun sank lower in the sky ….

And they danced.

THE PILOT SAID SOMETHING into the loudspeaker on the plane, but Tova had been reliving her weekend in Paris in such detail that she hadn't heard what he said.

"I'm sorry," she said to her seatmate. "What did the pilot just say?"

"Oh, he said we'll be landing in Tel Aviv in ten minutes."

Tova was dumbstruck. So deep had she been in her own thoughts that she hadn't even been aware of the four-hour flight.

Had she slept?

She pinched her cheeks, feeling as if she'd been dreaming.

Had she dreamed the whole weekend? What was real? What was not?

The whole weekend had been real. And when she leaned over to put her *Tehillim* into her carry-on bag that was under the seat, she drew something out. It was a pink sheet of construction paper, with a crude drawing of a flower on it. It was signed in a toddler's scrawl, *Naomie.*

Had the precocious child snuck her prized artwork from school that morning into her bag when she hadn't been looking?

Had she perhaps thought, in her childish naïveté, that it would be a way for Tova to remember her?

In which case, she needn't have bothered, for the little girl, and her father, had touched Tova's soul in a way that she wasn't likely to ever forget.

The plane touched down to a smattering of applause.

Tova was, at long last, in Eretz Yisrael.

CHAPTER SEVENTEEN

SHARI

SHARI WOKE UP EARLIER than usual and immediately realized that something was amiss. At first, still fighting off the murkiness of sleep, she couldn't remember what it was. But then she remembered all at once and bolted upright in bed. She looked over at Simcha, who was still sleeping soundly. Glancing at the small clock on the nightstand, she saw that it was only a little past five o'clock in the morning.

She laid her head back down on the pillow, but she knew that slumber wouldn't be forthcoming. There was too much on her mind ... Surely, there was no way she'd fall back asleep. So much had happened in the span of several weeks that she could hardly process it all. For starters, her first *shidduch* looked like it was about to come to fruition, and it gave her an inner sense of peace, for she knew that she had miraculously righted a wrong.

Pearl Marcus was about to become engaged to Uri Perlman, the son of Aunt Efrat's neighbors. They had hit it off right from the start, having much in common, and Pearl came over almost daily to apprise Shari of every new development. They'd be moving to New Jersey, where he was in dental school, and the way the whole thing had transpired around her own dining room table was nothing short of miraculous. In actuality, things had come full circle, since if Pearl had harbored any resentment toward her for any slights, real or imagined, it was forgiven. She would be the future Pearl Perlman and it had come about through the most unlikeliest of sources—Shari Adler.

And Shari couldn't have been happier about it.

The whole episode had taught her something, and she'd discussed it with Simcha only the night before.

THEY'D BEEN SITTING IN the living room late that night, wrapping the gifts she'd bought for the twins for their upcoming bar mitzvah, which was only two days away. They were just little gifts, mostly trinkets, but it was an exciting time, and her parents and Avi and Gavi were due to arrive the next morning. They would be staying by her Aunt Efrat and Uncle David on Ramat Hagolan, mere blocks away. They were getting together for dinner, and then the following day would be the actual bar mitzvah at the Kosel, followed by a *seudah* at a large shul in Rechavia.

Shari could recall every detail of their conversation the evening before.

"I must've been so self-centered to have ignored Pearl like that," she'd insisted.

"How many girls were in your seminary?" Simcha had asked.

"Probably around one hundred fifteen, or one hundred and twenty. Something like that."

"Well, it's very hard to be friends with everyone," he said kindly, giving her the benefit of the doubt.

"Yeah, I know," she said. "But Pearl obviously thought of me as her friend, and I didn't even know she existed. I must've hurt her feelings, and I'm so happy I now had the chance to make things right."

"Mmm-hmm," he agreed.

"People don't always get that chance," she reiterated. "To make things right."

Simcha had given her a *look.*

"Are you trying to tell me something?" he teased.

"I think you should call your mother."

His eyebrows lifted.

"What?"

"Look, I don't know what she said, Simcha, but it doesn't really matter—"

"Shari, I called her two weeks ago, remember?"

"Yes, but that doesn't count. It was only a five-minute phone call. I mean, I think you should call her and, and … I don't know."

"What?"

"I don't know." She hesitated. "Maybe invite her to the bar mitzvah?"

He stared at her, flabbergasted.

"Invite her?" he finally squeaked. "To Avi and Gavi's bar mitzvah? I can't even believe you're saying this."

"Neither can I," she admitted. "But I think it's the right thing to do. She's your mother, after all. I mean, the bar mitzvah is on Thursday, and tonight is Tuesday night. She won't come, of course, but it's the right thing to do—to extend the olive branch, or whatever."

He stared at her, finally breaking into an uncertain grin.

"I married a *tzaddekes.*"

She laughed. "I'm far from it, Simcha. But this … this cold

war is awful, and it's gone on too long. She hates me, I know, but at least you—I mean, you're her son! You should try to make amends, or whatever. Just do it."

Still staring at her, he picked up his phone and made the call.

"Hi, Ma," he said.

She'd gone into the kitchen to put away some things and give him some privacy. She couldn't tell how the conversation was going just from listening to his side, anyway. Before long, she'd rejoined him in the living room and was surprised to see him sitting on the couch, no longer speaking on the phone. He looked, well … dumbfounded.

"You spoke to your mother?"

He looked up at her. "That was not my mother."

"Who was it? Her secretary?" Shari was confused.

"No, it was my mother, all right," he said. "But it wasn't my mother."

Shari gave her husband a *look.*

"Simcha, you're talking in riddles."

He leaned back into the couch, smiling. "Riddles, inside a conundrum, wrapped inside an enigma—"

"What are you *talking* about?"

He grinned. "Just quoting my eighth grade science teacher. Never mind. No, what I'm trying to say is that I just spoke to my mother. Only she sounded very, very different than the mother I know. She sounded almost like a different person. It was weird."

She sat beside him. "Uh-oh."

"No, no … It was good! She sounded … I don't know. Happy. She was even laughing on the phone!"

Suddenly, Shari realized that she'd never heard his mother

laugh. She'd never seen her smile, either, not even in the photographs taken at their wedding three years earlier. The angles of her face had always been pointed, angular … There was no softness to her. Shari had always supposed it was due to the tragedy she'd endured, and the fact that her mother-in-law had never liked her, which was obvious in the extreme.

His mother … *laughing*? She could hardly picture it.

"Shari, she's coming," he said softly.

"WHAT?!"

He held up his hand. "Hold on, you can't tell me to invite her and then freak out. That's not fair. I just did what you said."

"Well, I know, but—"

"But you didn't think she'd come. I know, neither did I." He sighed.

"I mean, the bar mitzvah is in two days … The tickets must be costing her a fortune!"

"I guess she can afford it," he said. "But she's never thrown around money like this before. She said she doesn't care what it costs!"

Shari was quiet, thinking.

"She actually sounded a little mysterious. She said she wants me to meet the guy she's seriously dating, and they'll be here together at the bar mitzvah. They'll be coming to the *seudah* in Rechavia. Where is it being held, again?"

"At a shul on Ramban," she murmured. "You know, that big shul …" She couldn't believe what she was hearing.

And it wasn't as if she could complain, because it had all been her idea!

What had she been thinking*?*

"Don't worry, she's staying at a hotel, same as last time," he said.

"And her *chassan*? What was his name again?"

"They're not engaged yet," he reminded her. "But his name is Shmiel Goodman. Funny, though, when I asked her she kind of … changed the subject."

"What does *that* mean?"

"I have no clue. You know, when I last spoke to her she said something about … having two suitors. Or something like that. But she quickly changed the subject then, too. I really don't know what's going on."

Shari blanched. "*Two* suitors? What are you saying?"

He rubbed his eyes. "I don't even know what I'm saying. I guess we'll find out on Thursday! I'm so tired … these presents can wait until tomorrow, right?"

That had been the night before.

Shari had fallen asleep as soon as her head touched the pillow, but now here she was, wide awake, her tumultuous thoughts rioting in her mind.

Two suitors? She could scarcely believe that even one man would be interested in marrying her mother-in-law, let alone two. She knew it was a nasty thought, as her thoughts were always somewhat nasty when it came to Simcha's mother, but now that she'd had the insane idea of inviting her to the bar mitzvah, she would try her best to grit her teeth and bear it.

She'd learned her lesson from Pearl Marcus, she told herself. She'd try her best to be more … cordial, as hard it was. Still, she felt so nervous. Her stomach was doing somersaults at the mere thought of having to see her mother-in-law the very next day. She literally felt nauseous.

She laid her head back on the pillow and tried her best to relax. But before long, she realized that she couldn't. Her whole body was tense, and she truly felt sick.

She bolted from her bed and barely made it to the bathroom, vomiting for the first time in years. Truthfully, she'd felt a little funny ever since two days earlier, when she'd eaten sushi from a pop-up sushi stand around the corner.

Beads of sweat broke out on her forehead as she leaned back against the cool tiles.

I can't be sick now, she thought. *Not right before the bar mitzvah.*

Her parents were due to arrive later that morning, with the bar mitzvah boys themselves. She was so excited to see them, and she didn't want to be sidelined with a stomach virus.

Before long, her strength returned and she headed back to bed, where Simcha was still asleep. It was shortly after six, and she knew that he'd be up soon for minyan. She laid back down and felt her body relax.

Soon, she was asleep.

LATER THAT MORNING, SHARI woke up and was happy to discover that she felt much better. She tentatively got out of bed and went to the kitchen to check her phone. Sure enough, there were four missed calls from her mother and two missed calls from Aunt Efrat.

She called her mother.

"Shari!" her mother exclaimed. "Where were you? I tried calling you—"

"Sorry, Ima," she said. "I was sleeping."

"What? It's after eleven—are you okay?"

She glanced at the clock on the wall of the kitchen.

Eleven?

She was supposed to be at work over an hour earlier.

"Oh, no!" she groaned. "I overslept ... Ima, I think I have a little stomach bug. But I'm feeling better now, don't worry. When did you come in?"

"Around two hours ago ... Oy! Not before the bar mitzvah!" her mother wailed. "Oy, no matter, these things usually clear up quickly. By tomorrow, you'll be fine."

"I hope so. Look, Ima, I have to run to work now, but I'll come over to Aunt Efrat's house at around three, okay?"

"Perfect, we'll see you then."

Shari ran about, getting herself together before heading out to work. She'd never slept this late before, but she'd had a fitful night. Thankfully, she felt much better and more rested, so she'd still get to work that day, albeit a bit late.

THEY WERE ALL TOGETHER at dinner that evening—Simcha, her parents, Aunt Efrat and Uncle David, her cousins from Kfar Saba, her cousin from Beitar, and the toasts of the town themselves, Avi and Gavi. They'd grown taller since she'd last seen them, all gangly arms and legs, and their faces, so alike, were no longer babies' faces, but leaner and more mature. Shari's heart swelled with pride as she looked at them.

They were at a restaurant in Mamilla, the very same one they'd been at with Simcha's mother when she'd come to visit, but this time, Shari was able to relax and enjoy. The laughter around the table flowed like the wine that was poured, and everyone toasted the boys and showered them with *brachos*. Shari enjoyed herself so much that she was almost able to forget that the very next day she would be seeing her mother-in-law—and the only person she had to blame was herself.

"So," Aunt Efrat said with a wink to Shari's mother, "what do you think of my *shidduch*, Chana? The one me and Shari worked on together? You've heard about it, yes?"

"Of course, I think it's wonderful," Chana said. "More *shidduchim* should be made this way. Shari told me all about it."

"And the wedding will be in the summer, I'm assuming," Efrat continued. "So I guess I'll visit you in New York, yes?"

"Of course, we'd love to have you," Chana replied. "I'll take you everywhere … It's been a while since you've been to the States."

"David does all the traveling," Efrat said. "Me, I don't like to travel. I also don't like being a third wheelbarrow … I'll stay in a hotel, Chana."

She smiled. "Whatever you say, but you're welcome to stay with us. The boys will be in camp this summer and the house is going to be so quiet. Too quiet."

"Where will you be in camp, boys? In the mountains?" their aunt asked.

"Nah," Avi said. "We'll be in the Midwest."

"Best camp ever," Gavi added. "We've been going for three years already."

"In two years, we'll be junior counselors," Avi said.

Shari marveled at how much they'd grown up in the last year or so. Simcha clapped Avi on the back and commented, "That's a scary thought. Are you saying you guys are going to be responsible for other kids?"

At this, Gavi leaned over and pretended to pummel him, and Avi soon joined him. Shari realized that although they'd grown taller, they were still little boys, her husband included, and her heart filled with happiness.

THE NEXT MORNING, SHARI once again found herself awake at 5 a.m. At first, she couldn't understand why she was awake at that hour, until the nausea made itself known once again. She ran on shaky legs to the bathroom and then afterwards sat down on the tiled floor and tried to think.

When had she had that sushi?

It had been four days earlier.

It just didn't make sense. Last night, she'd felt perfectly fine. Unless she had some other bizarre virus, or unless she had some other strange germ … unless … unless ….

Unless …

What if ….?

She placed a protective hand over her stomach, wonderingly.

Could it be ….?

She'd seen the tests at the pharmacy, she even knew what shelf they were stacked on, though she'd never bought one.

She'd never thought that she'd have the need to buy one. She didn't want to buy one, just in case it really was some sort of virus.

Which, in all probability, it was.

She didn't want to buy the test and look at the negative reading.

She had a stomach bug, and she knew it was just a stomach bug.

Still …

She crept slowly and quietly back into her room, where Simcha was still asleep. She got dressed silently and walked into the living room, knowing that the pharmacy on Paran Street opened at six a.m.

It was ten minutes to six. She would be the first one there. No one would see her, and no one would know. And then she and Simcha would take a taxi and be at the Kosel at 8 a.m. sharp, just in time for the bar mitzvah.

She wouldn't even have time to feel disappointed, she told herself, because she'd be surrounded by her family's *simchah*. She had to *know*.

She let herself out of the apartment quietly. She didn't have time to think that maybe Simcha would awaken and panic, wondering where she was. She didn't have time to think that maybe it wasn't the best idea to do this right before she had to be at her brothers' bar mitzvah.

She didn't have time to *think*.

Before she knew it, she was standing outside the small pharmacy, her heart beating so loudly she was sure the entire Ramat Eshkol could hear it.

She opened the door, went inside, and walked toward the pregnancy tests in the rear of the store. She took one and, as if in a dream, put it on the counter. The woman behind the counter barely glanced at her. She quickly paid and left the shop, her purchase in a small plastic bag. The entire transaction had taken less than two minutes.

She sped home on shaky legs.

She was turning the key in the lock when the door opened. Simcha was there, holding the door open for her, a puzzled look on his face.

"Shari, what—"

"Oh, sorry, Simcha, I didn't want to wake you—"

"Are you okay? Where were you?"

She held out the bag and he took it, looking at the contents inside.

A light that she'd never before seen came into his eyes as he took in the meaning of what she'd done.

"Wh-why?"

"I threw up this morning. Again. I didn't want to wake you. It's probably a virus or something …."

He looked at her, keeping his voice level. "It *is* probably a virus, you know. That sushi was pretty nasty …."

"For sure. Total virus," she agreed.

With shaking fingers, she took the bag from him.

FIVE MINUTES LATER, SHE had the results.

Her husband was standing in the exact same spot as he'd been standing before, near the doorway to their apartment.

"It's just a virus, right?" he asked.

The tears came and she couldn't stop them from cascading down her cheeks as she whispered, "No."

He was by her side in an instant, his face trying to discern what had just taken place. "No? No, as in … it's not a virus?"

Now he saw that the tears were joyous tears, and she started to laugh and cry at the same time as she hiccupped and held up the test for him to see. "Simcha, look! It's not a virus at all!"

He stared at the small stick in the palm of his hand, which read one word ….

POSITIVE.

The tears that had been glistening in his eyes spilled over and the two of them stood there together, shaking and laughing and crying, offering up silent thanks to Hashem, humbled by the absolute miracle that He'd performed for them.

It was unbelievable.

It was a miracle.

They could hardly believe it.

They could hardly absorb it.

They could hardly process it, but there was no time. Before long, they had to get ready to leave.

The taxi was coming at seven-thirty to take them to the Kosel.

IT WAS A BEAUTIFUL bar mitzvah. Shari stood beside her mother the whole time, and they both cried joyous tears when the twins were called up to the Torah. Shari's heart was so filled with gratitude that she hardly knew what she was doing.

Everything that day seemed to be ... different, altered somewhat. Was the earth still spinning on its axis? How could it be? Even the sun shining on the stones of the Kosel looked brighter. The smiles on her family's faces seemed bigger. The *simchah* seemed to be heightened by the very private, extra joy that only she and her husband knew about.

She wanted to tell her mother but the timing wasn't quite right, aside from the fact that there were so many people milling about ....

After the davening and Torah reading had taken place, with the twins taking turns leining and doing a magnificent job, the whole party headed back to the shul for the bar mitzvah *seudah.*

Shari and Simcha shared a taxi together with Aunt Efrat and Uncle David, and her parents took a taxi with the twins.

Was it her imagination, or did her aunt keep glancing in her direction out of the corner of her eye, knowingly?

She couldn't possibly know. *Had she been smiling? Had the smile on her face given away her sweet secret?*

All at once, she remembered that Simcha's mother would be attending the *seudah*. She'd completely forgotten. But for the first time ever, the thought didn't fill her with anxiety.

She didn't dread seeing her like she had just a few months earlier. In fact, she even felt curious to meet the man whom her mother-in-law was dating. Simcha had said that she seemed like a different person on the phone.

What did *that* mean?

BEFORE LONG, THEY WERE walking up the stone steps to the shul on Ramban Street, where the *seudah* was being held. Her aunt's best friend, Livnat, was a well-known party planner, and she had organized the catered event in the party room. Aunt Efrat had told her that Livnat was talented, but nothing prepared Shari for what awaited them in the shul.

The room had been transformed from a typical shul party room to an absolutely stunning venue … It was remarkable what she'd done. Everything, from the tablecloths, to the candles on each table, to the lighting in the room, was in different shades of blue and silver. A huge, life-size cardboard cutout of the twins dominated the center of the room. Even the podium where Shari's father and Simcha would speak was draped in shimmery, blueish silver cloth.

Livnat had truly thought of everything.

The food looked appetizing and was beautifully presented, but Shari found that she really didn't have much of an appetite. In fact, with all the people milling about, the room suddenly became rather hot and claustrophobic. Shari fanned herself with a napkin, a thin bead of sweat breaking out on her upper lip, though no one else seemed to be uncomfortable.

It was Aunt Efrat who spied her first and took her aside.

"You know, my darling, there's a hallway outside ... maybe get some fresh air, away from the crowd, yes? Simcha, take your wife outside for a few moments, yes?"

She gestured for them to leave, but as Shari looked back, she saw her aunt wink at her, knowingly, her face wreathed in smiles.

She *knew* ... ?

And Shari knew that she knew.

It didn't bother her in the least, since Aunt Efrat was one of her favorite people and would keep her secret safe until she told her otherwise.

They had just entered the lobby, she and Simcha, where the doors were open wide and a fresh, cool breeze wafted through the building, when they stopped in their tracks.

Simcha's mother was just walking in, dressed as chic as ever, with impossibly high heels and an expensive looking dress. Next to her walked a tall man with a broad smile, a shock of messy hair, tortoise-shell rimmed glasses that were slightly askew, and an air of indiscernible confidence.

They were talking together and at first didn't even seem to notice Shari and Simcha standing there, gaping at them.

"Uh ... Ma?" Simcha said, bewildered.

"Oh, Simcha!" his mother replied exuberantly. "I didn't even see you standing there!"

Even her voice seemed different, more high-pitched and girlish. Simcha had been right—she seemed like a different woman.

A much happier woman, that much was certain. Shari looked at Simcha. He looked positively dazed, as if he was in a state of shock. Obviously, this man wasn't the accountant, Shmiel Goodman, whom he'd known all his life.

So who was he?

"Oh, Shari, there you are," her mother-in-law said with a smile. "You look lovely!"

Now it was Shari's turn to look dazed, since she had never before been complimented by this woman. But before she could say anything, her mother-in-law continued, "I'd like to introduce you two to a very special person."

They both stood there, speechless and waiting.

"This is Dr. Don Fischer, and I'm so proud to introduce you to him. I owe him … a lot. Everything."

Her eyes welled up with tears, but the smile never left her face, and he smiled down at her so sincerely that if Shari hadn't been there to witness it with her own eyes, she would never have believed that such a thing was possible.

Simcha shook Dr. Fischer's outstretched hand as if in a trance.

Shari looked from her mother-in-law to the doctor to her husband and back again, not knowing how to digest it all.

Was he the other suitor? What in the world … ?

Finally, after what seemed to be an eternity, Simcha found his voice.

"Uh … so how did the two of you meet?" His voice also sounded different than usual, a bit higher pitched.

"She walked into my office." Dr. Fischer grinned.

"Again," Eva added laughingly.

"I knew you'd be back," he teased.

Shari and Simcha stared at them, open-mouthed. They were like two giggly schoolchildren who had just found their best friend. It just seemed so … *impossible.* Things like this just didn't happen, did they?

Shari thought of the events that had transpired earlier that very same morning—and she knew that they, in fact, *did* happen.

Miracles happened each and every day, and especially when they were least expected.

"Simcha, I need to sit down," Shari said suddenly. She walked over to the chairs that were sitting near the entrance. So much had happened that day, and all at once her legs felt jittery and weak.

Her husband joined her in a flash, and if his mother thought the request was strange, she gave no sign of it. She and Dr. Fischer joined them as well, and the four of them sat together on folding chairs near the open double doors, as if this was a natural, everyday occurrence.

It was Dr. Fischer who spoke first.

"Simcha, can I call you that?"

Simcha nodded. "Of course."

"Well," he continued, "you must be a little surprised, I gather. Were you expecting Sam Goodman, I take it?"

What was the man, some sort of mind reader?

Simcha looked genuinely shocked by the man's candor.

How had he known about Shmiel Goodman? His mother wouldn't have told him, would she … ?

"Your mother told me, of course," he continued matter-of-factly.

Simcha's mouth was open in a perfect circle.

"So you're the second suitor?" he asked weakly.

Dr. Fischer grinned broadly.

"No, I'm guess I'm the third suitor," he quipped.

"Well, Shmiel rescinded his offer," Eva admitted. "So, if we're counting, it was just between you and Aaron Bergstein, and it wasn't even close …."

"Hold on … *Aaron Bergstein* … ?"

But Simcha never finished his thought because Aunt Efrat came over to them, saying in a rush, "The speeches are starting soon, my darlings. Can you come back inside?"

The four of them got up and followed her back into the room where the *seudah* was taking place. Shari felt a bit better and more like herself.

She couldn't help but stare wonderingly at her mother-in-law and Dr. Fischer, though. If there was ever a more unlikely pair, she couldn't imagine, but somehow it just seemed to … work.

They seemed so happy together.

And he seemed like a genuinely nice man, a good person, and …

Well. Her mother-in-law truly seemed like a different person, and Shari felt so grateful to the man just for that reason alone.

As they rejoined the others, she found herself wondering about their upcoming wedding plans. She recalled how she'd been afraid that her mother-in-law's wedding would coincide with Gali's wedding, but that was merely a few weeks away, in the beginning of June. Before, she'd dreaded this particular wedding, but now she felt cautiously optimistic.

So there were two weddings on the horizon, it seemed, and she found herself looking forward to both. Of course, she could hardly wait to dance with Gali, and she knew that Tova would be there, too. But now they were at the twins' bar mitzvah, and there was so much to be grateful for. She saw her father, who had just walked over to the podium and was about to address the crowd.

Not liking public speaking, he simply thanked everyone for coming and proudly introduced Simcha, his son-in-law, who then walked up to the podium.

And Shari, her heart filled with gratitude, settled into her seat and listened attentively to what he had to say …

EPILOGUE

TOMORROW

THE DAY DAWNED COOL and clear under the blue Jerusalem sky. It was the first week of June, and it would surely get warmer a bit later. But for now, there was a cool breeze that wafted off the balcony and into the suite where Gali was staying. It was still early, only a little past six o'clock in the morning, but she couldn't sleep.

Today was her wedding day.

Gali looked over at Tova, who was sound asleep in the corner of the large suite. She'd stayed overnight with her at the Waldorf. It hadn't been the long trip from the States for Tova as she'd originally thought, since she'd been working in Yerushalayim for the past several weeks. Apparently, her boss, Dan Davis, really needed her help in the office there and Tova had settled into a new routine and, most incredibly, a new life.

It warmed Gali's heart to know that soon Tova would be joined in Yerushalayim by Moshe Marciano, who'd be joining his family's business.

Permanently.

It was remarkable to think that the man Tova was seeing would be Shari's boss … Of all the people in the world, it was just so magically fitting. It was all so …

Orchestrated.

By the Master Conductor Himself.

Gali tiptoed out to the balcony and opened the door a little wider. The sun was shining under the most brilliant blue sky, and Gali breathed in the fragrant air of Yerushalayim. She wondered if Yigal was already up … He was always a very early riser, always punctual for Shacharis. Disciplined and conscientious, he took his Torah ideals seriously, he took his work seriously … he took his *life* seriously.

Gali knew that his life would always include her own happiness in it, and she was proud to become his wife. She was so humbled and grateful to Hashem for everything He'd done.

How well she remembered that day in Oxnard, California, when Yigal had first mentioned Yerushalayim as a possibility for their wedding. The idea had seemed so remote at the time, a destination wedding—but here it was. The day was finally here at last, sparklingly real, and now it was as if all the drama that had transpired since then was trivial and meaningless.

Gali knew in her heart that she'd daven for that girl as well, along with the list of names she'd been given.

Gali glanced at her watch, the beautiful watch that her *chassan* had given her. It was now almost seven o'clock in the morning. *How long had she been standing there, at the balcony, with such a feeling of contentment?*

All of the anxiety and worry she'd felt in the recent past seemed to be a distant memory, and now there was only joy.

Shari had said she'd be there at eight to join them. The hair and makeup team were coming at eight-thirty to get an early start.

Tova rolled over in her sleep and murmured something. Then suddenly, she bolted upright in her bed.

"Gali!"

"Yes?"

"Oh, you're up … I didn't want you to miss your wedding," she mumbled, her voice thick with sleep, before she lay back down and closed her eyes.

Gali laughed.

She looked at Tova, who was once again sound asleep, and her heart felt ready to burst with happiness, for she knew that one day soon it would be Tova's turn to walk down the aisle. Gali blinked back tears when she thought of the blessed day, which was rapidly approaching, when Moshe Marciano would be waiting for Tova underneath a *chuppah* of their own.

Once more, Gali quietly went out to the balcony. Her heart felt so full, she wanted to take some time to daven in solitude before the events of the day would engulf her. From her sixth floor balcony, the view was spectacular. The air was fragrant with the scent of bougainvilleas and the wide sky above was brilliantly blue, and she was content to gaze forever at the sun-drenched hills of Yerushalayim. Standing there, davening for their future, a peaceful serenity enveloped her … today, at long last, was her wedding day, and there were no nerves of any kind.

Only happiness.

MUCH LATER IN THE day, toward sunset, a radiant Gali, accompanied by her mother and future mother-in-law, with Shari and Tova following closely behind, walked together in a procession into the grand ballroom of the Waldorf Astoria.

The enormous room was swathed in white. Shimmering white draperies descended from the ceiling, iridescent white crystals hung from white birch branches, and white lights shone on the white pavilion under which Gali would sit to receive her guests.

Surprisingly, her gown was beautiful in its simplicity. Her blonde hair was only halfway pulled up under a diamond tiara, a less elaborate style that she'd chosen herself. Her makeup was also understated. Gali looked like a shining, yet modest queen, regal and demure.

The three friends sat together on the raised platform under the pavilion of so many sparkling lights, and Gali showered sincere *brachos* upon each guest who came over to her.

The wedding was exquisite and magical, and yet it was also a miraculous culmination of so many *brachos* that Hashem had bestowed upon each of them. It was, all at once, a perfect ending and a perfect beginning ....

Shari, who looked positively glowing with an inner serenity that hadn't been there mere months earlier, and whose hand rested protectively over her stomach ...

Tova, who only six weeks earlier had sadly lost the grandmother who'd made a home for her when she had none, but was now eagerly looking toward her own future and the home she'd build one day soon, right there in Yerushalayim ...

And Gali, whose happiness knew no bounds, who'd overcome obstacles that would have chased off other girls, but not her. She knew that Yigal was worth it all ....

And Moshe Marciano, who'd flown in from Paris that morning unbeknownst to Tova, and who'd come to the wedding, much to her delight ...

Gali was flanked on all sides by her mother, mother-in-law, sisters-in-law, and Shari and Tova, when she was surprised to see a woman who looked vaguely familiar come over to Shari and embrace her.

"Gali, this is my mother-in-law," Shari shouted over the loud music. "She's in town, apartment hunting, and I told her to come to the wedding!"

"Oh, so nice of you to come!" Gali said sincerely. "And *mazel tov* to you on your engagement!"

Eva Adler thanked her warmly, looking positively lit from within, and Gali noticed that her *chassan* stood nearby, his glasses charmingly askew, his face wreathed in smiles.

The music got louder, and the three friends … their eyes met.

Yigal was coming closer ….

In the excitement of the moment, they didn't think of the dark times and hardships they'd endured. They couldn't even recall how they each had yearned for a better tomorrow ….

Because tomorrow had come.

GLOSSARY

Abba—Daddy
Askan—community activist
B'seder—fine
B'ezrat Hashem—with the Almighty's help
Baruch Hashem— thank the Almighty
Beit din—Jewish court
Bentch—recite Grace After Meals
Brachah, brachos—blessing(s)
Bubby—grandmother
Challah—traditional braided bread eaten at Sabbath and holiday meals
Chassan—groom
Chavrusa—Torah study partner
Chessed—kindness
Chizuk—encouragement
Daven—pray
David Hamelech—King David
Emunah—faith
Eretz Yisrael—the Land of Israel
Frum—religiously observant
Gishmei brachah—rains of blessing
Hachnasat orchim—welcoming guests
Hashem—the Almighty
Hashgachah pratit—Divine providence

Hasmadah—diligence in study
Hatzalah—volunteer Jewish ambulance corp
Ima—Mommy
Ir Hakodesh—the Holy City
Ivrit—Hebrew
Kallah—bride
Kedushah—holiness
Kiddush—blessing made on wine to welcome the Sabbath
Kollel—institution of advanced Torah study
Kosel—the Western Wall
Leining—public Torah reading
Maariv—evening prayers
Makolet—grocery store
Mazel—fortune
Mazel tov—good luck
Middos—character traits
Minchah—afternoon prayers
Mirpeset—balcony
Mitzvah—Torah commandment
Nebach—an unfortunate person
Rabbanit—rabbi's wife
Rebbetzin—rabbi's wife
Rav—rabbi
Shacharis—morning prayers
Sefer, sefarim—Torah book(s)
Seudah—festive meal
Shabbat, Shabbos—the Sabbath
Shabbat Shalom—"a peaceful Sabbath," a traditional Sabbath gretting

Shadchan—matchmaker

Sheitel—wig

Shidduch—marital match

Shidduchim—the process of finding one's future spouse; marital matches

Shtuyot—foolishness

Shul—synagogue

Siddur—prayer book

Simchah—happy occasion

Tehillim—Psalms

Tefillos—prayers

Tzaddekes—righteous woman

Tzaddik—righteous man

Vort—engagement party

Yerushalayim—Jerusalem

Yad Hashem—the guiding hand of the Almighty

Yeshiva—Torah school

Yom Tov—holiday

Zechus, zechut—merit

Zeidy—grandfather